Blizzard at Blue Ridge Inn

PAT NICHOLS

Blizzard at Blue Ridge Inn by Pat Nichols
Published by Armchair Press
Copyright © 2024 by Pat Nichols
Cover Design by Elaina Lee
Edited by Sherri Stewart

Available in print from your local bookstore or online.
For more information on this book or the author visit:
https://patnicholsauthor.blog
Printed in the United States of America

Blizzard at Blue Ridge Inn is a work of fiction. Names, characters, and incidents are all products of the author's imagination or are used for fictional purposes. Any mentioned brand names, places, and trademarks remain the property of their respective owners, bear no association with the author or publisher, and are used for fictional purposes only.

Library of Congress Cataloging-in Publication Data
Nichols, Pat.
Blizzard at Blue Ridge Inn / Pat Nichols

Books by
Pat Nichols
Women's Fiction

Willow Falls series

The Secret of Willow Inn
Trouble in Willow Falls
Star Struck in Willow Falls
Bridges, Books, and Bones

Butler Family Legacy series

Big Secrets, Little Lies
Truth and Forgiveness
New Beginnings

Blue Ridge Series

Blizzard at Blue Ridge Inn
The Inheritance
The Wedding
More titles in 2025

Contemporary Romance

Jenny's Grace

To John Lavin, owner of the real Blue Ridge Inn, and all the guests who stay at the beautiful historic bed and breakfast.

Chapter 1

Rain pummeled the metal roof with a rhythm akin to a dozen jazz musicians striking snares with drumsticks. The sound sent a shiver cascading down Amanda Sullivan's spine. At least hurricane season had passed. She grabbed her phone off the dresser, pressed the weather app, and glared at the forecast for Blue Ridge, Georgia. Nothing about her destination had changed during the past twenty-four hours. Highs in the forties. Snow predicted tomorrow.

Amanda released a heavy sigh and tossed the phone on the bed beside her open suitcase. If Paul had bothered to ask where she wanted to celebrate their ninth anniversary, she would have suggested Miami or Key West—destinations more suitable for her New Orleans wardrobe. But then why would he consider her desires? Especially during the past two years when he hadn't been home long enough to engage in a meaningful conversation. She folded her warmest sweater and placed it in the suitcase atop outfits barely qualifying for cool weather, much less frigid temperatures—at least for a southern gal.

A lightning flash, and rain streaming in sheets down the bedroom window summoned images of the phone call that had sent her racing to the hospital emergency room ten years earlier. She closed her eyes to blot out the memories. Cradling her husband's hand as he exhaled his last breath and slipped into eternity. Telling her eleven-year-old daughter that her daddy had gone to heaven.

A shudder ripped through Amanda. If only her soulmate had stayed home that afternoon. But he hadn't, and now Paul shared her bed. A distant thunderclap forced her eyes open. Could spending an uninterrupted week alone with her second husband in a small Georgia town breathe new life into their marriage?

Amanda spun toward her dresser and opened her lingerie drawer. She folded back the layers of undergarments and fingered the lacy teddy she'd last worn the night of their one-year anniversary. Should she pack it for this trip? After all, at forty-three she could still pass for her mid-thirties. Plus, not one strand of gray invaded her red waves, which along with her green eyes, had first drawn Paul's attention. She tossed the garment in her suitcase and zipped the top closed before she could change her mind. With a few minutes to spare before it was time to leave for the airport, she grabbed her phone, lifted the bag off the bed, and pulled it into the hall.

Wooden planks creaked beneath Amanda's feet as she hauled her bag down the curved staircase to the foyer. The Saint Charles streetcar rolled past the hundred-year-old house her husband had tastefully furnished with priceless antiques. She ran her palm along a console's smooth marble top and caught her image in the gilded mirror. Truth was, the desire to provide for her daughter had motivated her to accept Paul's proposal a mere nine months after that drunk driver made her a widow. But now—

A familiar ringtone broke through Amanda's musings. She carried her phone into the formal living room, dropped onto the sofa, and pressed Facetime. "Hey, honey."

"Hi, Mom." Her daughter's hair—more auburn than red—cascaded over her shoulders. "Are you on the way to the airport?"

"I'll leave in a few minutes. How's everything going at LSU?"

"First semester finals begin Monday."

Amanda smiled, proud of Morgan's scholastic abilities. "You'll ace them as you always do."

"Hopefully, a couple more days of studying will do the trick." Her daughter paused. "I still can't believe Paul made reservations in a town miles from an airport. Why didn't he arrange his schedule to fly to Chattanooga with you, so you wouldn't have to drive alone?"

"The airport isn't that far from Blue Ridge."

"It's far enough, *and* snow's predicted—"

"Not until tomorrow." Even though Morgan understood how much she and Paul had drifted apart, she didn't need to worry this close to finals. "I'm looking forward to a change of scenery."

"You can't fool me, Mom. I know how much you dislike cold weather, and if you ask me, your husband is totally insensitive."

Amanda eyed the still life over the fireplace. How much was that one painting worth? A few thousand? "Have you forgotten how Paul rescued us after your father died, and he moved us into his beautiful home?"

"Away from the only home we loved."

"Which, by the way, ended up paying for your education. Besides, I'm counting on this trip to rekindle my relationship with your stepfather."

"If he even bothers to show up." A heavy sigh resonated through the phone. "Sorry for the snide remark. It's just you're a smart, beautiful woman who deserves more than a fancy house full of old furniture."

"Antiques, and please stop worrying about me. No matter what happens between Paul and me, you and I will always have each other."

"Always. I love you, Mom."

"I love you to the moon and back, honey." Amanda trudged back to the foyer, lifted her keys from a bowl on the console, and dropped her phone in her purse. Grateful the rain had eased a bit, she donned a lightweight, quilted jacket and pulled an umbrella from the stand beside the door. After activating the alarm, she rolled her suitcase across the front porch and dashed to her car parked in the driveway behind Paul's truck.

Ninety minutes after backing onto the street, Amanda stood at the airport terminal window and eyed the plane easing to a stop beside the jetway. She had only flown one other time—to Orlando to celebrate Morgan's tenth birthday with her best friend. They'd scrimped and saved for an entire year to accumulate enough money to pay for a week's stay at a fancy resort and to visit every Disney World venue. Despite their limited resources, those were happy times filled with love and laughter. Amanda's throat thickened.

Startled by Paul's ringtone, she spun away from the window and pulled her phone from her purse. "Hey."

"Have you boarded yet?"

"The plane just pulled up to the gate."

"The rental car's all set for you." He cleared his throat, hinting at the next words he'd utter. "I've run into a problem with this project."

Of course, he had. Amanda rolled her eyes. Just like every other project he tackled. Did he create chaos to avoid spending time with her, or was he incompetent?

"You'll have a couple additional days to relax before I meet you."

So much for celebrating their anniversary on its actual date. "I assume you're aware that snow's predicted."

"The room I reserved has a fireplace to keep you warm. Sorry about the delay, but you know how plans go awry on these assignments. Text me when you arrive at the inn."

Maybe she should cancel the trip and drive back home. Amanda squared her shoulders. No way she'd allow uncontrolled emotions to dictate her decision. "I will." She ended the call, slipped her phone into her purse, and focused on the arriving passengers. How many were locals returning home? How many were tourists or businesspeople visiting NOLA? When she returned from Blue Ridge, maybe she should go back to work. After all, New Orleans always needed good tour guides, and it wouldn't take long to brush up.

"Are you traveling for business or pleasure, Ms. Sullivan?"

Amanda's brow pinched as she turned and faced the man sitting behind her. "How do you know my name?"

He nodded toward her bag. "Your luggage tag."

"Oh." Was he flirting or meddling? She held up her left hand and tapped her wedding ring. "My husband and I are celebrating our anniversary."

"Congratulations."

He seemed harmless enough. "How about you?"

"Job interview. Chattanooga's a good town to raise a family—"

Amanda looked away and tuned out his chatter. What if they ended up in the same row? Hoping he'd take a hint, she pulled a book from her suitcase pocket.

He continued to carry on until the flight attendant called for business-class boarding. "That's me." He stood and grabbed his carryon. "Have a nice flight, Mrs. Sullivan."

Relieved his row was nowhere close to hers, Amanda tucked the book under her arm. When her section was called, she pulled her bag onto the plane and walked past him without making eye contact. In the main cabin, she hoisted her bag into the overhead bin, then slid to the window seat and laid the book on her lap.

The gentleman who settled into the aisle seat nodded at her, then tapped his earbud. Relieved her traveling companion seemed to possess the same mindset, she peered out at the low-hanging clouds. How safe was it to take off in foul weather? Her foot pumped of its own volition as the plane moved away from the gate. Maybe she should have insisted on driving to Georgia.

Amanda gripped the seat arms the moment the pilot pivoted onto the active runway. She held tight as the plane jolted through dense clouds and soared into a turbulence-free blue sky. Maybe this trip would help her and Paul break through the fog clouding their relationship. Whatever happened in Georgia, she'd find a way to make the most of it.

Chapter 2

Erica Parker set two plates on the kitchen island in her upscale Asheville home, then climbed onto a stool and rested her chin on her knuckles. She smiled at Abby's profile. Given her dark hair and expressive brown eyes, there was no mistaking the seventeen-year-old beauty as her child. Her friends claimed they looked more like sisters than mother and daughter.

Abby stopped tapping her phone and faced her mom. "What?"

"Are you positive you don't want me to ask Brian to postpone the trip until winter break so you can go with us?"

"Are you kidding?" Abby pinched a piece of bread off her sandwich and slipped it to her golden retriever, Dusty. "No way I'd want to spend an entire week doing all kinds of boring stuff with you two when I can hang out at my best friend's house. Besides, Dad scheduled the trip to celebrate you turning thirty-seven."

Erica scoffed. "A month before my actual birthday."

Abby bit into her sandwich. "Because his job will keep him away from home most of January."

Like every other month since she'd married him. Maybe his wanting to spend time alone with her less than a month before Christmas had nothing to do with celebrating her birthday. Erica glanced around the space four times the size of the kitchen in the tiny furnished apartment where she and Abby had lived before Brian came into their lives. A knot gripped her belly. If her escalating suspicions had merit, was divorce in her future? Or would her need for security force her to remain in a troubled marriage for her daughter's sake?

"When's Dad meeting you?"

Erica blinked. "He's scheduled to fly from New York to Atlanta and drive to Blue Ridge the day after tomorrow. Which means I could wait one more day before leaving."

Abby rolled her eyes. "You haven't been anywhere since we spent a week in Pigeon Forge a couple of years after you guys married. So stop feeling guilty and go do something fun until he shows up—like shopping or getting a manicure or a massage."

Erica released a sigh. "I suppose a relaxing massage would be a nice treat."

"No supposing about it." Abby grabbed her phone, then swiped and tapped the screen a few times. "There. You're all set for a one o'clock appointment tomorrow. I texted you the details. You can thank me by buying me a cute outfit."

"You're likely to come out ahead on that deal." Erica marveled at her daughter's take-charge approach—the polar opposite of her own reticence. Which was the reason she had stayed in her first poor excuse of a marriage far too long. What her child's father was up to or whether he had any idea of their whereabouts remained a mystery.

Abby finished her sandwich, then slid off her stool. After setting her plate in the dishwasher, she dashed out of the kitchen with Dusty padding behind her.

Erica wrapped her fingers around her iced-tea glass and imagined nine months in the future when her daughter would leave home to attend college. Maybe spending a week away from Abby now would help prepare her for their inevitable separation. At least her part-time job would help occupy her time and ease her loneliness.

Abby returned pulling a suitcase behind her. "Dusty and I are ready to go."

Erica set down her glass and forced a smile. "You have such a bright future, sweetheart."

"Are you getting all sentimental again?"

"You and I have struggled through so much together—"

"Until you married Brian, and he bought us this gorgeous house."

She couldn't blame Abby for adoring her stepdad. Especially since he appeared to treat her more like a daughter than a stepchild. Erica slid off her stool and embraced her child. "Have fun, sweetheart."

Abby kissed her cheek. "You too, Mom." She pulled away and headed to the door leading to the garage.

Erica followed and leaned against the doorframe. Abby hoisted her bag into the late-model sedan Brian had given her for her sixteenth birthday. His generosity was another reason he'd captured Abby's devotion. After Dusty sprang onto the back seat, Abby slid behind the wheel and lowered the window. "Call me after you check in, and don't forget your massage tomorrow."

"I'll call, and I promise not to forget."

Abby waved, then backed out of the garage.

Letting her only child go wouldn't come easy, especially if her suspicions about Brian proved valid. Erica returned to the kitchen and eyed her un-eaten sandwich. Should she wrap it up for the road or treat herself to lunch in a nice restaurant in Blue Ridge? Why not take full advantage of the trip? She stuffed the sandwich down the disposal.

After loading the dishwasher and wiping down the counter, Erica head-ed to the main bedroom and eyed her packed suitcase lying open on the king-size bed. Spending time alone with her husband in a romantic setting would either give credence to her doubts or prove them unfounded. She zipped the suitcase closed, set it on the floor, and glanced around the room. Before meeting Brian, she had never dreamed of living in such a luxurious home. Now she couldn't imagine living anywhere else. Somehow, she had to make sure this trip breathed new life into their relationship.

Erica pulled her suitcase to the kitchen, then ambled through the house to assure everything was in order. After checking the front door twice, she returned to the kitchen. Following one more glimpse around, she grabbed her fur-collared, wool coat, set the alarm, and carried her bag to the garage. She paused beside Brian's expensive sports car, which he rarely drove. One of these days she'd ask him to teach her how to shift the gears so at least someone in the family could enjoy the car.

Releasing a sigh, Erica stowed her bag and coat in her SUV, then slid behind the steering wheel and typed her destination's address into her phone's app. ETA two hours and thirty-six minutes. She backed out. After double-checking to ensure the garage door closed, she eased down the driveway.

While driving out of town, Erica's mind drifted to the day she and Abby first arrived in Asheville—that sense of freedom mingled with gut-wrenching angst. Now the further she drove from her normal routine, the more her shoulders tensed. She turned on the radio, hoping the nineties music would help her relax. What if she and Abby took a trip in June after she graduated from high school? Just the two of them to someplace fun. Maybe a Florida beach. Despite Brian's high-paying job keeping him away from home, it provided the means for a luxury vacation. By the time Erica reached the outskirts of Blue Ridge, she'd narrowed her options for a mother-daughter trip to three destinations. She'd leave the final choice to Abby.

Erica's stomach grumbled as she pulled into the parking lot behind the Blue Ridge Inn Bed and Breakfast. Why hadn't she packed that sandwich? After climbing out, she draped her coat over her arm, and hauled her suitcase up the porch steps. She paused beside Mountain Mama's Coffee Lounge, then continued to the inn's entrance and pressed the buzzer.

A middle-aged, attractive woman smiled as she pulled the door open. "Are you checking in?"

She nodded. "I'm Erica Parker."

"Welcome to Blue Ridge, Mrs. Parker, and happy birthday. I'm Faith, the assistant innkeeper. Your husband reserved the Sycamore suite for you."

The scent of fresh pine wafted through the hall as Faith led her past the elegantly decorated Christmas tree beside the staircase and the garland adorning the railing. After giving Erica a tour through the main floor and sharing tidbits about the historic inn's history, Faith escorted her to a door tucked behind a staircase.

Erica pulled her suitcase into the Sycamore suite's cozy sitting room and eyed a bottle of her favorite chardonnay on the coffee table.

"We're expecting a bit of snow, so the fireplace will keep you warm. Coffee's available in the dining room at seven, and breakfast is served every morning at nine. If you need reservations or recommendations for lunch or dinner, I'll be happy to help."

"Thank you."

"Our pleasure." Faith moved to the door, then paused. "One more thing, the front and back doors lock automatically, so take your key whenever you leave the inn."

"I will." Erica laid her coat on one of the wingback chairs flanking the couch, then lifted the card propped against the wine bottle. "Happy early

Birthday. Love, Brian. "A nice touch. So far, all seemed like the beginning of a romantic vacation.

Eager to check the first task off her list, Erica pulled her suitcase into the bedroom and transferred her clothes to the closet and dresser drawers. After stashing her toiletries in the bathroom vanity, she texted her daughter. "Arrived safe and sound. Checked into a two-room suite with fireplace."

Abby responded. "Perfect. Don't forget massage."

Erica responded with a thumbs-up and a heart emoji. She donned her coat and pocketed her key, then headed out to tackle task number two—find a place to alleviate her stomach's protest.

Chapter 3

Wendy Peterson pulled a pale blue sweater the color of her eyes over her head, then released her long blonde hair to cascade across her shoulders and down her chest. The twenty-three-year-old moved to the bedroom window in the tenth-floor Gulfport condo and gazed at the afternoon sun shimmering on the Gulf of Mexico. Growing up, she'd dreamed about living in a luxurious home. When she married Kurt, her dream became reality. A smile curved her lips as she pressed her hand to her belly. How long until she'd need a new wardrobe? A couple of weeks? Another month?

Her phone pinged a text, sending her dashing to the dresser. "Uber arriving in five minutes." Wendy slipped her phone into her purse, then pulled the suitcase and duffle to the contemporary living room. A warm sensation surged through her as she imagined bringing her little princess or prince home to her castle in the sky with a million-dollar view. Kurt promised she could furnish the rest of the condo after Christmas. She released a satisfied sigh, then headed out to the hall and on to the elevator bank.

Mrs. Jones, her inquisitive, elderly neighbor, greeted her while eyeing her luggage. "Where are you going?"

"To Blue Ridge, Georgia, so I can experience snow before our baby's born."

"I hope you packed plenty of warm clothes."

"There are lots of cute little stores in the town, so I'll buy whatever I need." Energized by the prospect of shopping to her heart's content, Wendy patted her belly. "Even though I won't be able to wear anything new much longer."

"I hope you have a wonderful time. And don't worry, I'll keep an eye on your place."

Of course, she would. Mrs. Jones had appointed herself as the resident watchdog.

"When are you coming home?"

The elevator door yawned open, beckoning Wendy to step inside. "A week from today."

Mrs. Jones followed and pressed the button for the ground floor "Do you know your baby's sex?"

Wendy shook her head. "Kurt is definitely leaning toward a boy. I'm hoping for a girl. Although, I suppose it doesn't matter as long as our baby is healthy."

The elevator eased to a stop.

"Enjoy your trip, and tell Kurt hi for me." Her neighbor waved over her shoulder as she stepped out.

Wendy strolled through the elegant lobby and exited the building seconds before a late-model sedan pulled under the canopy.

The middle-aged driver popped the trunk, then circled the car and opened the rear door. "Good morning, Mrs. Peterson. I'm Phillip."

"Good morning." Wendy slid behind the front passenger seat and stroked the leather armrest. Nice, but not as smooth as the leather in the high-end sports car Kurt had given her the week after they married. She loved driving with the top down, allowing the breeze to tousle her hair and warm her cheeks. After their baby was born, however, she'd drive Kurt's sedan. It seemed the right thing to do.

The driver stowed her bags in the trunk, then returned to his seat and pulled onto Beach Drive. He glanced over his shoulder. "Are you traveling for work or vacation?"

Wendy's chest puffed. Did the guy who drove people for a living actually believe she might be a businesswoman? Amazing he'd draw that conclusion, considering she'd only flown one other time. Waiting tables at high-end restaurants was the only job she'd ever held. "Vacation, in the Georgia mountains."

"Are you aware that snow's predicted for much of the country, including North Georgia?"

"That's why I'm going."

"Have you ever seen snow?"

"A couple of flurries years ago." Wendy peered at a luxury yacht cruising toward Biloxi. Maybe one day Kurt would buy a big fancy boat for her. "I grew up in Mobile and lived on the gulf coast my entire life, which is why I want to experience a winter wonderland. What about you?"

"I hail from Wisconsin. Every winter we ended up snowed in for days."

"Sounds like fun."

"Not when we lost power, and ten-foot snowdrifts kept us trapped indoors."

"I can't imagine that happening in Georgia." Wendy dug her phone from her purse and texted Kurt. "On my way to airport. Can't wait 'til you arrive." Assuming he was busy negotiating with a client, she dropped her phone back in her purse without waiting for a response.

The driver was peering at her in the rear-view mirror. Once her baby bulge appeared, would he still be looking? Phillip's eyes returned to the road. She fingered her engagement ring and diamond-studded wedding band. Would it even matter if men's eyes didn't follow her anymore? After all, she'd married a man with the means to provide a lifestyle she'd never imagined possible. Wendy peered out the window and focused on the passing scenery until they arrived at the airport.

After popping the trunk, Phillip opened the rear door and handed Wendy a business card. "Call me when you return, and I'll drive you home."

"Thanks, I will." She smiled while dropping the card into her purse, then entered the terminal and checked her oversized bag. Wendy's senses heightened as she made her way through security and headed to the gate. Maybe other passengers would also tag her as a businesswoman. She ambled to the window and snapped a selfie with the plane in the background.

"Your first flight?"

So much for coming across as a professional. Wendy faced the elderly woman. "Second. My first was to Las Vegas three years ago for my honeymoon." Her eyes drifted to a pregnant woman standing arm in arm with a man. Both appeared to be in their twenties, although, who could tell nowadays? Kurt could easily pass for ten years older than his actual age. Which, in her closest friend's opinion, made her his trophy wife. While flattered, Wendy had dismissed the notion as ridiculous.

The gate attendant began the boarding process, prompting Wendy to move beside the young couple. She caught the woman's eye. "When's your baby due?"

"In three months."

"My due date is six months away."

"Which means you must be right in the middle of morning sickness."

Wendy patted her tummy. "Other than a couple of days, I've escaped those symptoms."

"Lucky you. My sweet husband had to deal with three months of my nausea. I couldn't stomach the smell of food before noon."

They continued to compare notes until they stepped onto the plane. The woman's husband hoisted Wendy's duffle into the business-class overhead bin, then followed his wife into coach.

Wendy slid to the window seat. Maybe someone in the mood to chat would sit beside her. Or maybe not. A stern-looking, middle-aged woman dressed in a suit settled on the aisle seat and removed a laptop from her briefcase, hinting she intended to focus on work.

Wendy's shoulders slumped. How could she spend the entire flight with no one to talk to? She peered out at the overcast sky. During the flight to Vegas, she'd clung to Kurt's arm when they encountered turbulent air. Why hadn't he arranged his work schedule so he could fly with her? A businesswoman wouldn't worry about the weather, so why should she? Besides, she had her phone to keep her company. She inserted her earbuds and pulled up her song playlist.

The moment the plane backed away from the gate, Wendy gripped the armrest. She stared out the window and imagined Kurt sitting beside her, holding her hand. Her eyes remained focused on the passing scenery as the plane taxied down the runway and lifted off the ground. Grateful the turbulence was milder than she'd anticipated, she glanced sideways at the seatmate who'd replaced her laptop with a document in a blue folder.

Eager to appear busy, Wendy tapped her phone and scrolled through her social media messages. By the time the plane landed in Chattanooga, she was desperate for conversation. Her face lit up as she arrived at baggage claim and approached the female driver holding a sign bearing her name. "I'm Wendy Peterson."

"I hope you had a good flight, Mrs. Peterson. I'm CeeCee."

She seemed friendly. Wendy held out her hand. "It's a pleasure to meet you."

After pulling Wendy's suitcase off the carousel, her driver led her to a white SUV and stashed her luggage in the back. Time to find out if her escort was the chatty or silent type. "Is it okay if I sit up front with you? It'll be easier for us to talk."

"We have a ninety-minute drive, so I welcome the company."

While Wendy slid onto the passenger seat, her traveling companion hastened to the driver's side. "Even though you missed the fall foliage by a month, you're in for a lovely ride through the Blue Ridge foothills."

"Do you drive the route often?"

"At least once a week."

By the time they pulled in front of the three-story, white-framed build-ing, Wendy had made a new friend. "Why don't you let me treat you to dinner before you drive back?"

"Thank you for the invitation, but I'm scheduled to pick up a couple and drive them to Chattanooga." CeeCee climbed out and pulled Wendy's suitcase to Blue Ridge Inn's covered front porch.

Wendy followed carrying her duffle. "Thanks again for making the trip so much fun."

"You've been the most enjoyable fare I've had all month." She handed Wendy a business card. "If you're ever back in the area and need a ride, call me."

"I will." After CeeCee returned to her vehicle, Wendy pressed the buzzer beside the red door, then peered through the window framed with stained-glass squares.

A woman approached and pulled the door open. "Hello, I'm Faith, the assistant innkeeper. I assume you're Mrs. Peterson."

"That's me."

"We're delighted you're staying with us." Faith pulled her suitcase into the hall.

Wendy followed her and peered at the intimate sitting room to her right. "This looks more like a home than an inn."

"For good reason. This was a private residence for more than a hundred years." After sharing details about the inn's history, the manager hauled the suitcase to the second floor. "Your suite is all ready for you."

Wendy followed her into a room featuring dark green walls, a leather couch, and two antique chairs. Combination cabinets and bookshelves sandwiched a bench seat along the window wall. Not exactly her style but cozy.

"This library is part of the Tallulah suite."

"That fireplace is perfect for this weather."

"Actually, you have one in each room." Faith opened a door beside the fireplace and pulled Wendy's suitcase into a contemporary bedroom awash in shades of gray. She pointed to a box on the nightstand bearing "The Chocolate Express" label. "A gift from Mr. Peterson. Don't hesitate to let us know how we can make your visit special."

Wendy set her duffle on the floor beside the king-size bed, then plucked a dark-chocolate truffle from the box into her mouth. While savoring the rich taste, she texted Kurt. "All checked in. Thank you for remembering my favorite candy." Assuming he was still busy with work, she added a heart emoji, then slid her phone back into her purse and headed out to begin her next shopping spree.

Chapter 4

Clouds blanketed the night sky as Amanda steered her rental car into the parking lot behind the inn and parked beside a late-model SUV. Her eyes shifted from the Mountain Mama's Coffee Lounge sign painted on the side of the building to the Blue Ridge Inn flag fluttering from a porch pillar. At least she'd arrived at the right place. Her lightweight jacket failed to ward off the cold as she climbed out, hauled her suitcase up the porch stairs, and pressed the buzzer.

A woman responded through the speaker. "May I help you?"

"I'm Amanda Sullivan."

The door swung open releasing a waft of warm air. "Welcome to Blue Ridge, Mrs. Sullivan."

"Thank you." Amanda pulled her suitcase across the threshold, relishing the warm air.

"I'm Faith, the assistant innkeeper." She pushed the door closed. "I hope you had a pleasant drive."

"I did, thank you."

The wooden floors creaked as Faith escorted Amanda through the narrow hall. She paused beside a dining room. "Due to three weather-related cancellations, only two other guests will join you for breakfast tomorrow morning at nine o'clock."

Amanda's brow furrowed. "How much snow are you expecting?"

"A couple of inches. But don't worry. The snow's not forecast until tomorrow night. So, you'll have plenty of time to explore the town."

In this weather? Not a chance.

Faith led Amanda past a Christmas tree and through open French doors. She stopped beside a cozy sitting room. "Your husband reserved the room across the hall from our parlor."

Amanda peered at the parlor's dark blue walls and tall ceiling. A decorated tree stood beside the white fireplace surround. Festive garland and an array of candelabras created an elegant mantel display. "This building has obviously been here a long time."

"For more than a century. It was built as a private home in 1890 and converted to an inn in 1996."

Was that why Paul had chosen this place? "My husband is an antique aficionado."

"In that case, he'll love our cabinet of curiosities." Faith pointed to a cabinet. "That's our version of a gift shop with items that reflect the inn's history."

"No doubt Paul will find something to add to his collection."

After relaying the inn's historical details, Faith unlocked the door across from the parlor. "Welcome to the Rose room."

Amanda pulled her suitcase into the Victorian-inspired space and laid her jacket on the four-poster-canopy bed. "The room's lovely."

"And our most romantic. Have a pleasant evening, Mrs. Sullivan, and let us know if you need anything." Faith stepped out and pulled the door closed.

Amanda set her purse on a marble-top writing desk beside two flutes and a bottle of Paul's favorite Champagne. After going to the trouble of planning a romantic getaway, why had he allowed work to interfere with his arrival? Maybe a few days alone would give her time to reflect on her second marriage without comparing it to her first.

Eager to settle in, Amanda tossed her phone on the bed and peeled off her jacket. After unpacking and stowing her suitcase in the closet, she dropped onto a wingback chair beside the fireplace and called Morgan.

"Hey, Mom. I assume you arrived safe and sound."

"A half hour ago." Amanda fingered the chair's lush upholstery while describing the room.

"Sounds like the kind of place Paul would pick."

Ignoring her daughter's snarky tone, Amanda pushed to her feet. "After traveling for hours, I'm in the mood for a relaxing bath."

"And I have to run. My study partner just showed up. I love you, Mom."

"I love you too, honey." Amanda set her phone on the bedside table, then strode to the bathroom and drew a bubble bath. As she lowered herself into the tub and leaned back, the warm water and rose-scented bubbles began to release the tension from driving miles on dark roads.

She closed her eyes and summoned memories of her honeymoon with Paul. The historic New Orleans bed-and-breakfast—her choice so they wouldn't have to leave town and be far from Morgan. If he'd chosen this inn and this room to recapture the passion they'd enjoyed during those two days, perhaps she could find a way to love him as much as she had loved her first husband. Was it even fair to compare the two men who were as different as summer and winter? She forced her thoughts to shift from Paul to her daughter—the beautiful young woman with a keen mind and a bright future.

By the time the water cooled and the bubbles dissolved, the tension in Amanda's neck and shoulders had disappeared. After donning her warmest pajamas, she retrieved her book and climbed into the king-size bed. Halfway through a chapter, heavy eyelids forced her to set the book on the nightstand. She yawned, then turned off the light and drifted into a deep sleep.

Refreshed and eager for a quiet morning reading beside a fire in her room, Amanda pocketed her phone, then stepped into the hall and followed the rich scent of coffee to the dining room. She filled a mug from a carafe on a side table, stirred in cream and sugar, and carried her morning caffeine fix to the table.

Moments after she sat, a stunning, dark-haired woman dressed in jeans and a sweatshirt strolled in from across the hall. "Good morning."

Amanda smiled. "Good morning."

The woman filled a mug, then sat across the table from Amanda. "I'm Erica Parker, from Asheville."

Amanda Sullivan, from New Orleans."

"At least I drove south. What brought you this far north?"

"My ninth wedding anniversary."

"Congratulations."

"Thank you. What about you?"

Erica took a sip of her coffee. "My thirty-seventh birthday."

"So far, this seems like the perfect place to celebrate."

"I suppose."

Footsteps striking the stairs announced a new arrival. "Good morning, y'all." The blonde—who appeared close to Morgan's age—exuded enthusiasm as she breezed in. After pouring a glass of orange juice, she chose the chair at the end of the table. "I'm Wendy Peterson. Where are you ladies from?"

Erica introduced herself, followed by Amanda.

"Oh my gosh." Wendy's face lit as she caught Amanda's eye. "We're practically neighbors. I live in Gulfport. Are you as excited as I am about seeing snow?"

Hardly. "A flurry or two will more than satisfy my curiosity."

"We'll experience more than a few flurries." Erica cradled her coffee mug. "Blizzards forecast across much of the country have already cancelled flights."

"Including my husband's." Wendy's tone hinted of disappointment. "At least I'll have more time to shop. Although, yesterday I didn't find a single store that sells maternity clothes."

Amanda lifted her mug off the table. "How far along are you?"

"Three months. This is our first."

A woman wearing a chef's coat bearing the inn's logo entered from the kitchen and set a tray on the table. "Good morning, ladies. I hope you're hungry because I've prepared eggs Benedict for you. Later today, I'll stock the refrigerator with plenty of food in case the snow prevents me from driving over tomorrow."

Amanda's eyes widened. "What happened to the inch or two expected for this area?"

"The weather is known to change quickly up here." The chef set the plates on the table. "The latest forecast calls for snow to begin tonight and continue until morning. Based on all the years I've lived in Blue Ridge, I'm confident that will add up to more than a couple of inches. Don't worry, you'll be plenty warm inside." The chef carried the tray back to the kitchen.

"Seems I need to add a pair of snuggly boots to my shopping list." Wendy spread a napkin across her lap and grabbed her fork. "Are you two here with someone or alone?"

"Alone for now." Erica cut a piece of her eggs. "My husband's scheduled to arrive tomorrow, unless weather delays his flight."

Amanda speared a strawberry. "Work complications postponed my husband's arrival."

Wendy swallowed a bite. "Since the three of us are alone, let's go shopping, then have lunch. There's a cute restaurant right behind the inn."

While Erica's eyes remained trained on her plate and Wendy described the restaurant, Amanda scooted away from the table to top off her coffee. She could beg off. After all, traipsing around town with strangers wasn't her idea of a relaxing day. On the other hand, if she decided to shop for a heavier coat and bumped into either of them, they'd consider her unsociable. If the chef was right about tomorrow, and the two women ended up her only companions, refusing the offer would be a bad idea. Amanda returned to her seat and eyed Erica. "What do you think?"

"I have a one-o'clock massage. Although I promised to buy my daughter an outfit."

Wendy pointed her fork at Erica. "How old's your daughter?"

"Seventeen."

"I know the perfect place to take you. How about we shop until one, then meet for lunch after your massage?"

Erica shrugged. "I suppose that'll work, if Amanda's onboard."

Surrendering seemed a more accurate description than 'onboard.' "We might as well." Regretting her dispirited tone, Amanda forced a smile. "Actually, I can't think of a better way to spend our first day in Blue Ridge."

Wendy faced Amanda. "Do you have children?"

"A twenty-one-year-old daughter. Morgan's a senior at LSU. She's studying industrial engineering."

"Wow, she sounds smart, and she's only two years younger than me."

Great. Amanda resisted rolling her eyes. She'd committed to spending the day with a stranger barely out of her teens. At least Erica was closer to her age, so she might as well make the best of the situation.

Chapter 5

Twenty minutes after returning to her suite, a ping sent Erika rushing to the sitting room. She plucked her phone off the coffee table and read Brian's text. "Flight cancelled. Will keep you posted on new arrival schedule." At least he had a valid reason for a change of plans. Grateful she wasn't facing hours of idle time, Erica grabbed her coat and headed down the hall to Mountain Mama's Coffee Lounge. Breathing the rich scents of coffee beans and flavorings, she ambled to a wingback chair catercorner to Amanda relaxing on the dark brown couch. "The coffee smells delicious."

"It tastes even better." Amanda cradled a paper cup in both hands. "I chose bananas foster latte."

"The perfect morning dessert."

"And a pretty decent hand warmer."

Erica eyed the mural behind the couch. The multiple shades of blue seemed to depict rolling hills. "Is this your first trip to Blue Ridge?"

"It's my first trip anywhere this far north."

Erica's head tilted. "Why'd you choose this town to celebrate your anniversary?"

"Believe me, if I had made the reservations, I'd be soaking up the sun on a South Florida beach. No offense intended."

"None taken. In fact, I'd have made the same decision. For now, I'll join you and indulge in a hand-warming, decadent morning dessert." Erica strode to the counter and ordered a mountain-mama latte to go. While waiting, she turned toward the glass doors and peered at the overcast sky. Why hadn't Brian chosen a warm destination to celebrate her birthday? At least Blue Ridge seemed like a nice enough town with lots of shops and a tourist train. Maybe she and Brian could go for a ride after he arrived.

"Here you go." The barista handed over the latte.

Erica took a sip. "Oh my gosh, this is amazing."

"That's our most popular flavor."

Wendy breezed in from the inn. "Isn't this the most adorable coffee shop?"

Erica eyed her hooded, leather jacket. "You look ready to brave the weather."

"I bought this coat and a pair of gloves at the cutest little shop yesterday."

Amanda moseyed over.

Wendy's brow pinched as she fingered the collar on Amanda's quilted jacket. "You'll freeze in that lightweight jacket. I know the perfect place for you to buy a snow-ready coat."

"Seems like a waste to spend the money, considering I'll only be here for a week."

"Spending a couple hundred is better than freezing, or staying cooped up inside the entire time. So come with me." Wendy pivoted and led the way out to the porch and down the stairs.

A cold gust sent a shiver racing through Erica and forced her to pull her fur collar tight around her neck. "Definitely feels like snow."

Amanda shoved her bare hands into her coat pockets and fell in step beside Wendy. "Where's that cute little shop you mentioned?"

"Across from the train station."

The women headed up the driveway and stepped onto the sidewalk. Wendy slowed in front of a Victorian-style house. "This is Southern

Charm restaurant. It closes today at four. I hope you don't mind, but I made a two-thirty reservation for the three of us."

Erica's jaw tightened. Who appointed the woman barely old enough to vote as their travel agent? The moment she opened her mouth to voice her opinion, Wendy resumed her pace without waiting for a response.

Amanda leaned close to Erica. "It's easier to go along."

Erica hesitated. How had the woman she barely knew interpreted her expression? Unless Amanda shared the same impression. "I suppose you're right." They caught up with Wendy and turned left at the corner. Following a brisk walk between the train and a park, they crossed another street and turned onto the sidewalk. Christmas music and holiday decorations created a festive vibe. Halfway up the block, Wendy led them into a boutique.

The woman behind the counter grinned. "Welcome back. How do you like your new coat?"

"I love it." Wendy nodded toward Amanda. "Now, my friend needs to buy one."

"I'll be happy to help." The woman stepped from behind the counter and approached Amanda.

Erica unbuttoned her coat and ambled to a rack of jackets while Wendy headed to a table displaying an array of sweaters. She had to admit that their unofficial tour guide's enthusiasm and take-charge approach reminded her of her daughter. Maybe it was their youth, although at thirty-seven she still considered herself young. Even so, when she was Wendy's age, Abby had already turned three. An image from her first marriage released a shiver unrelated to Erica's cold hands.

Wendy rushed over and held up two sweaters. "Which color do you think looks best?"

Grateful for the interruption, Erica blinked. "Actually, they both complement your eyes."

"You're so sweet. Should I pick one or buy both?"

Was she asking for permission? Erica shrugged. "Whatever makes you happy."

"You're right, I should buy both. There's a gorgeous red sweater over there that would look fantastic on you."

"Red is one of my favorite colors, and I appreciate the suggestion. But today I'm shopping for my daughter."

Wendy patted her tummy. "If I have a girl, I'll dress her in the most adorable outfits. She'll look like a little princess."

Amanda strode over, a hooded sweatshirt draped over her arm.

Wendy's head tilted. "Couldn't you find a coat you like?"

"It doesn't make sense to spend money on something I'll only wear for a few days. Besides, this sweatshirt plus my jacket will keep me plenty warm." Amanda eyed Erica. "Did you find something you can't resist?"

Erica shook her head. "So far, nothing has reached out and grabbed me."

Wendy nodded toward the display. "Except that red sweater." She set her purchases on the counter and handed over a credit card. After fingering an earring display, she tucked her hair behind her ear. "Kurt bought me these diamond studs for my birthday. He promised to buy me a diamond tennis bracelet for Christmas."

The saleswoman faced Wendy. "I'm sorry, Mrs. Peterson." Her voice was barely above a whisper. "Your card was declined."

"There must be a mistake. Try running it again."

"I already tried twice."

"Oh my goodness. I must have spent too much yesterday. If you hold those sweaters for me, my husband will pay for them once he arrives."

Was their young friend suffering from compulsive-shopper syndrome? Erica exchanged glances with Amanda. Was their self-appointed shopping guide aware her companions had overheard the conversation?

Wendy turned away from the counter, her eyes downcast, her cheeks flushed.

Yeah, she knew they'd heard. Erica spoke up, "I have a great idea. Why don't we forget shopping and check out that art and antique store we passed on the way here."

"I'm game." After paying cash for her sweatshirt, Amanda donned her new purchase under her quilted jacket. "My husband has a penchant for antiques, although I still can't tell the difference between reproductions and the real thing."

"Neither can I." Erica nudged Wendy's arm. "What do you say we go antiquing, and try to guess what old stuff is really worth?"

Wendy shrugged. "Sure, why not?"

Following ninety minutes of browsing through two antique shops and a general store, Erica followed her new friends onto the sidewalk and typed an address into her phone's app. "I need to head over for my massage. Are we still on for lunch?"

"Absolutely." Amanda pulled up her hood. "My treat."

"All right then, I'll see you ladies at Southern Charm." Fifteen minutes later Erica lay face down on a massage table. Thankful for the female therapist's silence, she imagined the summer vacation she'd spend with Abby. Basking in the sun. Swimming in the surf. Chatting about her daughter's future. Why hadn't Brian ever suggested adopting her daughter? Erica flinched. Where did that question come from? She dismissed the thought as irrational and let her mind wander back to summer.

After dressing and tipping her therapist, Erica slipped into her coat and stepped out to the cold. She snugged her fur collar tight around her neck and headed back toward town. Following a brisk walk, she met her lunch companions at the restaurant's entrance.

"Right on time." Amanda lowered her hood as they stepped inside. "How was your massage?"

"Relaxing."

"Come with me, ladies. "The hostess led them through the half-empty room to a table beside a fireplace and handed them menus. After taking orders for hot tea, she returned with a basket of freshly-baked biscuits.

Wendy slathered apple butter on a biscuit and took a bite. "If the restaurants I worked in had served biscuits this yummy, I'd have made more tips."

Erica looked up from her menu. "You waited tables?"

"At high-end restaurants. That's how I met Kurt. One Sunday afternoon he sat in my section and left me a ginormous tip. Two days later, he returned and invited me on a date."

"Would you believe that's how I met Brian?"

Wendy's brows arched. "No kidding?"

"I waited tables at a downtown restaurant. Brian had traveled to Asheville for business."

"How long before he asked you for a date?"

Erica's mind drifted back to the fourth night he had shown up in her section and invited her to dinner. "He came to town two more times before I accepted his dinner invitation." She reached for a biscuit. "Six months later he proposed."

"Do you still work at that restaurant?"

Erica shook her head. "I work a couple days a week in a gift store. It doesn't pay much, but I enjoy the customers, and it keeps me busy."

After their server delivered the tea and took their orders, Wendy nudged Amanda. "How'd you meet your husband?"

"I worked as a New Orleans tour guide. Paul was one of the tourists."

Wendy stirred sugar into her tea. "I bet he couldn't take his eyes off your gorgeous red hair. Do you still work as a guide?"

"I stopped working when I married Paul. Occasionally, I do a little volunteer work."

"If Paul is anything like Kurt, he doesn't want his wife to work." Wendy's eyes lit. "Given that I'm a blonde and Erica's a brunette, our guys obviously have different taste in women, but they have the same idea about romantic getaways. When they show up, we need to have dinner together. Until then it's just us girls. After lunch, we should wait for the snow on the inn's front porch?"

Amanda wrapped her fingers around her teacup. "I've experienced more than enough cold weather."

"Then how about waiting in the parlor? That way, as soon as we see flurries, we can rush outside."

Erica's eyes shifted from Wendy's wide-eyed expression to Amanda's pinched brow. "It is fun to watch the world slowly turn white."

Amanda blinked. "You two are welcome to brave the cold while I observe nature through a closed window."

A grin lit Wendy's face. "In the parlor?"

She shrugged. "Sure, why not."

Erica stifled a bemused smile. It seemed she and Amanda had both fallen victim to the pretty blonde's power of persuasion.

Chapter 6

Amanda tossed her jacket and sweatshirt on the bed. If she begged off from hanging out in the parlor, she could curl up with her book. Except dishonoring a commitment—even one made in haste—didn't sit well with her conscience. She pulled her pinging phone from her jeans pocket. A text from Morgan—she'd aced her first final. She responded with a heart emoji. No messages from Paul. Not that she'd expected any.

Amanda set her phone on the desk beside the Champagne. Instead of waiting for her husband to show up, maybe she should share the bottle with Erica and Wendy. That wouldn't do because Wendy was pregnant. She walked out of her room and stopped beside the front door. Her fingers traced the stained-glass border on the window while she peered across the porch. Would the lamp in the front yard provide enough light to view a winter wonderland without venturing outside? She spun toward the floorboards creaking behind her.

"I brought reinforcements." Erica approached carrying an uncorked wine bottle, a bottle of ginger ale, and three wine glasses.

Did she also have second thoughts about giving in to Wendy's request? "Smart move." Amanda followed the brunette into the parlor and dropped onto a winged armchair.

Erica set the bottles and glasses on the coffee table, then settled on the dark-brown sofa and pointed to the upright piano beside the window. "Do you play?"

"I did until my mother died."

"I'm sorry. Did she pass away recently?"

Amanda shook her head, her eyes downcast. "Twenty-four years ago."

"I imagine you still miss her."

"All the time."

Wendy bounced in and plopped on the chair beside Amanda. "The weather channel is calling this a once-in-a-century blizzard." She pulled her phone from her pocket and tapped the screen. "Airports are closing all across the country."

"As far south as Tennessee." Faith strolled in carrying a deli tray. "The local forecast has changed significantly during the past hour. We could end up with five inches of accumulation by morning."

Wendy's eyebrows peaked. "Wow, we could be snowed in for days."

Amanda released an involuntary groan.

"A lot of people around here are expressing the same sentiment." Faith set the tray beside the wine. "Our chef isn't keen on driving in the snow, so she stocked the fridge with sandwich ingredients, and she prepared a breakfast casserole and a lasagna. Baking instructions for both are on the kitchen counter."

Erica's brows drew together. "That much snow could bring down power lines."

"Not a problem. Our backup generator kicks in whenever there's a power loss. I'll be here until five, so don't hesitate to let me know if you need anything before I leave."

Erica pressed her palms together. "Thank you for making us feel like guests in your home."

Faith's eyes lit up. "Our owner wants every visitor to experience hospitality at its finest and leave with beautiful memories."

Wendy looked up from her phone. "So far, everything's perfect."

"Excellent. I'll leave you ladies to enjoy happy hour."

As Faith disappeared around the corner, Erica filled the glasses and handed the ginger ale to Wendy.

Hoping to compensate for her earlier groan, Amanda lifted her glass. "Here's to making memories."

"And new friends." Wendy took a sip, then ran her finger around the rim. "The only foster parent who cared about me drank ginger ale."

Amanda swallowed a sip of wine. "Were you raised by foster parents?"

"From the time I was five until I turned eighteen, I lived in seven different foster homes in Mobile." Wendy's chin tilted down. "My mother did the best she could to take care of me. Until she left me alone one day and never came back."

Amanda's brow furrowed. "Do you know what happened to her?"

Wendy shook her head. "I never met my father, and my grandmother was too sick to take me in, so I ended up in the foster system."

Erica crossed her leg over her knee. "Did you ever consider trying to find your mother?"

"Sometimes when I was shopping with a foster parent, I'd see a pretty blonde lady and wonder if she was my mother. Then I'd remember she left because she didn't want me."

"Your baby is blessed to have two loving parents." Erica's tone was filled with compassion.

"Kurt teared up when I told him I was pregnant." Wendy lifted her chin. "I thought he was disappointed until he cancelled his business trip and stayed home for two weeks to celebrate."

Amanda peered at Wendy's profile. "What does he do for a living?"

"He's a salesman for a big software company. What about your husband?"

"Paul's a civil engineer."

Wendy's head tilted. "Since your daughter's twenty-one and you're celebrating your ninth anniversary, you've obviously been married before."

Memories of her first husband played in Amanda's mind. "I was. For fourteen wonderful years."

"In that case, I assume the marriage didn't end in divorce?"

How much should she reveal to women she'd met a mere seven hours ago? After a week she'd never see either of them again, so why not open up. Especially since they faced hours of idle time with nothing to do but talk. "He was killed by a drunk driver."

Wendy pressed her hand to her chest. "That's so sad."

Amanda stared at her wine as memories bubbled up and spilled out. "I was six years old when my father abandoned me and my mother. She was forced to work two part-time jobs to pay the mortgage and put food on the table. When she was diagnosed with cancer, I dropped out of high school to take care of her. We sold the house to pay the bills and moved into a small apartment. After she passed, I paid off the medical expenses and lived off the last bit of money so I could finish my senior year. Then I took a job as a New Orleans tour guide."

"Did your first husband rescue you?"

Such a strange question. "If you call falling in love rescuing, then yes." Amanda eyed the fringed lamp on the piano. "Even though we struggled financially, we were happy, and Morgan adored her daddy." Amanda hesitated. She'd opened the door, why stop now? "My daughter never warmed up to Paul."

"The opposite is true for Abby." Erica swilled her wine. "She's crazy about Brian."

"He must be a good dad."

"That's part of the reason."

Amanda peered at the sadness clouding Erica's eyes. Someone had definitely hurt her or her daughter. Was she reluctant to reveal too much to strangers?

"Oh my gosh, it's snowing." Wendy bolted to her feet and yanked her phone from her back pocket.

Erica turned toward the window. "Relax, they're only flurries."

Wendy huffed. "It's still snow." She dashed out the front door.

"Are you going with her?"

"Not until there's something to see." Erica plucked a cheddar cube off the tray. "Wendy's a lot like the teenage girls who hang out at our house."

"Enthusiastic and easily distracted?"

Erica grinned. "Which makes her charming and at the same time annoying."

"The exuberance of youth and young love." Amanda sipped her wine and imagined Morgan meeting a charming young man and falling head over heels. Just then a loud knock sent her dashing from her chair. She opened the front door. "Did you forget your key?"

"Yeah." Wendy rushed in clutching her phone. "Snow is so soft—"

"And cold," added Erica.

Wendy plopped onto her chair. "Did you grow up in Asheville?"

"Baltimore. Abby and I moved to Asheville after I divorced her father."

"So, he doesn't see his daughter very often?"

Erica's brows snapped then released. "He's no longer part of our lives."

Wendy patted her tummy. "My baby will grow up with a daddy who loves his child."

Amanda's shoulder's tensed as her eyes shifted to Erica's pained expression. Was Wendy oblivious to her comment's insensitivity, or had she suffered from too much childhood trauma to notice? Whichever the case, it was time to lighten the mood. "With Christmas a few weeks away, why don't we talk about holiday stuff, beginning with movies. What's your favorite Christmas movie, Wendy?"

"Definitely *Elf*." She tapped her finger on her chin. "Or maybe *Home Alone*. They're both hilarious."

"Mine's *It's a Wonderful Life*, which was also my mother's favorite. What about yours, Erica?"

"*Miracle on 34th Street*, the updated version. Abby and I watch it every year. It reminds her of me and her stepdad."

Wendy sandwiched a slice of cheese between two crackers. "Last year Kurt and I put up a real tree and decorated it with blue and gold ornaments. It was so pretty."

Amanda's shoulders relaxed as the conversation continued to center on Christmas traditions and favorite gifts. As dusk settled over Blue Ridge, the snowfall accelerated and sent Wendy racing back to the front porch. "Should we join her?"

"Absolutely." Erica lifted off the sofa. "After all, this is your first experience with a real winter."

"Since you put it that way." Amanda crossed the hall to the Rose Room and pocketed her key, then donned her sweatshirt and stepped out on the porch. The lamplight cast a warm glow on fat snowflakes blanketing the lawn. She held her hand over the railing, delighting in the flakes kissing her palm seconds before melting. As the world turned white, she understood why Paul chose this place to celebrate their ninth anniversary. Maybe the magical setting would breathe new life into their relationship after all.

Chapter 7

Heavy snowfall obscured the view, while wind whipped across the porch and sent shivers racing up Erica's spine. She shoved her hands into her jean pockets, already regretting venturing outside without her coat and gloves, "I don't know about you ladies, but the inn is beckoning me inside."

"That makes two of us." Amanda pushed away from the railing, unlocked the door, and stepped inside.

Wendy followed them into the hall. "Know where we should hang out now?"

Hoping to eliminate the goosebumps, Erica vigorously massaged her arms. "What's wrong with the parlor?"

"Nothing, except I have chocolate truffles upstairs, and the library's part of my suite."

Erica caught Amanda's eye. "What do you think?"

"The temperature's definitely too cold to venture back outside, and I'd enjoy seeing more of the inn."

"I'll grab the wine and glasses, if you'll carry the tray."

"You're on."

Erica followed the women upstairs into the cozy library. While Wendy disappeared into the adjoining room, she set the wine bottle on one of the combo cabinet and bookshelves flanking the padded window seat. "This is the perfect spot to curl up with a book."

Amanda laid the deli tray on the coffee table, then lifted a marble rook off the chessboard. "We have an antique chess set in our den. Since Paul never suggested I learn how to play, I assume he bought it to impress people." She set the piece down. "Although other than a few of my friends, we never entertain guests."

Erica removed a book from the shelf. "If Paul's anything like my husband, he works too many hours to socialize."

Wendy returned and set a box of truffles beside the tray. "Kurt promised to cut back on work and spend more time at home after our baby's born." She settled on the leather couch and plucked a truffle from the box. "It'll be fun to have him around more, as long as he continues to make a lot of money."

"Raising a child is expensive." Amanda refilled her wine glass and settled on a wingback chair. "Unless your husband is independently wealthy, you'll likely need to economize a bit."

Surprised by Amanda's bold comment, Erica returned the book to the shelf and dropped onto the matching chair. "She's right about the expense."

Wendy crossed her leg over her knee. "Just because my credit card bounced this one time doesn't mean I spend too much money."

Uh-oh, we touched a nerve. "Before and after my first marriage, Abby and I were forced to live on a tight budget."

"Same with me," added Amanda.

Wendy pumped her foot. "Yeah, well I've had my fill of being poor. Even though Kurt is older than other men I've dated, I didn't marry him because he has money."

How much older? Did Kurt consider Wendy his trophy wife?

The corners of Wendy's mouth turned up. "He loves me like crazy, which is why he wants me to have lots of nice things."

So much for the lesson on frugality.

Wendy's foot stopped pumping. "Why did you divorce your daughter's father?"

Erica's back stiffened.

Amanda glanced from Erica to Wendy. "That's not an appropriate question."

"Why not? Especially since you both seem to think I need money advice."

"I don't mean any disrespect." Erica paused. "The one thing the three of us seem to have in common is less than ideal childhoods."

Wendy's head tilted. "Were you poor?"

"If your definition of poor is growing up in a three-room apartment with a mother hooked on drugs and a younger brother who found solace in a violent gang, then yeah."

"Where's your brother now?"

Erica rose, ambled to the fireplace, and topped off her wine. "He was killed on our building's front stoop in a drive-by shooting. If I'd been sitting closer to him—" She took a sip, then pivoted. "The bullets missed me by inches."

Amanda gasped as she pressed her hand to her chest. "How old were you?"

"A month shy of eighteen. My brother had just turned sixteen. Jack Nelson was one of the police officers who responded to a neighbor's 911 call after the gunshots. Every day for the next two weeks, he came back to check on me and my mother. Three months later, Mom died of an overdose. Jack raised money to help pay for the funeral."

"Sounds like he was one of the good guys." Wendy popped another truffle into her mouth.

Erica returned to her chair and swallowed a sip of wine. "You asked Amanda if Brian had rescued her. Well, the fact is, Jack was *my* rescuer. We married ten months after our first date, and for the first time in my life I felt secure—"

"Because he was a cop?"

Erica hesitated, then took another sip of wine. "Mostly because we lived in a safer section of Baltimore, and I no longer had to worry about scraping together enough money to buy food."

Wendy's head tilted. "So, how come you divorced him?"

Amanda tucked her ankle under her knee. "You already asked Erica that question."

"I know." Wendy uncrossed her legs. "But she didn't answer."

Erica's eyes shifted from Wendy to the chess set. *Her move.* "After our honeymoon, everything was fine. Jack didn't want me to work, so I quit my waitress job." She cradled her wineglass and stared at the golden liquid. "I was eight months pregnant the first time he hit me."

Amanda's forehead creased. "Did you report the incident?"

"To who? His police buddies? Besides, he apologized and promised it would never happen again. And it didn't until Abby was seven months old. He blamed his lapse on job stress and promised to control his temper."

Wendy pressed her hand to her throat. "When my second foster father drank too much, he couldn't control his fists either. The social worker didn't believe me when I told her he beat us." Her voice cracked. "Until the day she showed up and found my foster mother with a black eye and me with a swollen lip. Two days later, I moved in with a new family."

Erica set her glass on the coffee table, then sat beside Wendy and slid her arm around her shoulders. "No child deserves to bear the brunt of an adult's anger."

Wendy sniffled. "Did Jack ever hit Abby?"

"Thankfully no. That, plus the fact that he didn't hit me all that often is the excuse I used to stay with him far longer than I should have." Erica withdrew her arm and leaned back as a memory found its way to the surface. "Everything changed on Abby's seventh birthday. After her friends left our house, I asked what she had wished for when she blew out her candles." Erica swallowed the pain attacking the back of her throat. "She looked up at me with the saddest eyes I'd ever seen and said, 'I prayed for Daddy not to kill you, Mommy.'" Erica's chin dipped to her chest as the guilt Abby's revelation had unleashed returned with a vengeance. "All those years I had allowed my insecurity to keep me in a relationship that traumatized my child."

"Fear of the unknown is a powerful and blinding force." Amanda's tone hinted of compassion.

"That night, Abby and I packed a few belongings and fled to a women's shelter. Four months later, Jack agreed to an uncontested divorce to protect his career." Erica lifted her chin. "Even though we no longer lived together, I didn't trust him. So the same friend who drove me to the shelter loaned me the money to buy bus tickets to Asheville and rent an apartment. For the next four years, I waited tables and poured all my energy into raising Abby and paying off that loan. Then one night my daughter marched into my bedroom and announced that she wanted a new daddy."

Wendy scoffed. "Didn't we all."

"Brian had come to town three months in a row, and each time he invited me to dinner." Erica reached for a truffle. "In my mind, Abby's comment gave me permission to accept his invitation. A year later we legally changed my daughter's name to Abby Parker."

"And now here you are commiserating with two more fatherless women who are also waiting for their husbands to show up." Amanda retrieved her wine glass. "Talk about irony."

Shocked she'd revealed guarded secrets to strangers, Erica bit into the truffle. How was it possible the three of them ended up stranded at the same inn during a snowstorm?

Chapter 8

The moment daylight nudged Wendy's eyes open, she climbed out of bed and pulled the sheer curtain aside. Anticipation mingled with excitement as she eyed the six-inch snowdrift blanketing the windowsill. She exchanged pajamas for jeans and a long-sleeved sweater, then grabbed her new coat and dashed downstairs.

Amanda spun away from the front door, cradling a coffee mug. "You look bright and cheery this morning."

Wendy hastened to her side. "Have you been outside?"

"Are you kidding? It's way below thirty degrees out there."

"You should've bought a coat yesterday instead of that sweatshirt." Wendy drank in the view across the front porch. "Isn't it gorgeous?"

"In my opinion, a winter wonderland is best viewed from inside a warm room."

"That's like staring at a mug of hot chocolate and never tasting it."

Amanda faced her. "Why do you find snow so fascinating?"

"I'll show you." Wendy tossed her coat across a parlor chair, then rushed upstairs. Inside her bedroom, she opened the nightstand drawer and fingered the drawing of a little girl standing at a log cabin door with her arms stretched toward a man approaching across the snow. She hadn't shown the book to anyone since she turned twelve, so why the sudden impulse to share it with strangers? Her eyes drifted to the windowsill. She swiped her hand in an arc across the condensation covering the window. Amanda and Erica would understand why it meant so much to her, and why this trip was important. She wiped her hand on her jeans, then carried her treasure to the first floor and rushed toward the voices drifting from the kitchen.

Erica was sliding a casserole into the oven and Amanda was removing a bottle of orange juice from the fridge when Wendy stepped in and held up her book. "This is why I wanted to experience snow."

Amanda raised a brow. "Your fascination with winter comes from a children's book?"

A crushing sensation gripped Wendy as she hugged the treasure to her chest. Why had she trusted strangers? "*Sugar Snow* was the last gift my mother gave me before she disappeared."

"Oh, honey." Amanda reached out and touched Wendy's arm. "I didn't mean to come across as insensitive."

Wendy's eyes shifted to Erica's fingers pressed to her lips. Why hadn't she explained before showing them the book? "Whenever I felt sad, I'd read the story and imagine living in a log cabin with a family who loved me. Sometimes I'd dream about my mommy coming back and my daddy finding me and taking us both home." Her vision blurred as tears filled her eyes. "But neither of them ever showed up."

Erica rushed over and embraced Wendy. "One day you'll read that story to your child and describe what it's like to experience snow."

Wendy sniffled as she blinked back tears. "You understand, don't you?"

"With all my heart." Erica released her. "The one treasure I have from my childhood is an angel snow globe. When our neighbor gave it to me, she claimed guardian angels watched over me every time my mother couldn't."

Wendy dabbed at the tears spilling down her cheeks. "Do you believe in guardian angels?"

A smile lit Erica's face. "With all my heart."

"After breakfast, will you go outside with me?"

"We both will. Right, Amanda?"

"Absolutely." Amanda nodded toward the counter. "For now, how about we find out what's in that box from The Sweet Shoppe." She lifted the lid and held the box out to Wendy. "First choice goes to the lady eating for two."

Thankful for the diversion, Wendy set her book on the counter and peered at six assorted muffins. She selected the chocolate pastry and peeled back the baking cup while catching Amanda's eye. "What's your favorite childhood treasure?"

"Actually, it's a memory. Baking oatmeal-raisin cookies with Mom."

Erica reached into the box. "Every Christmas, Abby and I bake sugar cookies to share with our friends and neighbors."

As her new friends relayed stories about raising their daughters, Wendy imagined the memories she would create with her child. Snuggling the teddy bear Kurt had brought home from a trip. Playing in the surf. Building sandcastles. While enjoying the chef's breakfast casserole in the dining room, she shared the *Sugar Snow* story about a late spring snow. "Maybe one day, Kurt and I will take our baby to a fancy ski lodge somewhere up north."

"Abby had a ball building snowmen until she turned sixteen and claimed she was too mature to engage in such childish activities."

"Children grow up too fast." Amanda wiped her fingers with her napkin. "I remember Morgan's first day at school. Now she's one semester away from earning a college degree."

"Kurt and I will give our baby everything I didn't have, including the best education money can buy." Wendy tossed her napkin on the table. "Right now, I'm going outside."

Erica pushed up. "I'll join you as soon as I grab my coat."

Wendy scurried to the parlor. After donning her new coat, her pulse pounded as she stepped out onto the porch. She pulled her phone from her pocket and snapped photos of sunshine sparkling on the front lawn until the clouds shrouded the beams. A cold breeze nipped her nose as she slid her phone back into her pocket and scooped a handful of snow off the railing.

Erica stepped out. "Unless you're looking to experience your first frostbite, I suggest you wear gloves before handling more of the white stuff."

A shiver surged up Wendy's arm as she brushed off the snow and wiped her hand on her jeans. "Did Brian help Abby build snowmen?"

"One time, when I'd come down with a nasty cold." Erica dropped onto a white rocking chair. "But not since."

Gripping a cup of steaming coffee, Amanda joined them. "Did either of you remember about the self-locking doors?"

Wendy removed her gloves from her coat pocket. "I forgot."

"So did I." Erica pulled her collar tight around her neck. "Please tell us you remembered."

Amanda held up her key. "Trust me, there's no way I'd step foot out here without being prepared to escape the elements before my skin freezes." She pocketed her key and settled beside Erica. "So, Wendy, are you planning on venturing off the porch to play in the snow?"

"Everything looks too perfect to mess up." She dropped onto the chair beside Amanda. "Besides, I want to save that adventure until I can share it with my baby."

Erica peered around Amanda. "You're going to be a wonderful mother."

Wendy's chin dropped to her chest. How was that possible? No one had ever taught her how.

Amanda set her rocker in motion. "The first time my baby moved inside me, I fell so deeply in love the world seemed to stand still. A child is God's gift to mothers."

"Not all mothers," Wendy mumbled.

Amanda stopped rocking and faced Wendy. "You can't allow what happened in your childhood to define you. Just being here proves you're a loving mother who already adores her baby."

Wendy lifted her chin. "I suppose you're right." A wind gust releasing a snow shower from trees beside the driveway sent a chill skittering up Wendy's spine. No way she'd let the cold force her to scurry back inside before her friends gave in. She pulled out her phone and tapped a message to Kurt. *Loving the snow. Can't wait to snuggle with you on the front porch.* She attached a photo of the lawn, then pressed send. Would he respond this time? She waited. A dark cloud floated overhead, dimming the sunlight. Maybe bad weather had knocked out the power, leaving Kurt stranded with a dead battery. Wendy pocketed her phone and tuned into the stillness disrupted by an occasional gust whipping through the trees. Enough bad thoughts. She closed her eyes and imagined rocking her baby on her condo balcony while listening to the surf lapping onto the shore.

"I think my husband's involved in an affair." Erica's voice was barely above a whisper.

Wendy's eyes popped open. *Where did that come from?*

"I knew when we married that Brian's job required him to work out of town. For the past few years, when he has been home, he's seemed more preoccupied than normal."

Wendy peered at Erica's downcast eyes. "If your husband was cheating on you, he wouldn't have planned this romantic getaway."

"Unless this trip is his way of easing a guilty conscience."

Wendy stopped rocking. "If you ask me, a husband who was cheating would compensate by giving his wife an expensive piece of jewelry."

Amanda scoffed. "Are you speaking from experience?"

Wendy bristled. Kurt would never cheat on her. "I'm just saying, unless Brian shows up with a diamond bracelet, Erica has nothing to worry about."

Erica splayed her left hand. Other than a diamond-studded wedding band, Brian had never given her jewelry. Not that she minded. After all, she'd take her beautiful home over diamonds any day. "I suppose stress over his job could explain why he's seemed distant."

Wendy set her rocker in motion. "What does he do?"

"He helps save struggling businesses. In a way he's a turnaround expert."

"Well, there you go. Like Kurt, Brian has an important job that keeps his mind preoccupied." Wendy snapped her fingers. "Know what we should do now? Create a family of snow people."

Amanda blew warm air on her fingers. "What happened to not messing up the lawn?"

"Not full-size snowmen." Wendy bolted off the rocking chair and scooped a handful of snow off the railing. She shaped the snow into a ball and set it on the cleared spot. After adding two balls atop the first, she stepped back. "Hmm." Wendy hesitated, then spun toward Amanda. "I need your key."

"Why? Are you giving up?"

"No way."

Amanda cocked her head.

"I can't unlock the door without it." Wendy held out her hand. "I promise to bring it back."

"All right." Amanda set her coffee mug on the table between her chair and Erica's, then fished the key from her pocket and handed it over.

After scurrying to unlock the door, Wendy stashed the key in her jeans pocket and disappeared inside.

"What do you suppose she's up to?"

"Your guess is as good as mine." Erica sidled to the railing. "What I do know, is the sooner we create our young friend's miniature snow family, the sooner we can all go inside."

"In that case, let the fun begin." Amanda joined her. After forming three snowballs, she rushed to the front door as it swung open. "Is the key still in your pocket?"

Wendy huffed as she brushed past Amanda and set a box of raisins, a jar of cherries, and a bag of pretzel sticks on the table. "I brought everything I could find to make our snow people look more real." She yanked the key from her pocket and dangled it in front of Amanda. "And I didn't forget, so you can close the door now."

Amanda pulled the door closed. "It's not that I doubted you—"

"Just because I forgot my key one time doesn't mean I'm irresponsible."

"Of course, you're not." Erica's shoulder and neck muscles tightened. "Amanda just wanted to make sure we wouldn't be stranded out here."

"I know." Wendy twisted off the jar lid. "Cherries will make cute little noses, don't you think?"

"Red nose snow people are definitely creative." Amanda sauntered to the railing and scooped a handful of snow.

The tension gripping Erica's muscles subsided as she opened the box and pressed two raisins into her miniature snowman's face. At least for the moment she had something to keep her hands busy and her mind off her suspicions about Brian. Besides, maybe Wendy's comment about pressures forcing him to focus on work instead of his family had merit. She'd probe that possibility soon after he showed up.

Chapter 9

M entally kicking herself for not buying gloves, Amanda stepped back from the railing and brushed snow off her ice-cold fingers. "I imagine this is the first time twenty-two snowmen stood at attention on the inn's railing."

"Or any railing anywhere." After endowing her final snowman with pretzel arms, Wendy crouched and snapped a selfie of her and her creation.

Erica pulled off her gloves and blew warm air on her fingers. "A picture for posterity?"

Wendy nodded. "And to share with my online friends."

Typical. "Are you a social-media fanatic?"

Wendy straightened and eyed Amanda. "What do you consider a fanatic?"

"Someone who...hold on." Amanda pulled her vibrating phone from her jacket pocket. "A message from my daughter. There's half an inch of snow on the ground in Baton Rouge, which is a big deal for southern Louisiana." She texted a photo of their handiwork along with an explanation. Her daughter's response triggered a laugh. "Morgan wants to know if we started happy hour early."

Erica tucked her hands into her coat pocket and headed to the door. "Right now, a steaming cup of hot chocolate would make me happy."

"Count me in." Amanda unlocked the front door and stepped inside.

Erica followed, then paused at the threshold and peered over her shoulder. "Hey, Wendy, are you coming with us, or do you plan to stay outside and stand guard over the Blue Ridge snow family?"

"No way I'm missing out on hot chocolate." She dashed past Erica and scurried down the hall.

Amanda shook her head. "If I'd known that's all it took to make you come inside, I would have suggested we indulge before my fingers turned into popsicles."

Wendy paused at the dining-room entrance and peered at Amanda. "That wouldn't have made a bit of difference."

"I suppose it wouldn't." Amanda peeled out of her jacket and sweatshirt as Wendy disappeared around the corner. "What is it about her that compelled two rational women to endure the cold for more than two hours?"

"Youthful enthusiasm." Erica slipped off her coat. "And a distraction from reality."

"There is that." Amanda headed into the Rose room and kicked off her shoes. After hanging her jacket and sweatshirt on the shower-curtain rod, she turned on the sink spigot. While holding her hands under warm water, Erica's comment about her husband's fidelity floated across Amanda's mind. Even though Paul had seemed distant, she'd never entertained the idea that he could be involved with another woman. For good reason—his career and antique collecting seemed to be his mistresses. What if she was wrong? She dismissed the notion, then dried her hands and made her way to the kitchen.

Wendy hummed while setting a saucepan on the gas flame.

Erica removed three mugs from a cabinet. "We found all the ingredients."

"Including whipped cream." Wendy stirred the liquid, sending a mouthwatering chocolate scent wafting from the saucepan. "This is what

I imagined university life would be like—talking about guys and sharing experiences with my sorority sisters. Did either of you go to college?"

Erica shook her head. "I wanted to but didn't have the resources."

Amanda's last day of high school before she quit to take care of her mother drifted to her mind. "I'd hope to save enough money from my tour-guide job to enroll in community college. Then I met my first husband and abandoned the idea."

"At least the three of us were smart enough to marry successful men." Wendy turned off the burner and poured the cocoa into three mugs.

After topping off the beverages with whipped cream, Erica lifted a box off the counter. "Hot chocolate and yummy muffins."

"The perfect lunch for the snow-family creators." Amanda gripped her mug and followed her companions to the dining room.

Wendy set her drink on the table and pulled her phone from her pocket. "Yay. A text from Kurt. He says, 'Sorry for weather delay. Glad you're enjoying the inn. Love you and our baby.' Isn't he the sweetest guy? I can't wait for you two to meet him."

Amanda stared at the whipped cream giving in to the hot liquid. Had she ever loved Paul as much as Wendy seemed to love her husband? She swallowed the lump rising in her throat. Was it possible her own feelings or lack thereof were the reason their relationship had cooled?

"You seem deep in thought."

Amanda blinked. Did Erica expect a response? Sharing her feelings didn't come easy, and yet here she was, stranded with two women who had opened up about their personal lives. Maybe verbalizing her thoughts would help bring clarity. Amanda filled her lungs, then slowly released the air. *Here goes.* "Losing my first husband to a senseless accident broke my heart into a million pieces. I married Paul hoping he could mend it. For months, I've blamed the rift in our relationship on his absence. Now I'm beginning to think at least some of the fault lies with me." Amanda eyed Erica's compassionate expression. She seemed to understand. "The truth is I never loved Paul as much as I loved my soulmate."

Wendy selected a muffin. "What's your soulmate's name?"

Amanda hesitated as her mind drifted to her favorite photo—her happy family of three celebrating Morgan's last birthday before the accident. Why did she always hesitate to speak his name? Because losing him was still painful. "Preston Smith."

"Funny." Wendy peeled the wrapper off her muffin. "You married two guys whose names begin with P."

Amanda shot the young woman an incredulous look. She'd just shared an intimate detail, and that was the only response the twenty-three-year-old could come up with?

Wendy's muffin halted inches from her mouth. "What?"

She obviously didn't have a clue, so why waste energy trying to explain. "Nothing." Amanda sipped her drink, then swiped whipped cream from her upper lip.

"If you ask me, this is the perfect place to show Paul how much you love him."

From clueless twenty-three-year-old to self-styled relationship expert in fewer than thirty seconds? Amanda failed to stifle a sarcastic laugh.

Wendy bit into her muffin, seemingly oblivious to the irony in Amanda's retort.

Erica cleared her throat as her focus shifted from Wendy to Amanda. "The forecast calls for warmer weather tomorrow."

Wendy's eyes widened. "Warm enough to melt our snow family?"

"Based on my experience in Asheville, probably not. At least not in the shade."

Relieved by the diversion, Amanda removed the last muffin from the box. As the lemon-filled center delighted her tastebuds, she pictured the lacy teddy tucked away in a nightstand drawer. Maybe Wendy was also right about the inn. She pulled her phone from her pocket and typed a text to Paul. "Looking forward to spending time alone with you." She added a heart emoji, then pressed send, hoping he'd eventually respond.

Chapter 10

Light peeking around the shade covering the front-porch window eased Amanda's eyes open. She lifted her phone off the nightstand. Seven-fifteen. A twinge of guilt pricked her conscience over last night's feigned headache to escape a second evening of chitchat. Avoiding Erica and Wendy this morning would be beyond the pale. If enough snow melted, she could brave the cold and take a long walk. Why hadn't she bought a pair of warm boots when she had the chance? Amanda trudged to the bathroom, turned on the shower, and stepped into the tub.

As the hot water flowed down her body, images of life with Preston floated up from her memory bank. Pushing Morgan's stroller while meandering beside the Mississippi River. Picnicking in the park. The shotgun house they'd mortgaged to the hilt, then spent every spare dollar to turn the rundown building into their home. If they had invested some of that money in life insurance, would she have married Paul? The unexpected question compelled her to squeeze shower gel onto a cloth and scrub away the second stab of guilt she'd experienced in fewer than ten minutes.

A half hour after waking, Amanda dressed in jeans and a pullover sweater, then stepped into the hall and peered out the front door. The clear blue sky stood as a stark contrast to the white world beneath. She glanced at her phone's weather app—thirty-six degrees with a high of forty by early afternoon. Her eyes drifted to the railing. How long before the snow family melted into messy puddles and relegated her and her cohorts to cleanup duty?

Amanda pivoted from the door and tuned into the silence. Were her companions sleeping in, or had they seen through her headache ruse and chosen to avoid her? The floor creaked as she tiptoed past the staircase and made her way to the kitchen. After brewing a pot of coffee, she filled a mug and carried it to the front parlor. She opened the piano lid and ran her finger along the ivory keys yellowed from age. After everyone awakened, maybe she'd find out how much remained of her piano-playing skills.

Amanda settled on the sofa and lifted *The Blue Ridge Scenic Railway* off the coffee table. She leafed through the book depicting a photographic history of the train. Preston would have loved riding along the Toccoa River, enjoying the view. Her pulse quickened as reality struck home. She had no idea whether or not Paul would find a train ride appealing. If she made a sincere effort to set their relationship on a new course, would Paul spend more time at home? At least it was worth a try.

Still wearing pajamas, Erica had just propped her feet on the sitting-room coffee table when the floor creaked in the hall outside the door. Must be Amanda, given she hadn't heard footsteps on the stairs. Had Amanda's headache been real or a mere excuse to avoid spending another evening with her and Wendy? Either way, she couldn't blame Amanda, especially since she'd retired to her own suite five minutes later. She'd spent the first half hour chatting with Abby and sharing pictures of their snow-inspired activities. Afterwards she'd changed into pajamas, climbed into bed, and channel surfed until she found a TV show that captured her attention then lulled her to sleep.

Erica sipped the orange juice she'd carried from the kitchen a half hour earlier, then checked her weather app. Frigid temperatures continued to keep the northern half of the country snowbound. She lifted Brian's 'happy birthday' note off the end table. Would he be disappointed she hadn't waited to share the wine with him? When the weather cleared, she could buy another bottle, or wait until after she'd discovered the real reason he'd scheduled the trip.

A stomach grumble compelled Erica to swallow the rest of her juice and head straight to the bathroom to turn on the shower. As she stepped under the warm water, a sinking sensation gripped her stomach. Had Amanda's headache and her own claim of exhaustion created a rift between the three women? What if they remained isolated for several more days? If she had stayed in Asheville longer, the snow would have prevented her from leaving home. But she hadn't, which meant she needed to make sure the relationship with her new companions remained intact, at least until their husbands arrived.

After towel-drying her hair, Erica donned yoga pants and a long-sleeved shirt, then stepped out to the hall. No one in sight. She followed the coffee aroma to the kitchen and poured a cup. Maybe after preparing the morning brew, Amanda returned to her room.

Erica dropped a slice of bread into the toaster and peered out the window. Snow still covered the sidewalk beside the building. How soon would it take for the sun to melt the snow atop the freestanding garage? What about the front-porch display?

After slathering butter and jam on her toast, Erica strode to the dining room and sat at the table closest to the window. If Brian was involved with another woman, would he prefer hanging out with her new friends and their spouses instead of spending time alone with her? She'd find out soon enough.

Nausea sent Wendy racing to the bathroom to splash cold water on her face. When the queasiness subsided, she peered at her pale skin. Had Amanda and Erica bailed because she was young enough to be their daughter, or were they jealous of the love she shared with her husband? Thankful she didn't have to worry about Kurt, she wiped the sweat from her forehead with a hand towel.

Another bout of nausea triggered dry heaves. Wendy gripped the vanity until the sensation passed. Hoping food would cure whatever ailed her, she donned her bathrobe, then trudged down the stairs and into the dining room.

Erica spun toward her. "Good morning."

"What's the best cure for nausea?"

"Ginger ale and crackers were my go-to cure for morning sickness." Erica followed Wendy into the kitchen and pulled a bottle from the fridge.

Amanda strolled in and set her coffee mug on the counter. "Dry toast always did the trick for me." She brushed hair away from Wendy's cheek. "Morning sickness is a bummer but harmless and short-lived."

Erica poured ginger ale over ice and handed Wendy the glass. "Sip it slowly."

As the cool liquid slid down her throat, the nausea subsided. "I'm starving, so how about we raid Mountain Mama's pastry case?"

Erica removed a box of crackers from the cabinet. "You should take it a bit slow. Besides, the lounge is closed."

"I checked last night, and the door from the inn is unlocked." Wendy swallowed another sip. "I'm feeling a hundred-percent better."

"That was one fast cure." Erica's brows lifted. "What do you think, Amanda?"

"Miraculous recovery."

Wendy planted her hands on her hips. "What about hanging out at Mountain Mama's?"

Amanda shrugged. "It beats going outside."

"Okay, then. I'll meet you two in the lounge in fifteen minutes." Wendy set her glass on the counter, then dashed to her room. Choosing to believe Amanda and Erica's excuses had been legit, she peeled out of her pajamas. Following a quick shower, she pulled her hair into a ponytail and peered at her image. Although Kurt called her a natural beauty, she always relied on a little makeup. After enhancing her features, she slipped into loose-fitting running pants and an off-the-shoulder sweater. She stole one more glance in the mirror, then stuffed her room key in her pocket and returned to the first floor.

Wendy eased to the front door and gazed at the sun glistening on the snow family. How long before every trace of the miniature village disappeared? She stepped onto the porch, propped the door open, and walked along the railing. Stopping beside the snow person she'd named Snowball, she lifted the miniature creation off the railing. Ice-cold hands sent her racing to the kitchen. She yanked the freezer door open and placed Snowball inside, then doused her hands with warm water. A smile formed as she dried her skin and scurried to Mountain Mama's. She sidled beside Erica standing at the counter. "Now that the temperature is above freezing, how fast will the snow melt?"

"In the direct sunlight, fairly fast." Erica removed a bagel from the pastry case, then set a five-dollar bill on the counter.

"When I was a kid, it was fun building sandcastles, but it was sad when the tide washed them away." Wendy eyed the pastry selection. "At least

Snowball won't fall victim to Mother Nature." She grabbed a muffin and carried it to the sofa facing the double-glass doors while Erica settled beside Amanda.

Pleased at the prospect of spending the day with her new friends, Wendy initiated a conversation about their childhoods. Every time a sad story crept in, she countered with a fun event—even though she exaggerated most of them. Hours after she devoured her third muffin, movement on the porch caught her eye. "Faith just climbed onto the porch with some guy. Maybe he's her husband or the inn's owner."

"We're about to find out." Amanda nodded toward the door.

Faith entered from the inn. "I'm glad you ladies are making yourselves at home."

Erica's head tilted. "Are you opening the lounge?"

"Not until tomorrow." Faith paused. "I'm here because a friend asked to meet with the three of you before the inn officially reopens."

Wendy scooted to the edge of the sofa. "Is he a reporter wanting to write an article about three ladies stranded at a romantic inn?"

"That would be a good story, but no. He's waiting for you in the dining room as soon as you're ready to join him." Faith spun around and hurried out the glass doors, making it clear the women were on their own.

"Why would some guy want to meet with us?" Wendy's brows arched. "Unless he's an author writing a book about Blue Ridge tourists."

"The way I see it, we have two choices." Erica pushed off her chair. "Either stay here and play twenty questions, or head over to the dining room and find out why the guy braved the weather to talk to us."

Chapter 11

Amanda's chest tightened as the memory of a life-changing phone call from years earlier skated across her mind. Was Faith's friend a police officer waiting to inform them about an accident? Except...if something had happened to one of their husbands, whoever waited for them would have requested a private meeting. She breathed deeply as common sense prevailed, and she followed Wendy and Erica to the dining room.

A good-looking young man stood at the end of the table. Dressed in slacks, an open-collared shirt and a sportscoat, he appeared both professional and approachable. Amanda's eyes drifted to a manila envelope lying on the table.

"Thank you for joining me." He motioned for them to sit. "Please."

Hoping his expression would reveal some sort of clue, Amanda studied the man's brown eyes as she and Erica settled beside each other.

Wendy opted for a seat on the opposite side of the table and turned toward the man. "Are you an author planning to write a story about three women stranded in an inn during a snowstorm? Or maybe you're a salesman looking to sell us some kind of vacation plan. My husband's a salesman—" Comments about Kurt's job spilled out as if Wendy were avoiding discovery of the reason they'd been summoned.

"I'm not a writer or a salesman." The man brushed his finger through his thick dark hair. "My name's Chris Armstrong. I'm an attorney with a local law firm."

"I don't understand." Erica's brow pinched. "Why are you meeting with us? Have we done something wrong?"

"Not at all." He made eye contact with each, then tapped his fingers on the envelope. "A week ago, I received this in the mail. There was no return address, which aroused my suspicions. However, a thorough investigation has proven the contents legitimate." He paused for a long moment. "There's no easy way to break the news, except to follow the sender's instructions." He removed three enlarged photographs from the envelope and laid them face up on the end of the table.

Cold fingers of fear skittered up Amanda's spine as her eyes scanned the pictures.

Wendy gasped while grabbing the photo closest to her. "Is this someone's idea of a cruel joke?"

The attorney swallowed. "I understand how difficult—"

"No!" Wendy sprang to her feet and bolted from the room.

"I can't deal with this right now." Erica's voice quivered as she lifted off her chair and staggered across the hall to her suite.

Amanda remained frozen. She stared unseeing at the kitchen door as words tumbled from the attorney's tongue and triggered a massive headache. How was all this possible? Unless Wendy's joke theory had merit. But why would anyone go to such lengths to fool three strangers?

"I realize this is a lot to take in—"

Amanda blinked. "This isn't some insane person's cruel prank, is it?"

"I wish it was, but unfortunately everything I've told you is true." The attorney handed Amanda a business card. "I've shared enough for now.

Call me in the morning if you and the other ladies are ready to absorb more details."

Amanda locked eyes with the attorney. "What do you mean by more?"

"We'll talk again tomorrow." Chris broke eye contact, then lifted the envelope off the table and walked out.

Amanda's heart pounded against her ribs as she gaped at the two remaining photographs. Only a psychopath could have pulled that off. In her wildest imagination, she would never have imagined such a demented act. Yet here she was, hundreds of miles from home, facing undeniable reality. She plucked the pictures off the table, then trudged to the front door. Her eyes focused on the melted snow dripping from the railings. How many hours before the frozen family ceased to exist?

Breaths caught in Amanda's lungs as she clutched the photos to her chest and whipped away from the view. The sudden impulse to crawl into bed and pull the covers over her head sent her rushing into her room. She dropped onto the chair and stared at the white rose print on the gray-green fabric adorning the window wall. Her eyes closed as she envisioned the dozen roses Preston had given her to celebrate their fourteenth anniversary—a week before his accident. If only she could turn the clock back to that fateful day and force him to stay home.

Cottonmouth triggered a cough and forced Amanda to her feet, sending the photographs fluttering to the floor. She rushed into the bathroom and filled a glass with water. After swallowing mouthfuls, she spun away from the mirror. Why had she stayed in the dining room after Wendy and Erica fled? Because someone had to hear the truth, that's why. Now the burden to relay those details rested squarely on her shoulders.

Amanda padded from the bathroom and dropped onto the chair. How long should she wait? An hour? Until morning? Heat flushed through her body as she scooped the photos off the floor and stole another glance. More time wouldn't change reality staring back at her from the pictures.

Clutching the evidence to her chest, Amanda forced her legs to carry her from her room and down the hall to the Sycamore suite. The door stood open. She stepped into the empty sitting room. "Erica?"

Silence.

She returned to the hall and eased to the staircase. Her heart drummed against her ribs as she climbed up to the second floor.

Erica faced the window at the end of the hall.

Amanda moved close. "Are you okay?"

"Some suspicions come from irrational fear and are nothing more than figments of the imagination. Others turn out to be far worse than imagined."

Amanda peered at the sunlight glistening on the front lawn. Blades of grass peeked through the snow at the edge of the sidewalk. "Have you talked to Wendy?"

"I wanted to, but I didn't know what to say." Erica wiped a smudge off the glass. "Those pictures are real, aren't they?"

"I'm afraid they are."

"If I had learned how to shift gears, I could've driven Brian's sports car here." A soft moan escaped as Erica's shoulders curled forward. "He rarely takes it out of the garage."

Amanda's stomach churned. What was her new friend talking about? What about Wendy? "The three of us need to talk."

Erica filled her lungs and slowly released the air. "I know."

Amanda squeezed her eyes shut hoping to summon enough courage to relay the details Chris Armstrong had revealed.

Chapter 12

Wendy hummed while scanning rows of books displayed in the library. If she started reading today, she could finish a few chapters before Kurt arrived. But which book? There were so many to choose from. Maybe one of the classics. Wendy stepped around a wingback chair, spun the antique globe displayed on the other bookcase, and imagined traveling to faraway places. After their baby was born, she and Kurt could take a trip to Italy or maybe Hawaii. Someplace exotic and fun.

A tap drew her eye away from the globe. She crossed the room and pulled the door open. "Perfect timing." The moment her friends settled on the sofa, Wendy scooted to her bedroom and grabbed the box of truffles off the mantel. She peered into the mirror over the fireplace. Were her pink cheeks a sign of the pregnant-lady glow everyone talked about?

Wendy returned to the library, set the box on the coffee table, and lifted the lid. "There are three left, one for each of us." She straightened and swept her arm in a wide arc. "Kurt's gonna love this cozy room. I'm thinking we should furnish one of our condo bedrooms as a library and buy lots of books." She dropped onto a chair and crossed her leg over her knee. "Do you suppose the restaurants will open tomorrow? Which one should we try next? I'm in the mood for spaghetti, or maybe a loaded pizza. Have you ever tried pizza with cheese stuffed in the crust? It's yummy."

Amanda's heart ached for the young woman sitting across from her. She had expected Wendy to display a bit of disbelief but not total denial. Somehow, she had to approach the subject with an abundance of compassion. "Pizza is one of my favorite treats." Keeping her eyes focused on Wendy, she laid the photographs she'd brought into the room facedown beside the truffle box. "I'm curious. What was your first thought when Mr. Armstrong showed us the pictures?"

Wendy tilted her head. "I wondered why anyone would send him my wedding photo. But when I brought it up to my room, I took another look and understood that Kurt had sent it as a hint."

Erica's brow pinched. "A hint about what?"

Wendy held up her right hand and splayed her fingers. "I think he's bringing me a new ring. Maybe with diamonds and emeralds."

Amanda's mouth fell open. Had Wendy ignored the other pictures, or had shock blocked the images from her mind?

"My sweet husband likes to surprise me. The last time he came home from a trip, he brought me an adorable white teddy bear for our baby's room."

Amanda swallowed against the dryness in her throat. This wouldn't be easy. "Know what? I'd like to take another look at that picture."

Wendy pumped her foot. "Why?"

"We can compare it to the other photos Mr. Armstrong showed us."

"I don't want to."

She's terrified to face the truth. "I understand, honey. But we don't have a choice. Is the photo in your bedroom?"

Wendy's foot pumped faster.

Erica glanced at Amanda. "I'll find it for her." She strode into the adjoining room.

Memories returned of comforting Morgan the night her seventeen-year-old boyfriend broke up with her. Today, Wendy needed ten times the strength she'd found to help Morgan deal with reality. "My daughter and I always sit together when we have something important to talk about." She patted the seat beside her. "Why don't you come sit here."

Wendy's foot stilled. "Kurt loves me. You'll see." She lifted off the chair, then grabbed her phone off the bookcase. After settling beside Amanda, she pulled up a photo. "This is a picture our neighbor took of me and Kurt on the beach in front of our condo."

Amanda stared at the man holding hands with bikini-clad Wendy.

"I found it." Erica returned and handed the photo to Amanda, then settled on the vacated wingback.

Drawing on her maternal instincts, Amanda slid her arm around Wendy's shoulders. "Let's begin with your picture." She placed the photo of Wendy dressed in a strapless wedding gown standing beside her groom on a beach. "Tell me what you see."

Wendy pressed her hand to her chest. "The most handsome and generous man. He bought me the cutest sports car. I like to drive it with the top down."

Amanda glanced at the young woman's profile, then turned the second photo face up. "Tell me about this picture."

Wendy tapped her finger on the photo. "That's you."

Amanda caught a glimpse of Erica's pained expression as she flipped the third photo over. "And this one?"

"That's Erica. If my baby is a girl, she might want to wear my wedding gown when she falls in love. Maybe she'll also get married on the beach."

How could she not see? "Take a close look at the men standing beside me and Erica."

Wendy's brow pinched. "Those are fake. Don't you know that people can do all kinds of things to make pictures look real?"

"You're right, honey. But these pictures *are* real—"

"That's not possible." Wendy tapped her phone, then held it in front of Amanda's face. "That's the last text from Kurt. He loves me and our baby."

"Stop ignoring what's right in front of you." Erica rose to her feet. "The man standing beside you in that picture on the table is the same man standing beside me and Amanda in the other photos."

"No!" Wendy closed her eyes and cupped her hands over her ears.

"I don't mean to come across as insensitive—" Erica dropped beside Wendy. "But no matter how painful it is, we need to face the truth."

Hoping to soften the blow, Amanda pulled Wendy close. "He claims his real name is Gunter Benson."

"I don't believe you." Wendy bolted to her feet, dashed to the bedroom, and slammed the door shut.

Amanda curled her left hand into a fist. "The man the three of us married is a con artist who preys on vulnerable women. All those weeks he claimed to be working, he was with one of his other families."

Erica's shoulders curled forward. "How could we have been so blind?"

"You and I both had suspicions—"

"That he might be involved in an affair, not that he's a polygamist." Erica grimaced. "What possessed him to marry three women, and why did he want us to meet?"

"All I know is there's a lot more to the story."

Sobs emanating from the bedroom sent Amanda rushing from the library. Failing to hold back tears, she knelt beside the unmade bed and placed her hand on Wendy's trembling shoulder. How could a man inflict so much pain on an innocent young woman he claimed to love? "Erica and I are here for you, honey."

As the sobs gave way to whimpers, Wendy pulled her knees up to her chest. "I want to go to sleep now."

Amanda lifted off the floor and pulled a blanket over the young mother. "We'll be next door if you need us." She followed Erica back to the library and settled on the sofa. "We shouldn't leave her alone."

"You're right." Erica grabbed the king off the chessboard. "The three of us are nothing more than pawns in some sort of sick game." She dropped onto the sofa. "A blonde, a redhead, and a brunette. The only one missing is a silver-haired wife."

"Based on our ages when he married us, he obviously prefers younger women." Amanda stared at the photos lying side by side. Other than the fact they lived in different states, why had he chosen the three of them? Last night...their stories. Her brows knitted together. "Our history is the answer."

"What are you talking about?"

"The reason he chose the three of us."

"I don't understand."

"The two factors Wendy, you, and I had in common when Gunter met each of us. We had no family to turn to, and we weren't financially stable. He chose women who needed what he claimed to offer."

"Stability and a comfortable lifestyle."

"So it seems."

"Which of the three jobs he claimed do you suppose was legit?" Erica held up the chess piece. "And how did he have enough money to support three families?"

"The attorney called him a con artist, which most likely means his job was cheating people out of their money." Amanda flipped the photos over and slammed them face down on the coffee table.

"He'd obviously perfected his game." Erica curled her fingers around the chess piece. "I don't know which is worse, marrying an abusive man or a criminal. How can I tell Abby the truth without breaking her heart?"

"At least Gunter Benson didn't father either of our daughters. As devastating as this nightmare is for the two of us, the truth is far worse for Wendy."

Erica set the chess piece back on the board. "Did the attorney explain why that man wants the three of us to meet, or why he chose this town to shatter our lives?"

"I've told you everything I know." A sudden wave of exhaustion wearied Amanda to her bones. She collapsed against the back of the sofa. "Hopefully, he'll answer all of our questions tomorrow."

Chapter 13

Hours after Amanda insisted Erica return to her suite, the pain attacking the base of her skull forced her awake. The ache intensified as she swung her legs to the floor and pushed off the library sofa. Soft snores in the bedroom made it clear Wendy hadn't awakened. Desperate for something to ease the pain, Amanda padded into the hall and followed the rich coffee aroma down the stairs and into the dining room. Had Faith or the chef placed the carafe on the side table? She filled a mug and headed toward her room.

"Were you able to sleep?" Erica called out from the parlor.

"Barely enough to function. What about you?"

"About the same."

"Did you make the coffee?"

"Two hours ago." Erica held up her mug. "This is my third cup."

"I'll definitely need at least one more dose of caffeine to face whatever the attorney has to share with us." Amanda took a sip. "Wendy's still asleep."

"Did she sleep through the night?"

"She cried out twice."

"I apologize for abandoning you."

"There was only room for one of us on the library sofa. Besides, I needed time alone to sort through my emotions."

"Did you make any headway?"

"I'll let you know after I shower." Amanda turned away from Erica and stepped into the Rose room. After swallowing two aspirin and taking a hot shower, she dried her hair and dabbed concealer on the dark circles under her eyes. At least the pain attacking the back of her neck had eased a bit. She pocketed her phone and the attorney's business card, then returned to the hall.

Erica stood peering out the front door. "Our snow village is in sad shape."

Amanda scoffed. "The perfect metaphor for three wives who've discovered they aren't legally married."

"Not even you?"

"Is my last name Benson?" Amanda's eyebrows gathered in. "I'm sorry for coming across as sarcastic."

"You don't need to apologize."

"Yes, I do." Amanda pivoted toward footsteps striking the stairs.

Wearing a pink yoga outfit and white sneakers, Wendy moseyed over. "I'm hungry."

How could she look so fresh following a tormenting night? She was twenty-three-years-old and pregnant, that's how. Amanda linked arms with the young woman. "How about we whip up some breakfast."

"Eggs and bacon?"

"Works for me."

Forty minutes later, Amanda swallowed her last bite of scrambled eggs and pushed away from the dining-room table. The three of them had barely spoken while preparing and consuming breakfast. She couldn't wait any longer to address the issue at hand. "The attorney who met with us yesterday is waiting for me to call him." *Was Wendy up to another meeting?* "If we're ready, he has more to share."

"Delaying the inevitable doesn't make sense." Erica pushed her plate away. "Unless Wendy wants to wait."

The young woman's eyes remained downcast. "Kurt will take care of me and our baby."

Conflicting thoughts collided in Amanda's brain. Would more details help Wendy accept reality, or would they send her spiraling toward a mental breakdown? Maybe the truth coming from a man would open her eyes. "I'll contact Mr. Armstrong now." She walked out of the dining room to make the call, then returned. "He'll meet us in the coffee lounge in half an hour."

"Which gives us enough time to clean up." Erica gathered the plates and carried them to the kitchen. Amanda followed and brewed another pot of coffee. Wendy poured a glass of orange juice, then ambled to the window. By the time Amanda carried the full carafe to Mountain Mama's and filled two mugs, her headache had intensified instead of abated with the aspirin.

Erica chose the chair beside Wendy and stirred sugar into her coffee.

Silence hung heavy as the minutes ticked by. Amanda peered at Wendy's fingers wrapped around her glass. Was the truth creeping into the young woman, or was she still wallowing in denial? A rap on the glass door drew her attention. "I'll let him in."

Amanda's pulse accelerated as she hastened to the door. "We're ready for you." Her eyes zeroed in on the two manila envelopes tucked under the attorney's arm. Had he brought more pictures or something more daunting? She led him to the table. "Would you like some coffee?"

"Please." He took a seat and laid down the envelopes as Amanda filled a mug. "Thank you for agreeing to meet with me this morning." He made eye contact with each of them. "First, I want to answer any questions you have."

Wendy tilted her head. "Do you know when my baby's daddy is coming here?"

Amanda flinched as she turned toward the attorney. "I told my friends what you shared with me yesterday, Mr. Armstrong."

He proffered an understanding nod. "Since I'm also here as a friend, are you ladies okay if we use first names?"

Amanda and Erica nodded. Wendy chewed her fingernail.

"All right. To begin, the man you married claims his real name is Gunter Benson."

"Do you believe him?" Wendy's eyes remained downcast.

"That he isn't Paul, Brian, or Kurt? Yes. Because he's a master at deception, I had my doubts about his real identity. Anyway, he called me the day after I received the photos and claimed he grew up with his grandfather, who worked as a custodian in a high-end Atlantic City hotel."

"Which means there's no paper trail?"

"Not of his history. After his grandfather died, Gunter was left to fend for himself. He worked odd jobs until he turned twenty-one and became a casino blackjack dealer. That's when his addiction began."

Erica's brows pinched. "Addiction to what?"

"He quit his job and became a full-time gambler. Other than the reservations he made at the inn for you three, that's all he told me. Everything else I discovered on my own and with the help of a private detective." Chris paused and eyed each of them. "For the next ten years, he drifted from casino to casino and won enough money to sustain a meager lifestyle."

Wendy faced Chris. "Then he landed a job as a software salesman and bought a condo in Gulfport, right?"

Amanda shot the young woman an incredulous look. Did she continue to deny reality because the truth was too painful to bear?

"The condo part is true." Chris cleared his throat. "As I was saying, Gunter existed on his winnings until he found another source of income—a sixty-two-year-old childless widow worth millions. Eleanor Harrington fell victim to Gunter's charm and accepted his marriage proposal."

Erica gasped. "Are you saying he married a woman that old?"

Chris nodded. "Eleven years ago."

"The silver-haired wife." Amanda's tone mocked.

Wendy's eyes rounded. "Is that why Kurt is rich?"

Amanda glared at the blonde sitting across from her and slapped her palm on the table. "His name isn't Kurt. It's Gunter."

Wendy's bottom lip trembled.

Amanda immediately regretted her comment which only intensified the pain attacking her own head. "I'm sorry for my insensitive outburst, Wendy."

"Hearing painful truth affects everyone differently." Erica's tone hinted of compassion. "Amanda's anger needed an outlet."

Wendy blinked. "Kurt...I mean Gunter isn't going to show up here, is he?"

Was reality finally setting in? Amanda shook her head. "No, honey, he isn't."

Chris crossed his arms on the table and leaned toward Wendy. "Do you want me to continue, or should we finish this conversation tomorrow?"

"I'm okay." Her voice faltered. "You can stay."

"To answer the question you asked a few minutes ago, Eleanor's money fueled Gunter's gambling addiction and his vanity." The attorney turned toward Amanda. "He assumed the Paul Sullivan identity to take full advantage of his newfound wealth. Gunter was frequenting the New Orleans casinos when he met you and bought the house on St. Charles Avenue."

Amanda's breath caught in her throat. "He was Eleanor's husband when he married me, wasn't he?"

"Yes."

"You're telling us that Gunter conned an old woman out of her money to fabricate false identities?"

"In a sense."

"What do you mean by 'in a sense'?"

"Eleanor died the year after he married you and left everything to Gunter. Which is how he was able to continue gambling and assume the Brian Parker and Kurt Peterson identities."

Erica's eyes narrowed to a slit. "So he could marry two more women?"

Chris nodded. "Each in a town with a casino Gunter frequented. Eventually his penchant for high-stake gambling made him an esteemed guest at half a dozen Las Vegas hotels. His obsession with the perks his lifestyle afforded him intensified when his gambling addiction began to spiral out of control. After he burned through Eleanor's cash and investments, he sold her home." Chris paused to take a sip of coffee. "When that money ran dry, he mortgaged the New Orleans house."

Amanda's jaw tensed. "How could a man with a false identity and no legitimate source of income secure a mortgage?"

"High interest rates from shady lenders."

"How much did he borrow?"

Chris hesitated. "The maximum."

Amanda heaved a sigh.

"Gunter's persistent losing streak, plus the mounting debt, forced him to mortgage the max on the Asheville and Gulfport properties. When that money ran out, he made the worst possible decision. He borrowed from loan sharks. Which brings us to three weeks ago, when Gunter gambled away his last dollar."

Erica flinched. "The sharks went after him, didn't they?"

"Yes."

Wendy's face paled. "Did they hurt him? Is that why he's not coming?"

Chris took a deep breath. "The man you know as Kurt isn't coming to Blue Ridge because he fled the country to escape the lender's wrath."

Amanda slammed her fist on the table. "Leaving Erica, Wendy, and me to pay the mortgages on our homes."

"Unfortunately." Chris paused for a long moment. "All three houses have gone into foreclosure." He removed three documents from an envelope and gave one to each of them. "That's how much he owes in back payments on your homes."

Erica's breath hitched.

"I don't understand." Wendy's brows drew together. "How could he do that without me having a clue?"

Amanda eyed Wendy. "Who pays the bills in your family?"

She shrugged. "Kurt."

"Have you ever seen any of those bills?"

Wendy shook her head.

Amanda's eyes grew lightning fierce. "There's your answer."

"I always assumed Brian paid everything online." Erica's face paled. "I never questioned why nothing came in the mail."

"That's how he kept us in the dark, and most likely explains why your credit card was rejected, Wendy."

"Because he didn't pay the bill?"

"Erica and I are probably in the same predicament." Amanda's eyes narrowed. "To sum it all up, the coward fled to escape the consequences of his behavior and left three women he professed to love with nothing but debt."

"Something else I don't understand." Erica's brows snapped together as she faced Chris. "If Gunter spent his last dime at a casino, how did he pay for the three of us to take this trip?"

"Good question. I don't know the answer."

"Are the bad guys gonna come after us now?" Wendy's voice quivered.

"They can't because you aren't legally married to Gunter."

Suppressing the urge to hurl her coffee mug across the room, Amanda faced the attorney. "What else did Gunter send you, and why did he choose this town to break the news?"

"To answer the first part of your question, he sent a letter. About the rest of your question, he created a last will and testament naming the three of you as his beneficiaries."

Amanda's nostrils flared. "Beneficiaries of what? Houses that are mortgaged to the hilt?"

"What about the car Kurt gave me and everything in the Gulfport condo?"

"One bit of good news, whatever he didn't use as collateral for loans and is in your possession belongs to you."

Hoping to ease the pain that had returned with a vengeance, Amanda pressed her fingers to the back of her neck. When would this nightmare end?

Chapter 14

E rica propped her elbows on the table, squeezed her eyes closed, and pressed her fingers to her temples. How much more gut-wrenching news could she bear without breaking down? Images of her daughter's seventeenth-birthday slumber party flashed in her mind—a dozen of Abby's girlfriends laughing and munching on junk food until dawn.

The income from Erica's part-time job barely qualified as pocket change. There was no way she could pay the past-due house payments, much less take on a pricey mortgage. What would happen to Abby's college dreams? The pain behind her eyes strengthened. First she'd married an abuser, then a fraud. Her choice of husbands was seriously flawed.

A hand touching her arm startled Erica. She opened her eyes and stared at Wendy. Was the young woman who struggled to face reality trying to comfort her?

Chris placed his hand on one of the envelopes. "I can save the rest for tomorrow—"

"No." Erica faced the attorney. "I'm okay."

"Are you sure?"

"Yes. Please continue and tell us why that man sent all three of us to Blue Ridge."

The attorney's eyes remained locked on hers. "You're here because Eleanor Harrington has history in this town." He removed two photographs from the envelope beneath his hand, then laid them on the table and tapped the larger picture. "Thirty years ago, Mr. Harrington built that home for his wife. They vacationed here during the summer months. When he fell ill, they stopped coming. The house has remained vacant and unattended for more than two decades."

Amanda examined the picture. "What does that house have to do with us?"

"Gunter willed both properties and everything in them to the three of you."

"I don't understand." Erica pulled the photo close and eyed the three-story, Victorian-style house. "Why didn't he sell it for gambling money?"

"Because he didn't know it existed until a month ago when the county tracked him down to collect delinquent property taxes, which he didn't pay."

Erica glared at Chris. "Are you telling us that in addition to saddling Amanda, Wendy, and me with mortgaged homes, he dumped another house on us?"

"I wouldn't call it dumping."

"Why not?" Amanda scoffed. "How much is the tax bill?"

"After Mr. Harrington died, Eleanor had set up an account to pay the annual taxes until the money ran out." He removed a sheet of paper and handed it to Amanda. "This is how much he owes."

"Are you kidding me?"

"You have forty-five days to decide what to do before the properties are sold to pay that bill."

"Unless Erica or Wendy have cash hidden in a mattress somewhere, there's no way we can come up with that amount of money." She slid the paper across the table.

Erica gawked at the number.

Wendy pointed to the other picture. "What's that?"

"The house on the adjacent lot. Mr. Harrington bought it with the intention of turning it into a guesthouse. For some reason that never happened. The tax bill is for both properties." Chris paused. "I understand that nineteen thousand is a lot of money—"

"That's a major understatement." Amanda folded her arms across her chest.

"True. However, I urge the three of you to visit the properties before you consider your options."

"The fancy house looks expensive." Wendy's head tilted. "We could sell it and split the money."

"The tax bill is due in fewer than two months." Amanda's eyes narrowed. "Do you have any idea how long it takes to engage a realtor and establish a reasonable price? Not to mention the shape that house is most likely in after twenty years of neglect."

Wendy sulked. "Why are you being so negative?"

"I'm drawing on my experience to face reality. Years ago, Preston and I bought a house for thousands under market value because it needed a ton of work. The same is likely true for the Harrington properties."

"I still think you're a pessimist."

Erica bristled at the tension between the two women. "In my opinion, it won't hurt at least to look at the houses."

"You owe yourselves that much." The attorney tapped the larger photo. "If you'd like, I'll arrange for an agent to quote a price for you."

"Please." Erica eyed Amanda, then Wendy. "That is if my co-owners agree."

"I do." Wendy's tone hinted of optimism.

Amanda unfolded her arms and heaved a heavy sigh. "Might as well."

"By tomorrow, the roads should be clear enough to drive you to the property. There's one more item to discuss." Chris removed a folded document from an envelope and held it up. "This is the letter Gunter wrote to the three of you. Although his instructions are to read it to you together, I'll leave the final decision in your hands."

Amanda reached for the coffee carafe. "I assume you've read it."

"I have."

She refilled her mug. "Is it a confession?"

"To some extent." He pulled his phone from his belt clip. "You ladies decide what you want me to do while I take this call." He pocketed the letter, then pivoted away from the table.

Erica's eyes followed the attorney until he disappeared into the inn. "Why do you suppose Gunter wants us to hear the letter together?"

Amanda rolled her eyes. "Because he's an egotistical creep."

"I know Kurt made some mistakes, but he promised to take care of me and our baby."

"Gunter married three women on purpose, not by mistake." Amanda locked eyes with Wendy. "Don't you understand that his promises are as worthless as our marriage licenses?"

"Maybe you're just jealous because he loves me."

"Look—" Amanda puffed her cheeks and blew a long stream of air. "No matter how difficult, the three of us have to face the truth."

Wendy tapped her finger on the table. "I want to hear what Kurt—I mean, Gunter wrote."

"We all do." A burst of air escaped Erica's lungs as she pushed off her chair.

Wendy looked up at her. "Are you leaving us?"

"I'm going for reinforcements." Erica headed straight to the pastry case, then returned and set four donuts on the table.

Amanda snickered. "The universal comfort food."

Wendy grabbed the chocolate donut. "My favorites have icing and sprinkles." She took a bite. "I think Chris should read the letter to the three of us at the same time."

Amanda eyed Erica. "What's your opinion?"

She broke eye contact and stared at her half-empty coffee mug. "I still have the last birthday card my brother gave me before he died. The note he wrote inside said, 'no matter what, we have each other.' As members of a bizarre wives club, the same applies to the three of us." She reached for a donut. "I agree with Wendy. We should hear what he has to say together."

Wendy swallowed a bite. "Kurt planned to join the most exclusive country club in Gulfport."

"Instead he created one so exclusive it only has three members." Amanda grabbed a donut and pinched off a piece. "At least as far as we know."

Wendy's eyes widened. "Do you think he has more wives?"

"Until yesterday, we didn't know he had more than one."

Erica frowned at Amanda, then touched Wendy's arm. "If Gunter had married other women, don't you think they'd be sitting here with us?"

Wendy shrugged. "I guess so."

Chris returned and removed the letter from his pocket. "What have you ladies decided?"

Erica eyed Amanda. "Wendy and I have voiced our opinion. Now it's your turn."

"Are you looking for consensus?"

"It would help."

"All right." Amanda turned toward the attorney. "Would you prefer your donut before or after you read that letter?"

"After."

Chapter 15

W endy fingered her wedding rings as her eyes shifted from Amanda to the letter the attorney held in his hand. Kurt had lied about his name and his job. Had he also lied about loving her? Her mouth was so dry a cough threatened. She grabbed her glass and guzzled the last of her orange juice.

Erica bolted from her chair and rushed to the inn. Moments later she returned and set a fresh glass of juice in front of Wendy.

She swallowed a mouthful. "Thank you." Startled by her raspy voice, Wendy took another sip.

Chris leaned forward. "Do we need to take a break before I read Gunter's letter?"

Doubt clouded her thoughts. Would her baby's father have claimed to love her in his last text message if his feelings weren't real? Why had he written one letter instead of three?

Erica touched her arm. "We can wait and hear what he wrote tomorrow."

What if his letter expressed how much Kurt loved her? "I don't want to wait." She faced Chris. "Go ahead and start reading."

"All right." The attorney unfolded the document and laid it on the table. "It begins with 'Dearest Amanda, Erica, and Wendy.'"

Wendy caught her bottom lip between her teeth. Had Gunter named her last because she was number three, or because he loved her the least?

Chris cleared his throat. *"By now you're aware that I have four different identities. My intention was never to deceive you. Instead I wanted to share the abundance of love I had stored up in my heart during my deprived childhood. I married Eleanor to give her a measure of happiness during her final years. She rewarded me by sharing her wealth."*

Amanda sneered. "What a load of horse manure."

Chris eyed her for a moment, then continued reading. *"But Eleanor couldn't satisfy my desire to have a young, beautiful woman share my life. Then I met you, Amanda. Everything about you attracted me. Your beauty. The way you described the sites during the tour through New Orleans. I began falling in love with you on our first date. When I met Morgan, I knew I'd found the family I had always longed for."*

A gut-wrenching cough forced Wendy to grab her glass and swallow mouthfuls of juice. As soon as she recovered, she faced Chris. "Please keep reading."

"Are you sure?"

"Positive."

"All right." His eyes returned to the letter. *"By that time I had perfected the art of beating the odds at casinos. I also understood that revealing my profession would create unnecessary worry for you and Morgan. Which is why I told you I worked as a civil engineer. After we married, I accepted the fact that you would never love me as much as you loved Preston. He was, after all, the father of your child. Although I'm not blaming you, my desire to be fully loved by a woman tempted my loyalty."*

Amanda slapped her palm on the table. "Infidelity couldn't possibly have been his fault. Oh wait, the guy's a genius con artist who's perfected the art of lying."

Wendy bristled at her friend's mocking tone.

Chris eyed Amanda. "Do *you* want me to stop reading?"

"And deprive us of hearing more of Gunter Benson's masterfully concocted, so-called confession?"

Wendy crossed her arms over her chest. "He's just trying to be honest."

"The man doesn't have an honest bone in his body." Amanda heaved a heavy sigh. "Don't take my comments personally, Wendy."

"Then stop being so mean."

"Do you ladies need a break?" Chris's tone hinted of impatience.

Amanda laced her fingers on the table. "Just keep reading."

"Thank you." Chris's tone hinted of frustration. "*Then during one of my trips to Asheville, you waited on my table, Erica. My first intention was to enjoy the company of a stunningly beautiful woman while visiting your town. When I fell deeply in love with you, I knew I had the means to support a second family. Again, because I wanted you and Abby to feel confident about my ability to provide for you, I fabricated a different job. The biggest surprise about marrying two women was the thrill of juggling two lifestyles without raising any suspicions or compromising my identity.*"

"No suspicions?" Erica's face reddened. "I've suspected his infidelity for months."

Amanda unlaced her fingers and gripped her coffee mug. "The man's obviously delusional."

"Erica didn't tell him she suspected anything." Wendy glared at Amanda. "So how would he know?"

"What do you think he would have done if she had told him about her suspicions? Confessed to being a bigamist or continued to lie?"

"Look, I understand how difficult it is to listen to this letter." Chris made eye contact with each of them. "However, if you ladies will hold your comments, maybe I'll manage to read all the way to the end."

Amanda leaned back and crossed her arms.

Erica shrugged.

Wendy faced Chris. "Keep reading. I want to hear what he says about me."

"Here goes." Chris returned his focus to the letter. "*The fact is, I never intended to pursue a third marriage until you showed up at my table and flashed your engaging smile, Wendy. You were the most beautiful woman I had ever laid eyes on—so young and playful. I knew I'd been chosen to give you the life you deserve.*

"*The reason I arranged for the three of you to meet is because you are all my family, and you have made me a very happy man. Although my destiny has changed, please know that I will always love you and hold a special place in my heart for each of you. I'm leaving you the Blue Ridge properties to give you the opportunity to move on with your lives and take care of your families. Your loving husband, Paul, Brian, and Kurt.*"

Tears pooled and tracked down Wendy's face as Chris folded the letter. "He didn't say anything about our baby."

"You know what I think?" Erica squeezed Wendy's hand. "Of the three of us, I believe he loved you the most."

Wendy swiped her fingers across her cheeks. If Kurt had met her first, he wouldn't have needed to marry Amanda and Erica.

"The narcissist failed to mention two relevant facts." Amanda unfolded her arms and leaned forward. "His failure as a gambler and the mountains of debt he left behind. Although in his warped mind, I suspect he believes he didn't leave the three of us worse off than when he found us."

Wendy sniffled. "Except he gave us Eleanor's houses."

Amanda eyed Wendy. "If he'd known about Eleanor's property six months ago, chances are he would have sold it to further enrich his favorite casino venues."

"Maybe if he'd had that money, he would have started a winning streak and changed his destiny."

"But he didn't." Erica reached for Wendy's hand. "And now the three of us need to find a way to move on with our lives."

Wendy's eyes met Erica's. "I don't know how."

"Amanda and I will help you. After all, whether we like it or not, Gunter Benson made us family."

Chapter 16

After Chris left them alone, Amanda's mind reeled as she glared at the evidence of Gunter's shams and betrayals lying on the table. In the amount of time it would have taken to watch a television drama, the man they'd married had turned the lives of three women upside down.

Wendy trudged from the table to the sofa facing the coffee-lounge entrance. Like a mother hen watching over her chick, Erica followed the young woman and settled beside her. What would happen to Wendy when their stay at the inn ended? Did she have anyone in Gulfport to turn to for support?

Amanda put the pictures of the two houses side by side. Wendy was right about selling the properties and splitting the proceeds. More than likely it would take the full forty-five days for a realtor to find a buyer and close the deal. Fortunately, she had money in the joint checking account she had shared with Preston, and Erica had income from her job. But what about Wendy? Did she have any cash? With a maxed-out credit card, how would she survive until the sale finalized?

Gloom permeated the coffee lounge as the minutes ticked by. Resisting the urge to escape to her room and crawl into bed, Amanda plucked Gunter's letter off the table. At least she could attempt to lighten the mood. She moved to the wingback facing Wendy and Erica. "I've been thinking." She held up the letter. "We could earn a sizable chunk of change for this oddity if we put it in a fancy frame and sell it to *Ripley's Believe it or Not!*"

Erica managed a half grin. "Or we could use it to start a Gunter Benson's Wives Club scrapbook."

"Both ideas are more creative than burning it and flushing away the ashes." Amanda tossed the letter onto the coffee table. "What do you think we should do with it, Wendy?"

The young woman was staring into space. "One of my foster mothers said only God, dogs, and babies love unconditionally. That's why I'm gonna buy a puppy when I get home."

Amanda exchanged glances with Erica. How long would Wendy be stuck in denial?

Erica faced the young woman and stretched her arm across the back of the sofa. "Abby's golden retriever was a puppy when we rescued her from the pound, and Dusty loves my daughter unconditionally. However, it took both of us to housebreak the dog and teach her not to chew the furniture. And then there were the vet bills, and the cost of Puppy Chow. In a way, buying a dog is a lot like adopting a baby who never grows up."

"I'll buy my puppy a fancy doggie bed and walk him on the beach every day." Wendy tilted her head. "One of my neighbors pushes her dog in a stroller. Do you think I should buy a little dog or a big one?"

Forget about dogs. "It's time for the three of us to check out our snow family—that's what I think."

Wendy lifted off the sofa. "I'll grab my new coat and meet you on the front porch." She scurried to the inn.

Erica released a sigh. "Gunter's third wife won't be able to move forward until she faces reality. We need to find a way to help her."

"I know." Amanda scooped the letter off the coffee table. "Maybe we can use the melting snow family as a metaphor."

"How?"

"I haven't figured that out yet." Amanda gathered the items the attorney had left behind, then carried them to her room and set them on the desk beside the Champagne. Erica was right about helping Wendy. Hoping for some divine guidance, Amanda whispered a short prayer. After bundling up, she slid her room key into her jeans pocket and returned to the hall.

Erica stood peering out the front door. "Our snow creations are in sad shape."

Amanda eyed what remained of the frozen family. "An appropriate symbol for the three of us."

The stairs creaked, followed by rapid footsteps. "The snow on my windowsill is all melted."

"Sunshine always comes after a storm." Amanda pulled the door open as an idea began to form.

Wendy followed her friends onto the front porch. A water droplet slid off the railing and splashed onto the puddle below. "Our snow family's dying."

The idea blossomed in Amanda's brain. "Actually, they're transforming from a frozen to a liquid state." Amanda lifted a cherry off the railing and held it up. "What gave them each a unique personality remains. The same is true for the three of us."

"Amanda's right." Erica stepped beside Wendy and slid her arm around her shoulders. "Even though our situations have changed, we are still the strong, capable women we were before Chris broke the news about Gunter."

Wendy plucked a limp pretzel stick off the railing. "Kurt Peterson doesn't exist, does he?"

"No, sweetie, he doesn't."

Wendy pulled away from Erica. She dashed to the front sidewalk, scooped a handful of snow off the lawn, and shaped it into a ball. "Gunter Benson lied about everything." Wendy hurled the snowball at the lamppost.

Was she finally moving beyond denial to anger? Amanda formed her own snowball and heaved it at a porch pillar. "Gunter is a seriously disturbed man."

Erica sent her snowball crashing to the sidewalk. "No matter what, we'll find a way not just to survive, but to thrive." She scooped another handful of snow off the lawn.

Wendy's shoulders drooped as she dropped to her knees. "Gunter made me pregnant, but he isn't good enough to be my baby's daddy." She traced half a heart in the snow. "I rescued one of the snowmen."

Erica knelt beside Wendy. "And God is in the midst of rescuing us."

"One day I'll fall in love with a good man." Wendy completed the heart. "Someone who will never lie or cheat." She sat back on her heels. "Maybe he'll have a dog."

Erica opened her hand and let the snowball slide off her fingers. "Maybe he will."

The front door swung open. Faith stepped onto the porch. "Well now. This explains the snowman in our freezer."

Wendy rose to her feet. "I hope you don't mind me putting him in there."

"That's definitely the most unique item a guest has ever stored in our fridge." Faith grinned. "Our chef will return in the morning, and most of the restaurants will open tomorrow. In the meantime, I brought you ladies lunch and dinner."

Amanda brushed snow off her hands. "After lunch, the three of us will clean up the mess we made."

"You mean the creative snow-art display? You ladies relax and enjoy your vacation. Our staff will handle the cleanup tomorrow. For now, bowls of homemade chili and egg-salad sandwiches are waiting for you."

"Two of my favorites." Erica stood and brushed the snow off her knees.

The succulent scents of tomatoes and chili powder greeted Amanda as they followed Faith to the dining room. Her eyes drifted to the end of the table where Chris had first revealed the truth about the man she'd known as Paul—the criminal whose bed she'd shared for nine years. Her body tensed as reality hit home. To satisfy his sick delusions, Gunter Benson would no doubt pick up where he left off and continue luring unsuspecting women in whatever country he'd fled to.

After they carried their lunch to the dining room, Erica pulled her phone from her pocket and eyed Abby's text. A lump formed in her throat as she stared at the picture of her daughter and Dusty standing beside a snow creature wearing a strand of pearls and a fancy scarf. How could she explain that the man Abby lovingly called Dad was a fraud, and the lifestyle they enjoyed was built on lies? If a realtor managed to contract a decent price for Eleanor's properties, maybe she'd have enough money to send Abby to college. How long before the mortgage company forced them to leave their home? Except it wasn't their home.

Amanda's eyes met Erica's. "You're wondering how to explain all this to your daughter, aren't you?"

"The truth will break her heart."

"Morgan's strained relationship with Gunter makes my task a bit easier than yours. Although she'll be angry enough to spit nails."

Wendy fingered her sandwich. "I don't know if I should tell my baby the truth about her father."

"You'll have plenty of time to decide what to do." Amanda dipped her spoon into the chili. "We should find a way to prevent Gunter from hurting any more women."

Wendy's spoon stopped halfway to her mouth. "How? We don't even know what country he ran off to."

"Good question, and at the moment I don't have a clue how to begin."

"Even so, I agree with Amanda's idea, but not because I want revenge." Erica set her phone on the table. "What if his next victim discovers the truth, and in a moment of passion, she shoots Gunter? She could end up being convicted of murder. Stopping him before something like that happens could save two lives. But it won't be easy."

Amanda swallowed a mouthful of chili. "Doing the right thing seldom is."

"Want to know what I think?" Wendy lifted her sandwich off her plate. "We should decide what to do with those two houses Gunter left us before we try to figure out how to punish him."

Erica stared at Wendy. She obviously needed more time to come to grips with the truth about her child's father. "Agreed, we'd best focus our energy on our immediate needs. Right, Amanda?"

"For now." Gunter's New Orleans wife pointed her spoon at Erica. "After we put the pieces of our lives back together, we need to stop the man who tore them apart."

Chapter 17

Following a restless night punctuated by nightmares of confronting Gunter's defense attorney in a courtroom packed with angry women, Amanda trudged to the bathroom. Had anger or the desire for revenge compelled her to insist they bring the con man to justice? Didn't the three of them already have enough to deal with without adding another complication?

After showering and donning her warmest sweater, Amanda followed the scent of coffee to the dining room.

Erica spun away from the window. The puffy skin under her eyes hinted she'd also struggled through a restless night. "What time is Chris picking us up?"

"Ten o'clock." Amanda filled a mug and stirred in a packet of sugar. Should she mention her qualms about stopping Gunter, or let that dog sleep for now?

"Abby and I lived in a tiny two-bedroom apartment before I married her stepdad." Erica set her coffee on the table and pulled out a chair. "I guess since our marriage was illegitimate, he was never qualified to fill that role."

Amanda sat across from her. "It seems Wendy might be the only one of the three of us whose primary motivation to marry Gunter was love."

"What does that make you and me?"

"Mothers who care deeply about their daughters' welfare."

Erica's forehead creased. "Are you second guessing your suggestion to go after Gunter?"

"Once we leave Blue Ridge, we'll all be busy trying to put our lives back in order."

"What about doing the right thing?"

Amanda trilled her lips. "That's what makes the idea a conundrum."

Wendy strode in and poured a cup of decaf. "What idea?"

Amanda eyed Erica, then faced Wendy. "What to do about the properties we inherited."

"We should definitely sell them. When my baby's born, I'll need money to pay what Kurt's insurance doesn't cover. Except—" Her shoulders slumped as she dropped onto the chair beside Erica. "He didn't work for a company, so he probably doesn't have insurance."

The sweet scent of cinnamon accompanied the chef as she entered the dining room carrying a large tray. "Which one of you ladies created the miniature snowman I found in our freezer?"

Wendy scooted her chair close to the table. "That one's mine."

"It's adorable." The chef set the tray on the table. "And deserving of the inn's specialty—mountain blueberry French toast soufflé."

Despite the delicious breakfast fare, gloom permeated the dining room. Avoiding eye contact with the other victims, Amanda mentally debated the Gunter-quandary pros and cons. Given the difficulty of the task and the likelihood of failure, she landed on the only decision that made sense. Unless another bombshell landed in their laps, it was best to dismiss the idea of bringing the criminal to justice.

At ten o'clock, Amanda and Erica settled in the back seat of Chris's late-model luxury sedan while Wendy slid into the front. As they drove out of town, Amanda peered out at the patches of snow resisting the sun's rays. Unlike the bustle of New Orleans, there was a peacefulness about the countryside. She imagined spring bursting onto the scene and turning the rolling hills into a lush green oasis.

Shortly after turning off the main road that cut through dense forests, Chris eased up a steep driveway beside a wide swath of cleared land. The remaining snow failed to mask the weed-infested front lawn. Amanda's shoulders curled forward as her focus shifted from the naked spots on the turret roof and a broken front window to the massive tree branch lying across the side-porch. Years of neglect had transformed the once grand, three-story Victorian home into a sad eyesore.

Chris parked beside the sidewalk leading to the front porch. Amanda breathed deeply as she stepped onto the uneven pavement. The once thriving shrubs appeared to have died from neglect long ago. Stains and mildew marred the building's white façade. Broken balusters left wide gaps in the balcony railing over the arched entry to the front porch.

Amanda's eyes raked over the peeling paint as she climbed the cracked concrete steps and followed Erica and Wendy into the massive foyer. Her nose scrunched at the stench of stale air and mold. A sinking sensation weighted down her chest at the sight of dilapidated furniture and curled wooden floorboards in the living room. How many gallons of rainwater had blown through the broken window over the years?

Chris pulled a spiderweb off the double doorframe, then led the way into the turret room on the opposite side of the foyer. Wendy pointed to a long string of cobwebs stretching from the chandelier to the fireplace. "This looks like a haunted mansion inhabited by a family of creepy ghosts."

Erica's nose crinkled as she brushed a web away from her face. "It definitely smells like something died in here."

Amanda sighed while eyeing water spots on the ceiling. "It already appears to be in worse shape than the shotgun house Preston and I bought." The prospect of getting a decent price for the property diminished as they trudged to the first-floor bedroom suite overlooking the backyard patio and the free-standing, three-car garage at the end of the driveway.

They continued through the remaining rooms ending in the massive kitchen. The back staircase creaked as they climbed to the second story. A rodent skittered across the floor in the fourth empty bedroom and disappeared through a hole in the baseboard.

Droppings on the floor in the elegantly furnished front-bedroom suite made it clear critters had claimed the space as their habitat. Amanda's confidence in the home's value plummeted further as they crossed the hall and peered at the collapsed ceiling in the seventh bedroom—evidence of the missing turret shingles. The gaping hole revealed what appeared to be an unfinished third floor. Her shoulders slumped. "This is what happens to a house after years of neglect."

"Unfortunately." Chris cleared his throat. "Do you ladies want to take a look at the other property?"

"We might as well." Erica backed away from the door. "It can't be in worse shape than this one."

Chris led the way down the grand staircase and out the front door. They retraced their steps to the driveway, then walked across a cleared path to the double carport extending from the side of a brick, ranch-style house. "This property dates back to the sixties." He opened the back door.

Amanda stepped onto the yellowed linoleum curled at the edge in the galley-style kitchen that shared the carport's back wall. She swiped a swath of dust off the speckled yellow Formica countertop.

Erica opened a cabinet. "The kitchen's dated, but appears in half-decent shape."

Amanda followed Erica and Wendy into the paneled den anchored by a brick fireplace and bookshelves. Her nose crinkled at the musty odor as her eyes drifted upwards. "At least the ceiling hasn't collapsed. Not yet, anyway." Her tone failed to mask her frustration.

Wendy ambled to the dirt-encrusted, sliding-glass doors leading to a patio and peered at the wooded, fenced-in backyard. "A family with a dog probably lived here a long time ago." She pivoted from the window. "Why do you suppose Eleanor and her husband didn't fix this place up?"

"Maybe they weren't all that eager to entertain guests." Amanda followed Chris through an arched opening into a narrow foyer open to a compact living room. They continued down a hall and peered into four decent-sized bedrooms and two bathrooms filled with spiderwebs, dead-bug carcasses, and years of accumulated dust and grime.

Erica sneezed. "At least this house is in a lot better shape than the big one." She faced Chris. "Have you contacted a realtor?"

He nodded. "She'll evaluate both properties after lunch." Following one more walk through the unfurnished house, Chris led them back to his vehicle.

Amanda climbed onto the back seat beside Erica and buckled her belt. No one uttered a word until Chris parked at the inn and peered over his shoulder. "I'll contact you as soon as I have the realtor's assessment."

"Thank you." Desperate for time alone, Amanda climbed out of the sedan and headed to the street. When she reached the sidewalk, she glanced over her shoulder. Grateful no one followed her, she strode past Southern Charm restaurant and turned at the corner. She stopped on the railroad track and peered at the massive train engine nosing the sidewalk. Had the scenic railroad turned Blue Ridge into a tourist destination?

She resumed her walk and turned onto East Main. With Morgan away at college, she could make do in a small apartment. Would she be able to sell Paul's...Gunter's truck since it was registered in his name? What about his passion for antiques? How much would an estate sale raise? Amanda's body tensed as she trudged past the train station. How could she have lived with a man for nine years without having a clue about his true character? Because Gunter Benson had mastered the art of deception, that's how. She continued walking until cold air and exhaustion forced her to return to the inn.

Amanda climbed onto the front porch, surprised that someone had cleared every bit of evidence that the snow family had ever existed. An overwhelming mixture of sadness and anger hunched her shoulders as she unlocked the front door and crept to her room. Hoping a bath would ease the chill and wash away the rage boiling inside, she tossed her jacket and sweatshirt on the bed, then headed straight to the bathroom and turned on the spigot. As soon as steam fogged the mirror, she slid into the water, leaned back, and closed her eyes. As the warmth engulfed her, visions of the rundown, shotgun house she and Preston had transformed into a home skated across her mind. Somehow she had to summon the strength to rebuild her life once again. This time without a man by her side.

Chapter 18

The sudden onset of nausea sent Wendy scurrying from Chris's passenger seat. Rushing past Erica, she sprinted up the back steps, and unlocked the back door. Inside the inn, she dashed upstairs to her suite's bathroom. She pressed a damp washcloth to the back of her neck until the queasiness subsided, then traipsed to the library and dropped onto the sofa. The soft leather conjured up images of the white couch facing the wall of windows in her Gulfport living room.

She lifted her wedding photo off the coffee table and traced her finger over her groom dressed in casual white slacks and a button-down white shirt. Wendy closed her eyes and pictured the twenty-six guests gathered to celebrate their surfside ceremony—all friends from restaurants where she'd worked. Kurt had claimed that no one he knew showed up because he'd neglected to mail the invitations. Was the real reason because con artists only had victims, not friends?

Wendy's eyes popped open as the photo slipped from her fingers. She pulled her knees to her chest and wrapped her arms around her shins. Everyone had envied her for snagging a rich husband who owned an expensive home with a million-dollar view. She couldn't let her friends or her nosy neighbors believe Kurt had abandoned her, or that he didn't love her. Wendy blew out a breath. When she returned home, how would she explain why her husband didn't come back to Gulfport, or why she had to move out of the condo?

Wendy breathed deeply to fight off another wave of nausea. She closed her eyes again and envisioned her life before the trip to Blue Ridge, when she'd lived under the illusion that she was married to a rich software salesman. Kurt Peterson had given her a life she'd never dreamed possible. Gunter Benson had yanked that life away from her with total disregard for the child she carried inside. Her mind drifted to the day she'd aged out of the foster system and moved to Gulfport. Somehow, she had found the courage to make a life for herself without a lick of help from anyone.

A sudden impulse compelled Wendy to unwrap her arms and lower her feet to the floor. Without a second's hesitation, she grabbed the wedding picture and ripped it in two. As the groom half fluttered to the floor, she vowed to find the courage to survive, maybe even thrive as a single mother who loved her baby with all her heart.

Thankful Wendy had dashed straight to the stairs without uttering a word, Erica sought refuge in her suite. After hanging her coat in the closet, she dropped onto the sitting-room sofa. Leaving the three women he'd married two dilapidated properties added a whole new layer of insult to the injury Gunter had already inflicted.

The sudden urge to delve into a task sent Erica rushing back to the bedroom. She sat at the desk, then removed a sheet of stationery and a pen from the drawer. How much was the sports car in her garage worth?

Enough to keep from losing the house? A shudder ripped through her. What about the credit card Gunter had given her?

Erica lifted her phone off the desk and dialed the number on the back of her card. After following the prompts, she gasped at the past-due balance. One more trip to the grocery store would put her over the credit limit. At least she had enough cash on hand to buy gas if she ran low during the trip home, and she could use the debit card for her personal account and her monthly paycheck to buy food. Sweat erupted on Erica's upper lip. What about utilities and cell phones? Were those services also in danger of being shut off?

Responding to the overwhelming desire to return to Asheville, Erica dropped the pen and dashed to the closet. Her body froze the moment she grabbed her suitcase. It wouldn't be right to abandon Amanda and Wendy before they came to some kind of agreement about the properties they shared. Not to mention the fact that she needed another day to figure out how to break all the bad news to Abby.

Erica returned to the desk and jotted a list of responsibilities to tackle after she left Blue Ridge. The satisfaction of completing the task awakened the desire to feel the sun shining on her face. She pulled her coat from the closet and made her way to the front porch. Damp spots on the railing remained as the only evidence the snow family had ever existed.

She stepped off the porch and lifted her chin. As the cold air filled her lungs, two disturbing questions sent a chill racing through her. Could she find it in her heart to forgive Gunter Benson, and could she ever trust another man enough to fall in love again? A blue jay soared from a tree beside the driveway and landed on the porch railing. The bird took flight the second the front door swung open.

Amanda stepped out and stood at the porch railing. "Have you recovered from the shock?"

"I was single for nearly five years after I divorced my first husband. If Abby hadn't asked for a new dad, I probably wouldn't have gambled on a second marriage."

"Was the word 'gamble' intentional or subliminal?"

"Either way, it's appropriate." Erica joined Amanda on the porch. "The credit card Gunter gave me is past due and a few dollars from being maxed out. If I'd had the slightest inkling about his deception, I wouldn't have cancelled the card I used before I married him. What if—" Erica grabbed a porch pillar to counter the sudden onset of dizziness.

Amanda gripped her arm. "Are you okay?"

"What if I'm responsible to pay off that credit card?"

"Is your name on the account?"

Erica shook her head. "As far as I know, just Brian's."

"Considering you weren't legally married, I doubt you'll be held accountable."

"I hope you're right."

"For both our sakes, so do I."

Erica pulled her hand away from the pillar. "You're in the same boat, aren't you?"

"I checked the account I use a few minutes ago. If the bill at Southern Charm had been twenty dollars higher, I'd have exceeded the credit limit. Which makes me wonder—" Amanda paused, then unlocked the door and motioned for Erica to follow her.

"Where are we going?"

"To find Faith." Amanda led the way to the inn's office and tapped on the door. Responding to the invitation to enter, Erica followed Amanda into the compact space. Faith pointed to two straight-backed chairs facing the desk. "What can I do for you ladies?"

Amanda dropped onto the chair beside Erica. "We hope you can answer a question about our husband's reservations."

Faith's brow pinched, then released. "What do you want to know?"

"How he...I mean...they paid."

Faith's expression tightened as her eyes shifted from Amanda to Erica, then back to Amanda.

Was the assistant innkeeper debating the ethics of disclosing the information? She was aware Chris had met with the three of them, so she had to suspect something was going on. Erica leaned forward. "I discovered an issue with my credit card and want to make sure there isn't a problem with my bill."

Amanda's brow pinched as if questioning the sanity of Erica's explanation.

"Since they're your husbands', the information isn't confidential." Faith tapped her keyboard. "Mr. Sullivan paid through a cash account." She tapped again. "So did Mr. Parker."

Erica forced a smile. "That's a relief."

"We appreciate you checking." Amanda stood. "And thank you for your gracious hospitality."

"Our pleasure."

Faith's revelation played havoc with Erica's emotions as they made their way to the Sycamore suite. She stepped inside, left the door ajar, and ambled to the fireplace. "Three rooms reserved for a full week obviously cost Gunter a bundle."

"Plus, the price of the two airline tickets and rental car, which means he had plenty of cash stashed away." Amanda settled on the sofa and crossed her leg over her knee. "Either he hit a lucky streak before the loan sharks caught up with him, or he conned another victim."

The door swung wide open. Wendy shuffled in and sat beside Amanda. "How many of Gunter's friends came to your weddings?"

Of all the problems they faced, that's the question foremost in her mind? Erica dropped onto the chair beside the fireplace. "We were married at city hall, with my daughter as our only witness."

"Same here," added Amanda. "Why are you asking?"

"None of his friends came to my wedding, most likely because he didn't have any." Wendy propped her feet on the coffee table. "I'm thinking of moving someplace new. Maybe Florida."

"Hold that thought." Amanda pulled her phone from her pocket. "Chris sent me a text. He wants us to meet him at Harvest on Main at three o'clock today."

"I can't imagine he'd have real-estate quotes this soon. Unless—" Erica pressed her lips tight.

Wendy's eyes probed Erica's. "You were gonna say unless he has bad news, weren't you?"

Why had she let that one word slip out? "Whatever he has to tell us might not be so bad."

Wendy pinched her chin between her thumb and forefinger. "Maybe the real-estate lady already found a buyer."

Erica peered at the young woman who seemed to exist somewhere between reality and fantasyland. No point bursting her bubble until they learned the actual reason for Chris's invitation.

Chapter 19

A manda's stomach churned as she spotted Chris waiting at the top of the stairs on the restaurant's lodge-like front porch. Had he arranged to meet their three-member wives club in public to soften the blow of devastating news? His impassive expression failed to offer a clue about his motivation.

"Right on time." Chris escorted them through the nearly empty dining room to a private space. He set a folder and a small manila envelope on the table, then remained standing until Erica and Wendy sat on one side of the table and Amanda on the other. "The food here is excellent, and lunch is my treat."

Because he took pity on them? Amanda's chest tightened. Was the news worse than she could have imagined?

A waitress breezed in. "Welcome to Harvest on Main. I'm always happy to serve Mr. Armstrong's clients."

"Sherri is one of the best waitresses in Blue Ridge."

The pretty young woman's face beamed as she handed over menus.

Amanda attempted to focus on the food options. If treating clients to a meal wasn't out of the ordinary, maybe whatever Chris had to share wasn't all that devastating.

"What do you recommend?" Erica's tone hinted of anxiety.

"Depends on how hungry you are." While Chris rattled off his favorites, Amanda eyed the envelope lying on top of the folder. It appeared to conceal items thicker than paper. Should she give in to her curiosity and ask about the contents or exercise a modicum of patience? The waitress returned with their drinks. After Sherri took their food orders and left them alone, patience lost the battle to curiosity. Amanda pointed to the smaller envelope. "What did you bring us?"

Chris lifted the distraction off the table. "Although this was mailed from Las Vegas nine days ago, it didn't arrive until this morning." He opened the envelope and emptied three keys taped to three index cards onto the table. "These unlock post-office boxes in New Orleans, Biloxi, and Asheville." Chris handed each the card from their town.

Amanda stared at the handwritten address scribed beside the key. "Secret post office boxes must be how the scumbag kept us from discovering the truth about his financial catastrophes."

"So it seems." Chris reached for his glass. "You should each check the contents as soon as you return home."

Erica laced her fingers on the table. "I'm curious. How did Gunter pay you for the work you've done on our behalf?"

"He included fifteen one-hundred-dollar bills in the envelope with the wedding photos."

"Based on my experience when I divorced my first husband, I suspect that amount hasn't come close to paying for the hours you've already invested in us."

"You're right. However, I would have handled your case even if he hadn't paid me." Chris withdrew three envelopes from his coat pocket and handed one to each of them. "Which is why—even though the money is a pittance compared to the cost of Gunter's fraud—I'm splitting that cash between the three of you."

Erica's eyes widened. "You're working for free?"

"Our firm doesn't have the opportunity to take on pro-bono cases all that often."

After counting the cash in her envelope, Wendy leaned toward Chris. "Are you married?"

Amanda stared wide-eyed at the young woman. Was she already on the hunt for husband number two?

"No. Why do you ask?"

Wendy's head tilted. "Because you'd make someone an awesome husband."

A bemused grin curled the attorney's lips. "Thanks for the compliment."

She offered a perky smile. "You're welcome."

Sherri returned with their food and disrupted whatever bizarre flirtation was going on between the pregnant lady and the good-looking, young attorney.

The conversation during lunch steered clear of anything relating to Gunter. By the time their waitress cleared the table, Amanda could no longer ignore the two-ton elephant in the room. "You didn't invite us to lunch just to hand out post office-box keys, did you?"

"You're right." Chris pulled the unopened envelope close. "The agent prepared estimates on the Harrington properties." He paused as if debating how to break the news. "The first would require full restoration of both houses. The second considers the as-is conditions as well as the current state of the real-estate market in this area. Keep in mind that what I'm about to show you is based on finding buyers who would be willing to tackle fixer-uppers, which could take six months to a year." He removed a sheet of paper from the envelope and handed it to Amanda.

Her stomach clenched as she glared at the number. "I assume the price would decrease if we decided to sell quickly."

"That is correct."

Amanda pushed the paper across the table.

Erica's shoulders drooped as she eyed the document.

Wendy's brows pinched. "That's a lot less money than I expected."

Chris planted his forearms on the table. "The agent suggests putting both houses on the market for a few weeks before making any adjustments. Who knows, maybe you'll get lucky."

Erica scoffed. "Counting on luck is what put the three of us in this predicament in the first place."

"She's right." Amanda fingered a crumb left behind. "Gunter has a better chance at beating the odds in casinos than we have at securing a decent profit from our inheritance."

"Regardless of the odds, the three of you need some time to consider your options."

"Seems we have a lot to talk about." Amanda pushed away from the table. "Thank you for lunch, Chris."

"You're welcome. Text me as soon as you arrive at a decision, and I'll bring the contracts to the inn." He escorted them to the porch, then turned left at the bottom of the stairs.

Wendy's eyes followed him as he strode away. "You two meet me in the inn's library in twenty minutes." She spun away from Amanda and Erica, then scurried up the sidewalk.

"What do you suppose she's up to?"

Erica shrugged. "At least she turned in the opposite direction from the attorney."

They fell silent as they made their way to the inn. After unlocking the back door, Amanda headed straight to the Rose room. After tossing her phone on the bed, she peeled out of her jacket and peered around the space that had been home for the past six days. The room she'd believed the man she'd known as Paul had reserved to celebrate their ninth anniversary. Gunter's illegal wives had one more night before returning home to deal with the consequences of his deception. She filled her lungs as realization arrested her thoughts. Her relationship with Erica and Wendy wouldn't end when they drove away from Blue Ridge.

She dropped onto the bed and eyed the array of art displayed on the wall beside the door. Her eyes drifted to Gunter's gift holding center stage on the desk—one more statement of his deceit. Should she dump it down the drain? Erica and Wendy had shared their wine and truffles before they'd discovered the truth. So why waste a perfectly good bottle of Champagne?

Amanda pocketed her phone, grabbed the bottle and flutes, and made a quick stop in the kitchen before heading upstairs. Voices drifted from the library as she approached the open door. "This time, I brought reinforcements." She placed the glasses and an ice bucket cradling the Champagne and a bottle of ginger ale on the coffee table beside a new box of dark chocolate truffles, then settled on a wingback. "Looks more like a party than a serious business meeting."

"Blame the sweets on my craving for chocolate." Wendy reached for a truffle. "Besides, why not make the most of our last night together."

"Good point." Erica eyed Amanda. "How much time does the Champagne need to chill?"

"Maybe thirty minutes?"

Wendy swallowed, then licked her lips. "Wasn't Chris sweet to give us the money Gunter sent him?" She lifted another truffle from the box. "I'm gonna sell my sports car and keep Gunter's SUV. I'll need the back seat after my baby's born."

Amanda flattened her palms on the chair's arms. "Unless your name is on the title, you'll need legal help to make that happen."

"Not a problem. I'll call Chris."

Amanda resisted rolling her eyes. Wendy's little game of flirtation had definitely been premeditated. "Before we pop that Champagne cork, we need to discuss the real-estate estimates."

"One fact is certain. Restoration is off the table." Erica slipped her boots off and tucked her left foot under her knee. "How much do you suppose the price would need to decrease to sell fast?"

Amanda drummed her fingers on the chair's arm. "After a professional inspected the shotgun house, Preston and I convinced the seller to lower the price by twenty percent. Since the three of us are joint owners, we'll all have to agree to a prospective buyer's final offer."

Wendy removed the ginger ale from the bucket. "In that case, I vote we stick with the higher price on both houses."

"Let's say we go with that plan, and if after two weeks we don't have a single nibble—" Erica fingered her sock. "Before lowering the price on the ranch, we could pay a crew to clean the place up, so it at least looks and smells more appealing."

"There's still the issue of the inspection. Even though the ranch didn't look bad compared to the Victorian, there's likely a long list of problems that go beyond the appearance."

Wendy's brow pinched. "What kind of problems?"

Amanda held up her index finger. "Chances are the heating and air conditioning unit doesn't work." She lifted a second finger. "It's likely the water heater has also gone kaput." Finger number three. "Then there's the issue of the kitchen appliances that sat idle for twenty years—"

"No need to continue." Erica sighed. "We get the point."

Wendy huffed. "Amanda's being a pessimist again."

"It doesn't matter what you call me—unless we're willing to wait for who knows how long, we'll likely be forced to dump both properties."

"I still say we need to start with the higher prices."

Erica's eyes shifted from Wendy to Amanda. "I suppose it won't hurt to wait a couple of weeks and see what happens."

"All right. Two weeks from today—"

Wendy snapped her fingers. "You mean from tomorrow."

Amanda drew in a deep breath, then slowly let it escape. "Fourteen days from tomorrow, we'll talk and decide our next step." After texting their decision to Chris, Amanda lifted off the chair and removed the Champagne from the bucket. "I believe this beverage has chilled long enough." She pulled the cork, filled two flutes, and handed one to Erica. "Let our farewell party begin."

Erica clicked her glass to Amanda's, then to Wendy's. "To my new friends who perhaps one day will share more than a scumbag husband."

Chapter 20

Amanda's sense of trepidation heightened as she folded her new sweatshirt and placed it atop the rest of the clothes in her suitcase. Returning to the house she'd shared with a criminal wouldn't be easy. Especially after she revealed the truth to Morgan. At least she had more time to prepare for that conversation.

A stomach grumble forced Amanda to pocket her phone and walk out of her room. Unfamiliar voices drifted into the hall as she strode past the parlor and the Christmas tree and stepped into the dining room. The gray-haired gentleman sitting beside a woman and across from Erica turned toward her. "Good morning. We're James and Esther Wright from Jacksonville."

"Welcome to Blue Ridge. I'm Amanda—" The last name she'd been using for the past nine years stuck in her throat. "Smith, from New Orleans." She filled a coffee mug, then chose the chair beside Erica. "When did you folks check in?"

"Yesterday around suppertime. Your friend has been telling us about your adventures during the snowstorm."

Amanda stole a sideways glance at Erica. How much had she shared?

"I explained how you, Wendy, and I arrived as strangers and are leaving as friends."

"Extra-special friends." Wendy wandered in. She poured a glass of juice, then sat beside Amanda and eyed the newcomers. "Are y'all celebrating a special occasion?"

"My wife's birthday."

"Same as Erica, except her actual birthday is next month."

Unsure what details Wendy might reveal next, Amanda steered the conversation to the details she'd learned about the town.

The chef stepped in from the kitchen, grinning ear-to-ear. "Good morning, folks." She set an array of platters on the table and described each dish. "Enjoy."

James passed a platter to his wife. "Breakfast is one of the amenities we love most about this inn."

Erica reached for a plate. "James and Esther have visited numerous times. Sometimes to celebrate her birthday and other times their anniversary."

Wendy transferred a sausage patty to her plate. "Amanda, Erica, and I need to come back one day for a reunion to celebrate our adventure. You two need to check out the miniature snowman I put in the freezer. I wish I could take it back to Gulfport and show all my friends."

James chuckled. "A frozen snowman is definitely worth a look."

The conversation focused on the town and the iconic railroad. Grateful they'd made it through breakfast without revealing the real reason for their Blue Ridge experience, Amanda swallowed her last bite and wiped her fingers with a napkin. "I've enjoyed chatting with you folks, but now I need to finish packing."

"So do I," Erica and Wendy said in unison.

James grinned. "You three ladies must have a lot in common."

More than he'd ever know.

"Enjoy the rest of your stay." Amanda returned to her room and brushed her teeth. After packing her toiletry bag, she zipped her suitcase closed and set it on the floor. She tucked her purse under her arm and took one last look around. Would she ever return to Blue Ridge or to this inn? Maybe one day she and Morgan would visit and ride the train. Amanda set the room key on the desk, then pulled her suitcase down the hall and out the back door.

Erica stood between her car and Amanda's rental. She embraced Wendy then Amanda. "I miss you both already."

Amanda struggled to keep her emotions at bay. "Maybe we should take Wendy's reunion suggestion seriously."

"Why don't you both come to Asheville next summer. We'll spend a couple of days visiting the Biltmore estate and dream about being rich." Erica's voice cracked. "Until then we need to stay strong and take one day at a time."

Amanda nodded. "Remember our commitment to talk about the properties we own."

"Two weeks from today." Wendy sniffled as she faced Erica. "Thanks for being my friend."

Erica stroked Wendy's cheek. "Always." She stashed her suitcase in the back seat, then slid onto the driver's seat and drove out of the parking lot.

Amanda stole one more glance at the inn. The day she'd pulled into this parking space, she'd hoped to revive her marriage. Today she was leaving as a single woman, uncertain what else she might learn about Gunter Benson's deceptions. After sliding behind the steering wheel and waiting for Wendy to close the passenger door, Amanda backed up and drove out of the lot. She passed by Southern Charm as images of their first meal together came to mind. At the stop sign, she turned left.

As they approached the railroad track, Wendy peered around Amanda. "I wish we'd have had a chance to ride that train. When my baby's old enough, I'll bring her back here and stay at the inn. Maybe my snowman will still be in the freezer."

"You're definitely a wide-eyed optimist."

"Sometimes—" She turned away. "But not always."

After heading out of town, Amanda's breath hitched as she passed the road leading to the Victorian mansion and ranch house. Would the three of them come to a consensus about the sale? During the drive to Chattanooga, long stretches of silence prevailed, interrupted by random bits of conversation. By the time they arrived at the airport, a palpable gloom had settled over them.

After returning the rental car, Amanda waited while Wendy checked her suitcase. "At least the weather is more suitable for flying than it was the day we arrived."

Wendy's shoulder drooped under the weight of her duffle. "Will you walk me to my gate?"

Amanda linked arms with her young friend. "Of course."

When they arrived, Wendy strode to the window and set her duffle on the floor. "I don't have a lot of close friends." Her voice faltered. "I'm glad it was you and Erica who Gunter...you know."

"I'm glad as well, and as a member of an exclusive wives club, you have two life-long friends."

Wendy sighed as the flight attendant called for the first passengers to board. "That's me."

"Business class." Amanda forced a smile. "Impressive and well deserved. Do you have a ride back to your condo?"

"I'll call the nice guy who drove me to the airport." Wendy's bottom lip caught between her teeth as her eyes welled up. "What if I need to talk to you before two weeks are up?" Amanda embraced her. "You can call me anytime. And as you said the day we met, we're practically neighbors."

"Is it okay if I sort of consider you like my mom?"

Amanda swallowed the lump forming in her throat. "Of course. Besides, Morgan always wanted a sister." Her eyes filled with tears as she released Wendy. "You should board before we both start bawling."

Wendy wiped her fingers across her cheeks. "Thank you." She spun away from Amanda and plodded to the jetway.

Still reeling from the young mother's request, Amanda silently prayed for Wendy to find the strength to move on with her life. With an hour to hang out before her departure, she ambled to her gate and removed a book from her suitcase. Halfway through a page, her mind drifted to Morgan. In addition to telling her they'd been living with a fraud for nine years, she'd have to explain that one of Gunter's wives had unofficially adopted them as her family.

Chapter 21

T he closer Erica came to downtown Asheville, the faster her heart
raced. In less than an hour, Abby would park in their garage and
dash into the kitchen with Dusty bounding behind her. She'd enthusi-
astically share snippets about her week-long stay with Carrie, her closest
friend, before asking about the Blue Ridge trip.

Erica braked for a red light. Waiting until tomorrow to break the news
would force her to skirt the truth and risk damaging their relationship.
Somehow, she had to summon the courage to tell Abby what she'd discovered about the man they'd known as Brian.

Six blocks from home, Erica pulled into the post office parking lot. She
gripped the steering wheel and stared at the key and index card lying on
the passenger seat. How much more shocking news could she bear? She
peeled her fingers off the wheel, then grabbed the card and trudged into
the building. After locating the box, she stared at the number. How many
times during the past six years had Gunter stood in this spot? She breathed
deeply as she summoned the courage to thrust the key into the slot and pull
the door open. A gasp escaped. The sheer volume of mail packed into the
box indicated he hadn't bothered to show up for weeks, maybe months.

After forcing the contents out of the box, she tossed what appeared to
be junk mail in a trash bin, then carried the remaining stack to her car and
stashed it in the back of her SUV. She already had enough to deal with

today. Searching through all that mail would have to wait until tomorrow while Abby was in school.

Erica made one more stop before driving home and opening the garage door. A knot gripped her stomach as she pulled beside Gunter's sports car. Did he own the vehicle outright, or was it financed? What about her vehicle? And Abby's? She forced the questions aside and carried her suitcase and the box of donuts she'd purchased into the kitchen. A week ago her daughter had lived with the illusion that her mother could afford a massage. And now...

Her phone pinged a text from Abby. "Picking up Dusty, home in five."

Nausea threatened to erupt as Erica rolled her suitcase from the kitchen and eyed the door leading to the main bedroom. Unable to bear the thought of spending one more night in a criminal's bed, she spun away from the door and pulled her suitcase to the guestroom. At least here she'd be on the opposite side of the house and close to Abby's room. Erica returned to the kitchen seconds before a car pulled into the garage.

Her daughter breezed in, tossed her bookbag on the island, and climbed onto a stool while Dusty bounded from the room as if on a mission to scope out his house. "I had the best time, even though Carrie's mom is stricter than you. Would you believe that every day except the weekend, she took our cell phones until we finished our homework? At least you allow me some down time before making me study. Do I smell donuts?"

Erica forced a smile. "All your favorites."

"Either you had a super good time, or you're softening me up." Abby opened the box and selected a cream-filled donut with chocolate icing.

"Where's Dad?"

Erica's pulse pounded in her ears as all the speeches she'd rehearsed during the drive home ran through her head at warp speed. Not a single one would ease the pain she was about to inflict on the person she loved more than anyone in the world. "He isn't here."

"Did he fly off to save another company?"

Dusty returned and plopped on the floor beside Abby's stool.

"Not exactly." Erica poured two glasses of milk, then settled beside Abby. "Sometimes people aren't who we think they are."

"I know. You won't believe what Taylor did when she found out I was staying at Carrie's house."

Erica tuned Abby out as she rattled on about her second-best friend. When her daughter stopped talking long enough to take a drink, she summoned the courage to break the news. "There's something I need to tell you about Brian. His real name is Gunter—"

"If I were a guy, and my parents had stuck me with that name, I also would've changed it to Brian."

This wouldn't be easy. "There's more. His last name isn't Parker." Erica swallowed. "It's Benson."

"Is Brian Parker an alias because Dad's some sort of undercover CIA agent hunting down bad guys? That's way more exciting than turning companies around."

"He's not a secret agent, sweetheart."

Abby's head tilted. "Then what is he?"

Erica placed her hand on her daughter's arm. "The man we know as Brian sent me to Blue Ridge to meet two women he had also married."

"Before he met you?"

"Not before. At the same time."

Abby's brows gathered in. "I don't understand."

Erica breathed deeply, then slowly emptied her lungs. "Gunter Benson has three aliases...and three wives. He's a con artist—"

"No!"

Dusty sprang to his feet with his tail tucked.

Abby's face paled. "That's not possible."

"I understand how difficult this is to accept, sweetheart. But the truth is, Gunter is a master at deception who gambles for a living."

"What makes you think that's true?"

Erica swallowed against the pain attacking the back of her throat. "He sent wedding pictures and a letter to an attorney."

"How do you know they were real?"

"Because he failed to show up in Blue Ridge—"

"The blizzard grounded his plane."

Erica curled her fingers around Abby's hand. "He didn't show up because he left the country."

Abby's eyes shot daggers at Erica seconds before she jerked her hand away and dashed from the kitchen with Dusty bounding behind her.

Anger punctuated with heart-wrenching regret sent Erica's fist slamming on the granite. She winced at the stab of pain triggered by the blow. Despite the unknown future, she had to remain strong for her daughter. She gathered her courage, then strode to the hall and slipped into Abby's room.

Abby curled into a fetal position with Dusty stretched out on the twin bed beside her. Erica knelt on the floor and stroked her daughter's arm as the minutes ticked by. Did Gunter have one ounce of remorse for the misery he'd inflicted on five innocent victims?

Abby sniffled. "Everything you told me is true, isn't it?"

"I'm afraid it is."

"Where do Gunter's other wives live?"

"Wendy lives in Gulfport. She's pregnant. Amanda's in New Orleans. Her daughter's an engineering student at LSU."

Abby uncurled and turned toward her mother. "You aren't really married to Brian, are you?"

"No, sweetheart, I'm not."

"Why did he decide to tell the truth?"

"Because he lost a lot of money gambling and borrowed cash from some loan sharks. He fled to some foreign country because he couldn't pay them back."

Abby remained silent for a long moment. "Would you have married him if I hadn't asked for a new daddy?"

Erica couldn't allow her daughter to shoulder one ounce of blame for Gunter's deception. At the same time, she didn't want to lie. "He charmed his way into my heart and into our lives."

"What are we gonna do, Mom?"

"We'll start figuring that out tomorrow. For now, let's order a pizza and spend the rest of the afternoon binge-watching your favorite series. Then we'll indulge on hot fudge sundaes."

Abby sat up and swung her legs to the floor. "You haven't told me everything, have you?"

"I'm still trying to put all the pieces together." Ignoring the anxiety building up inside, Erica lifted off her knees and slid her arm around her daughter's shoulders. "No matter what happens, we'll face the future together as two strong, capable women."

Tears pooled and spilled down Abby's cheeks. "I love you, Mom."

Erica pulled her close. "I love you too, sweetheart, with all my heart."

Chapter 22

Amanda heaved her suitcase into the overhead bin, then tapped the gentleman sitting in the aisle seat on the shoulder. "Pardon me."

He looked up from his phone, then stood and stepped into the aisle.

Amanda slid to the window and tucked her purse under the seat in front of her. Hoping to send the message she wasn't in the mood for conversation, she peered out at skycaps loading baggage into the plane's belly. Had any other passengers endured anything close to what she and the other wives club members had suffered through?

A teenaged boy plopped onto the middle seat, earbuds jammed into his ears. Assuming her seatmates would remain silent, she closed her eyes. Moments after the plane taxied down the runway and lifted into smooth air, Amanda drifted to sleep.

The flight attendant announcing the approach to the Louis Armstrong International Airport forced Amanda's eyes opened. She lifted her chin off her chest and peered out the window. Returning to her hometown triggered a bundle of emotions. By the time the plane landed and taxied to the gate, one overwhelming desire consumed her.

After deplaning, Amanda rushed to her car and drove to town. She continued past the French Quarter and parked in front of the shotgun house she and Preston had lovingly restored before Morgan was born. The tree they'd planted in the four-foot-wide front yard had somehow survived multiple hurricanes. Two rocking chairs sat behind the porch railing.

Tears trickled down Amanda's cheeks as memories bubbled up. Replacing damaged walls and ceilings. Stripping and refinishing the wooden-plank floors. Gutting and redesigning the kitchen. Replacing shutters and shingles. The work had been dirty and difficult, yet deeply satisfying. Partly because she and her soulmate had labored together, and partly because they'd transformed a dilapidated eyesore into the most beautiful house on the block—the perfect home for their little family of three. If Preston had survived that accident, she would have pulled into the driveway, unlocked the front door, and walked into her living room.

A young mother pushed a stroller toward the river. How many times had she walked baby Morgan along the same path? Amanda closed her eyes. She leaned forward, rested her head on the steering wheel, and imagined Preston's arms wrapped around her. That fateful day had shattered her vision of growing old with the man who had captured her heart. Startled by a knock on the passenger window, she opened her eyes.

An old man leaned down and stared at her. "Are you okay, Miss?"

"Yes." She lowered the window and nodded toward the house. "I was remembering the years my family lived there."

"I hope they were good times."

"The happiest of my life." She stole one more glance at the home, then smiled at the stranger. "Thank you for checking on me."

"I just wanted to make sure you were okay. You take care now and drive safe." He stepped onto the sidewalk and waved as she pulled away from the curb.

Blocks away from her home, Amanda braked at a red light and eyed Harrah's Casino stretching across an entire block. The day she'd met Gunter he'd claimed to be in New Orleans on business. If she'd had the slightest inkling that his business was playing blackjack and poker, she never would have agreed to go out with him. Unfortunately, he'd already mastered the art of deception.

A horn honking from behind forced her eyes back to the road. Ten minutes later, she drove onto her driveway. Surprised to find Morgan's car parked behind Gunter's truck, she popped the trunk and climbed out. The streetcar passed by as Amanda pulled her suitcase to the front porch. Jazz music and the succulent aroma of spaghetti sauce greeted her the moment she stepped into the foyer. She strode into the kitchen. "I didn't expect you home until tomorrow."

"My roommate drove to Shreveport this morning, so I decided to surprise you and Paul with a home-cooked meal."

Amanda's heart jumped to her throat. She had counted on more time to prepare before breaking the news. "It smells delicious."

"Your signature recipe."

Amanda set her purse on the island beside a bottle of red wine, then slid onto a stool. "It'll just be you and me tonight."

"Let me guess. Your husband landed then immediately boarded another plane to fly off to some obscure job site. Not that I'm the slightest bit disappointed. In fact, now's the perfect time to begin happy hour." Morgan cut the foil, then pulled the cork and poured two glasses. "To us."

Amanda clicked her glass to Morgan's. "The best mother-daughter team in the country." Hoping a glass or two of wine would pave the way to explaining the real reason she'd returned home alone, she took her first sip. "How'd your exams go?"

"I'm pretty sure I aced all of them." Morgan sipped, then set down her glass. "I have a date tomorrow night."

"Someone I know?"

Morgan shook her head. "Kevin's a senior mechanical engineering student. His family lives in the Lakewood district."

"Smart young man, most likely from a good family."

"He's also gorgeous and has a great sense of humor. Anyway, I met him a month ago." Morgan continued to tout Kevin's attributes while preparing the pasta. After ladling sauce over the noodles, she placed two plates on the island, sat beside Amanda, and waited for her mom to bless the food. "I've nearly talked your ear off, so now tell me all about Blue Ridge."

Amanda twirled spaghetti around her fork. Maybe she could wait until tomorrow to break the bad news. "The inn was quaint and the company fun." Careful to avoid any mention of husbands or the real reason for the trip, she shared stories about creating the snow family, the town, and Wendy's childhood treasure.

Halfway through her second glass of wine, Amanda paused and ran her finger around the rim. "I stopped by our old house on the way home from the airport. Other than a tree doubling in size, it hasn't changed."

Morgan laid her fork across her plate. "After all these years, I still miss Dad."

"So do I, every day."

"Dad was your soulmate, wasn't he?"

"In every way possible."

"That's why Paul will never replace him." Morgan jerked her head away from Amanda. "Someone's in our driveway." She slid off the stool and dashed to the window. "A tow truck is backing up to your car."

Amanda sensed the color draining from her face as she raced out the back door with Morgan at her heels. A burly man stood beside the truck while lowering the ramp to ground level. Praying he'd made a mistake, she cleared her throat. "Excuse me, sir, but I believe you're at the wrong house."

"Sorry, ma'am. This is the right house, and I'm just following orders."

Amanda's brow pinched. "What orders are you talking about?"

"See for yourself." He fished a paper from his pocket and handed it over. Amanda's throat constricted as she read the document from a leasing company with orders to repossess the car for nonpayment.

Morgan grabbed the paper from her hand.

The driver nodded toward the car. "You need to clear out your personal stuff.

Amanda's heart pounded against her ribs as she retrieved an umbrella and a sunshade.

Morgan's brow pinched. "What's going on, Mom?"

Forget about waiting until tomorrow. "We need to talk." Amanda led the way back to the kitchen island. "There's a valid reason why you've never warmed up to Brian."

Morgan stared at her. "Because he isn't Dad?"

"Partly." Amanda slid onto her stool. "But also because Paul isn't who he claimed to be. His real name is Gunter Benson." Struggling to remain calm, she shared every detail she'd learned about the man, his deception, and what he'd left behind.

"The man's a monster." Morgan's eyes grew lightning fierce. "He needs to pay for his crimes."

"There aren't enough police officers to pursue dangerous criminals, much less a bigamist who enriched casinos, then fled to who knows where."

"He cheated an old woman out of her money, Mom."

"Gunter and Eleanor were legally married."

"But you weren't." Morgan's cheeks reddened. "How long before you're kicked out of this house? And what about my car? Will another tow truck back into our driveway and haul it off too?"

"Maybe we'll find answers to those questions in his post-office box." Amanda breathed to keep her voice calm. "I understand why you're so upset—"

"Upset?" Morgan shot her an incredulous look. "I don't understand why you aren't seething with anger."

"I've had a few days to let it all sink in." Amanda touched her daughter's arm. "When I stepped back and viewed the situation rationally, I realized I have two choices. Let anger consume me or move on and begin a new chapter in my life."

"What about justice?"

"For who?"

"You and the other women he deceived."

"To what end? Revenge? Self-satisfaction?" Amanda topped off her wine. "At this point, all he's taken from me is my pride and a house and a car that were never mine in the first place."

"That doesn't matter. You need to take action and turn the scumbag in."

"I appreciate your advice, honey. But, unless something even more shocking surfaces, I need to forge ahead and take back control of my life. Starting tonight when I sleep in the guestroom."

"In the bed you and Dad shared."

Amanda's heart ached as memories bubbled up. *The same bed where her daughter's life began.*

Chapter 23

Grateful no one sat beside her during the flight from Chattanooga, Wendy avoided eye contact with other passengers as she made her way from the gate to baggage claim. She glanced around the space and spotted Phillip pulling her suitcase off the carousel. How much should she tell her driver if he asked questions about her trip? She approached him.

He grinned. "Welcome back to the sunny south."

"Thanks."

"I'll carry that bag for you."

She handed over the duffle and walked beside him as they made their way to his car, then settled behind the driver's seat. Her entire world had been turned upside down since he'd driven her to the airport.

After setting her bags in the trunk, Phillip slid behind the wheel and started the engine. "How was your first snow experience?"

Surprised yet pleased he'd remembered, she laced her fingers in her lap. She had to tell him something without raising suspicion. Wendy relayed the snow-family story while he drove away from the airport.

"Sounds like you had a blast."

"Not the whole time." She winced. Had he noticed her tone? Hoping to discourage him from asking questions she didn't have a clue how to answer, Wendy leaned her head back and closed her eyes. How long could she avoid running into friends or neighbors? She didn't know anyone in

Asheville. Maybe she should have gone home with Erica. Except her car and everything she owned was in Gulfport. She'd take the rest of the day to come up with better answers as well as a logical story about coming home alone. Whatever Gunter had left in the post-office box could wait until tomorrow.

"You're home, Mrs. Peterson."

Hearing the last name of the fraud she'd married sent a shockwave through Wendy and released a crop of goosebumps. She opened her eyes as the driver pulled beneath the canopy.

He removed her luggage from the trunk, then opened her door. "Do you need help carrying the bags inside?"

"No thanks. How much do I owe you?"

He responded.

She had included a generous tip when she used a credit card to pay for the first trip. What would he think if she tipped him less now that she had to use cash? Did it matter? Yeah, it did. She fished bills from her purse, added a bigger tip than before, then climbed out and handed the payment over. "Thank you for the ride."

"My pleasure. Please call me any time."

Now that she was back home, she wouldn't need to pay someone to drive her around. Grateful the lobby was empty, Wendy rode the elevator to her floor and scurried down the hall. Her pulse pounded as she unlocked the door and entered the condo she'd called home for the past three years.

After depositing her luggage in her bedroom, she trudged to the kitchen, set her purse on the island, and ran her fingers along the granite countertop. How much would it cost to lease a small surfside apartment in Biloxi? Too close to Gulfport. What about the Atlantic side of Florida? Chances are she wouldn't run into anyone she knew that far away. After she sold her sports car, she'd have enough cash to make the deposit and pay rent until she landed a job.

Wendy padded to the living room and eyed the white leather contemporary sofa. If Chris was right about everything in the condo belonging to her, the rooms Kurt had furnished would provide more than enough furniture for her own place—at least until her baby arrived.

She skirted the sofa, opened the sliding-glass door, and stepped out to the balcony. A cool breeze tousled her hair as she breathed in the salty sea air. The setting sun illuminated storm clouds gathering off the coast. Rain was coming. She ran her fingers along the railing. A first or second-floor apartment would be safer for a toddler. Was the Atlantic Ocean as calm as the gulf?

Door chimes drew Wendy back inside. She tiptoed to the foyer and peered through the peep hole at her inquisitive elderly neighbor. Was Mrs. Jones checking to find out if she'd returned home? Whatever compelled her to ring the bell could wait until tomorrow.

Wendy remained at the door until the neighbor left, then headed to the kitchen and switched on the under-cabinet lights. After counting her remaining cash, she took quick stock of the food in her fridge and pantry. At least she could wait a few days before making a trip to the grocery store. Tomorrow she'd figure out how to sell her car without raising suspicion about returning home without a husband. Tonight she'd do what she had done so many other nights when she'd been left alone. Wendy turned on the television and scrolled through a streaming service for her favorite chick flick. After grabbing a throw, she curled up on the sofa and let *The Princess Diaries* transport her to fantasyland.

Hours after the movie ended and she'd drifted to sleep, a thunderclap startled her awake. Wendy wrapped the throw around her shoulders and moved to the open balcony door. She marveled at the lightning show playing out over the gulf. How many times had she stood here alone—waiting for the man she'd known as Kurt to come home? A wind gust sent a shiver through her limbs. Had he ever loved her, or was she nothing more than his third secret trophy wife?

Wendy's muscles quivered as she dashed to the bedroom and pulled the silk spread onto the floor. She yanked the sheets off the bed, grabbed a pair of scissors, and cut the linens to ribbons. When finished, she knelt beside the pile. Tomorrow she'd stuff the rags into a trash bag and send it spiraling down the garbage shoot, like Gunter had done to her life. She returned to the living room, curled up on the sofa, and waited for the sound of rain striking the balcony floor to lull her back to sleep.

Chapter 24

After spiraling into a deep sleep a few hours before dawn, an alarm shocked Erica awake. She lifted her phone off the guest-room nightstand and pressed the off button. This morning marked the beginning of the second day of her return to the role of a single mother. She had to maintain her composure and some sense of normalcy to help Abby deal with their new reality.

Erica lifted her shoulders off the pillow and forced her legs to swing over the side of the bed. After trudging to the bathroom and donning her favorite bathrobe, she slipped into her daughter's room and turned on the nightstand lamp between the twin beds. Dusty yawned, then leapt off Abby's bed and stretched.

Squinting, Abby shaded her eyes with her hand. "What time is it?"

Abby's phone alarm sounded. "Six-thirty on the dot. I'll fix us pancakes while you shower. Our new tradition—Saturday breakfast on a weekday." Hoping her tone belied the anxiety churning inside her gut, Erica brushed her daughter's hair away from her cheek. "So rise and shine, sleepyhead, and get ready for school."

"Ugh." Abby rolled her eyes as she climbed out of bed and headed straight to her ensuite bathroom—one of the luxuries Gunter's deception had provided.

While making her way through the dark hall, Erica heaved a heavy sigh as she imagined sharing a bathroom in a two-bedroom apartment. She flipped on the kitchen lights and opened the back door for Dusty. After filling a mug with coffee and stirring in sugar, she gathered the ingredients for Abby's favorite breakfast—chocolate-chip pancakes with a side of crisp bacon.

Responding to the scratch on the back door, Erica let Dusty back inside. Her daughter's faithful companion sprawled on the floor until Abby wandered in and plopped onto her stool.

Erica set a plate on the island, then poured a glass of milk while Abby smothered her pancakes with syrup. Respecting her daughter's resistance to engage in early-morning conversation, she leaned against the counter and sipped her coffee while breathing in the sweet and smoky aromas wafting across the space. What were the chances she'd find an affordable rental in the same school district? Maybe she could pick up extra hours at work and pay the mortgage company enough to allow her to stay in the house until the end of the school year.

"Thanks for breakfast, Mom."

"You're welcome, sweetheart."

Abby slipped off her stool and walked out with Dusty at her heels.

Erica rinsed her daughter's plate and placed it in the dishwasher, then gazed out at the backyard. Slivers of sunlight peeking through bare branches had begun to turn the black sky to shades of dark blue. What new revelations would the mail stashed in her SUV reveal? She already knew about the maxed-out credit card. Erica turned away from the window. At least the lights and heat hadn't been turned off.

Abby returned with her bookbag slung over her shoulder. She patted Dusty's head, then ambled to the garage.

Erica followed and stood at the door while her daughter backed out of the space and disappeared down the driveway. Thus far, it seemed Brian's deception hadn't traumatized Abby to the point she'd require serious counseling. What would happen when she shared the rest of the news? Erica's eyes drifted to her car parked in the middle slot. Somehow, she had to summon the courage to face the daunting task ahead. She closed the door, returned to the kitchen, and dropped a slice of bread in the toaster.

After forcing two bites down, Erica tossed the toast in the sink. Sheer will forced her legs to carry her to the garage. Gunter's sports car seemed to mock her as she trudged between the vehicles. Her chest tightened the moment she opened her rear hatch and eyed the post-office box contents scattered across the floor. She scooped the mail into a pile and carried it to the kitchen desk. What shocking news hid inside those envelopes? Did she have any other choice but to look?

The overwhelming urge to shower sent Erica dashing to the main bathroom. She turned on the spigot, peeled out of her clothes, and stepped under the rain head. While the hot water eased the tension gripping the back of her neck, the heat failed to alleviate her anxiety.

After drying her hair and donning jeans and a sweatshirt, Erica traipsed to the kitchen and refilled her coffee. Her breath came in short spurts as she glared at the post office-box contents. She couldn't postpone the inevitable any longer.

A sour taste invaded her mouth as she settled at the desk and eyed the top envelope—a letter from a mortgage company addressed to Brian Parker. She slit the envelope and unfolded the notice-of-payment default dated four months earlier. The ninety-day window to pay the past-due balance had passed weeks ago. Sweat invaded her neck and armpits as she pulled every mortgage-company letter from the stack and arranged them in chronological order. The top envelope had been postmarked two days ago. Her fingers trembled as she ripped the envelope open and unfolded the letter. Her heart pounded against her ribs.

Erica sprang to her feet, sending her chair crashing to the floor. Dusty jumped to all fours. Desperate to talk to someone who would understand, she hurried to the guestroom and plucked her phone off the nightstand. She hesitated. It was an hour earlier in New Orleans. Dusty sat beside her and plopped his head on her lap. Erica stroked his muzzle. Hoping her friend wasn't sleeping in, she pressed the number.

Amanda answered after the second ring.

"I hope I didn't wake you."

"You didn't. I've been awake since six. How's your daughter taking the news?"

"Better than I expected. But I haven't told her everything." Erica eyed the print on the wall above the headboard—one of the garage-sale items she'd purchased for her and Abby's apartment. "I emptied the post-office box yesterday." Tears erupted and tracked down her cheeks. "We have four weeks to move out before our home is sold out from under us."

The pain in Erica's voice sent Amanda's hand flying to her chest and tears to her eyes. "I'm so sorry."

Erica sniffled. "Have you emptied the New Orleans post-office box?"

"Morgan and I plan to drive over this morning." What other surprises had Gunter's secret Asheville stash divulged? "Did you open all the mail?"

"Just the mortgage-company letters."

Amanda quashed the urge to blurt details about her repossessed car. Why burden her friend with news that might not affect her. "Whatever happens, we're strong women capable of weathering the storm."

"Our daughters didn't do anything to deserve this."

Amanda sighed. "Neither did the three of us."

"Have you talked to Wendy since she returned to Gulfport?"

"Not yet."

"She might not have anyone other than you and me to talk to."

"Which is why I'll reach out to her later today." Amanda lifted off the kitchen stool and moved to the window. Gunter's truck and Morgan's car remained in the driveway.

"Let me know what you find in the post-office box."

"I will." Amanda ended the call, then returned to a stool and set her phone on the island.

Morgan wandered in, yawning.

"Did you sleep okay?"

"Barely." Morgan poured a cup of coffee. "What about you?"

"I've had better nights." She couldn't tell her daughter she'd cried herself to sleep. "Erica called a few minutes ago." Amanda shared the auction details.

"Four weeks? Based on what you told me yesterday, we're likely facing a similar situation." Morgan carried her coffee mug to the window. "At least we still have two vehicles."

"Since your car is five years old and Gunter's truck is older, they're obviously not leased."

"He could have used them for collateral." Morgan spun around. "How about I scramble us some eggs."

"Fuel for our trek to the post office?"

"It's too early for wine."

"Good point."

After eating and showering in the guest bath, Amanda wrapped a towel around her and stepped into the main bedroom. Knots gripped her belly as she skirted the bed and opened the closet door. This afternoon she'd move her clothes to the guest bedroom.

Morgan stood at the door. "We could burn that bed."

"Or donate it to a homeless shelter." Amanda slipped into a pair of jeans then pulled a sweater over her head.

"How much do you suppose Gunter's old furniture is worth?"

"Assuming they're legitimate antiques, probably a good bit."

Morgan scowled. "Given everything was purchased by a con man, that's one big assumption." She followed her mother out of the bedroom.

"We need to find out how much time we have until this house is auctioned off before debating Gunter's furniture choices."

"It wouldn't surprise me to learn he'd stolen half the stuff."

"I doubt theft is one of his crimes." Amanda led the way down to the foyer and lifted her purse off the console. "Are you ready to raid Gunter Benson's private mailbox?"

"My car's behind the truck, so I'll drive." Morgan grabbed her keys from the bowl and walked out to the front porch.

Amanda followed, then slid into the sedan and buckled her belt. As her daughter backed onto St. Charles Avenue and headed away from downtown, images of Morgan's sixteenth birthday floated up. Her squeal of delight when she climbed down from the school bus and found the car parked in their driveway with a pink ribbon wrapped around the hood. Even after her stepfather's generosity, she'd failed to warm up to him. Maybe at some deep level, Morgan understood that her mother hadn't married a good man.

When Morgan stopped at a light, Amanda's eyes focused on a fly landing on the windshield. Since Gunter had cared enough to give her daughter an expensive car, maybe his affection had prevented him from putting the gift at risk.

The light turned green. Morgan pulled forward.

A car sped toward the intersection.

Morgan slammed on the brakes.

Amanda jolted forward. Her seatbelt locked.

"Idiot driver." Morgan continued through the intersection.

Amanda sucked in air to slow her pounding pulse. Her daughter's quick reaction prevented them from t-boning the red-light runner.

Amanda reached across the console and touched her daughter's arm. "Perfect reaction time." She kept her eyes glued to the road until they pulled into the post-office parking lot.

After pulling dozens of envelopes from the box, they returned to the car and remained parked. Amanda leafed through the envelopes and tossed the junk mail on the floor.

"What's left to open?"

"Mortgage and utility-company letters." She pulled out the latest mortgage envelope and ripped it open. Her nostrils flared. "We have a week less than Erica before Gunter's house is sold at auction."

Morgan gripped the steering wheel. "I don't have to return to campus until January, so I'll help us find a new place to live."

Amanda opened a letter from the power company. "We might need to make that happen sooner than the sale date."

"Let me guess, the power bill is past due."

"Two months."

"What a shocker!" Morgan's tone screamed of contempt.

"Stop by my bank on the way back. I need to withdraw some cash."

Ten minutes later, they drove up to an ATM. Morgan slid her mother's debit card into the slot, typed the pin, then pressed a cash icon. The machine spit out three twenties and a slip of paper. Her jaw clenched as she handed both over.

Amanda blinked, hoping her eyes had deceived her.

Chapter 25

A cool breeze and sun streaming through the open door nudged Wendy's eyes open. She massaged her arms to ward off the chill, then uncurled and pushed off the sofa. After heading straight to the guest bathroom, she traipsed to the kitchen and poured a glass of orange juice. Eager for the sun to warm her skin, she strode to the balcony and set her glass on the table. She eased to the railing and gazed at white caps dotting the surf like lacy ribbons. Even though watching the world turn into a winter wonderland was wonderful, nothing compared to waking up to the gentle swish of surf kissing the beach.

The doorbell chimed. Wendy spun from the railing. Had her nosy neighbor returned? A second chime. She eased to the foyer and peered through the peephole. Mrs. Jones knew she'd planned to return yesterday. Ignoring her again might raise suspicions. Wendy reluctantly pulled the door open. "Hi."

"Welcome back." The woman held a covered casserole-dish carrier in one hand and a folded newspaper in the other. "I assumed you wouldn't want to cook your second day back." She held out the carrier. "So I fixed you spaghetti casserole. All you need to do is heat and serve."

Was she just being neighborly? Wendy accepted the gift. "Thanks. It sounds yummy."

"May I come in for few minutes?"

Denying the request would make her suspicious. "Sure. Do you mind if we sit on the deck."

"The perfect place for a chat."

A chat about what? Wendy set the carrier on the round glass dining-room table, then led her uninvited guest out the sliding-glass doors.

Mrs. Jones lowered onto a chair and placed the paper in her lap. "Did you enjoy your trip?"

What's with the newspaper? "Uh-huh. Especially the snow." She couldn't give her a chance to ask questions. Wendy launched into the story about her new friends' snow family.

"After my husband retired, we moved here from up north to escape the snow and ice." Mrs. Jones fell silent.

Wendy glanced sideways at the woman's profile. Maybe she was just being a good neighbor.

"Most young folks today find their news online." Mrs. Jones paused as if waiting for a response. "My husband is old-fashioned; he prefers print." She held out the newspaper. "Which is how he found this."

Wendy clutched the paper in both hands and struggled to focus on the words circled in red. Pain attacked the back of her throat as reality rocked her brain. The home she had lived in for the past three years was scheduled for public auction one week from tomorrow.

"You and Kurt are such nice folks. Is he another victim of company layoffs?"

Wendy's eyes remained glued on the red circle. Her husband losing his job was a logical explanation and far less humiliating. In a sense it was true, since gambling was Gunter's occupation. "I'm afraid so."

"Where is he now?"

"He's um...interviewing for a job in another town."

"You'll obviously need to move out before next week. Do you have someplace to go?"

Wendy's mouth was so dry it triggered intense thirst, forcing her to grab her glass. She swallowed mouthfuls of orange juice.

"Don't feel bad." Mrs. Jones tone hinted of compassion. "Losing a job is nothing to be ashamed of. Lots of good folks have been hurt by the slow economy. If you need a place to stay, you're welcome to sleep in our guestroom until Kurt returns."

"I...thanks for the offer." Sweat erupted and trickled down Wendy's back. "I have plans."

"Let me know if I can help you in any way." Mrs. Jones stood. "I'll show myself to the door. You stay here and enjoy the view."

Grateful she hadn't added 'while you still can,' Wendy gasped to control her breath. She barely had enough cash to buy groceries. How could she possibly move into a new place and find a job in less than a week? Unless she sold her sports car to give her more time. Rejuvenated by a sliver of hope, Wendy dashed to the bedroom she had shared with Kurt and stepped around the bag filled with shredded sheets. Tomorrow she'd stuff that eyesore down the garbage chute.

After showering and dressing, she grabbed her car keys and rode the elevator to the lobby. How many thousands was the convertible worth? Would she need to call Chris to help her work out the details? Impatient to complete her mission, she entered the parking garage and dashed toward their reserved spots. Wendy stopped dead in her tracks. Her heart pounded against her chest as she gawked at two empty spaces.

The second her daughter parked in their driveway, Amanda rushed to the back door and tossed her purse on the kitchen island. After booting her laptop, she pulled up her bank account and scrolled through the transactions. She slammed her fist on the granite. "That's how the slimeball paid for the trip to Blue Ridge."

Morgan sat beside her. "With your money?"

"He wrote two checks to himself, forged my signature, and took everything except the cash we withdrew and the three dollars left in my account."

"How much did he steal?"

"More than three grand."

"Check forging is a felony, Mom." Morgan's jaw clenched. "You can't let this go."

Amanda's face flushed with heat. "You need to check your account."

Morgan opened her laptop and tapped the keys. "The money's still there. If the scumbag had known I'd opened my own account, he would have wiped me out too."

"I never should have told him about mine." Amanda pulled her ringing phone from her purse. "It's Wendy." She pressed the speaker icon. "Are you okay?"

"Last night a thief stole both our cars. I need to sell mine so I can move out before my condo goes to auction next week." Wendy's voice screamed of panic.

"Slow down and take a deep breath."

A sigh resonated. "If I call the police, maybe they'll find the cars in time."

Amanda's right hand curled. "They weren't stolen. They were repossessed."

"How do you know?"

"Because the same thing happened to the car Gunter gave me."

Wendy whimpered. "My money's almost gone, and my neighbor thinks Kurt is coming back to help me move. I don't know what to do."

"Where are you?"

"In my living room."

"Sit tight, and I'll call you back in an hour." Amanda ended the call.

Morgan propped her elbow on the island and rested her chin on her knuckles. "What are you going to do, Mom?"

"Warn Erica about the bank account, then figure out what we need to do to rescue Gunter Benson's youngest wife."

Chapter 26

Desperate to ease the spinning sensation, Erica pressed her fingers to her temples. How long before Amanda was forced to vacate her house? What about Wendy? How could she tell Abby they were a month away from losing their home? As Amanda's comment about weathering the storm resonated, the spinning subsided. If she sold Gunter's sports car, maybe she'd have enough money to pay the past-due balance and avoid moving until her daughter graduated.

Erica sucked in air and forced her legs to carry her back to the kitchen. The unopened mail taunted her. Summoning the courage to continue tackling the task, Erica set the desk chair upright and opened the latest power company envelope. Assuming Gunter hadn't paid the bill, she jotted the current plus the past-due amounts on a sheet of paper. After adding numbers from the water, gas and phone companies, she stared at the final number. At least she had enough cash in her personal bank account to keep the lights on until she figured out how to sell the sports car.

The tension gripping her shoulders and neck traveled to the base of her skull and triggered a tsunami-sized headache. Careful not to send her chair crashing to the floor again, Erica rose and removed a bottle of over-the-counter pain medication. After washing down two pills, she bit into the one donut left from yesterday. Hoping a warm bath would accelerate the painkillers and give her the courage to open the rest of the mail, she headed straight to the guest bathroom.

After soaking for a half hour, the meds kicked in and reduced the pain to a dull ache. Erica wrapped a towel around her, then traipsed to the closet she'd shared with Gunter and exchanged the towel for clothes. Later today, she'd move everything she'd need to the guestroom. For now she had to continue the task at hand.

Seconds after Erica stepped into the hall, a chime sent Dusty scrambling to the foyer. Erica followed and halted three feet from the door. Should she answer, or wait for the uninvited visitor to leave? The bell chimed a second then a third time. Curiosity won out over irritation, compelling her to respond. She yanked the door open and stood face-to-face with a portly man sporting a scruffy beard. "Can I help you?"

"I'm here for your cars, ma'am."

Erica's brow pinched. "Excuse me?"

He handed over a sheet of paper. "The lease company is repossessing the SUV and sports car."

Her fingers curled forcing her nails to sink into her flesh.

A smug expression hinted of the man's scorn. "Either you open the garage door, or I'll call the cops."

Dusty's growl forced Erica to uncurl her fingers and grip the dog's collar. "There's no need to call the police." A full-blown headache returned with a vengeance as she rushed to the garage. She grabbed a hammer and glared at the sports car. Stunned by the overwhelming urge to smash the windows, she released her grip, letting the hammer slip from her fingers and crash to the concrete with a loud bang. She wouldn't let Gunter steal her dignity and turn her into a criminal.

Sweat invaded her upper lip as Erica removed personal items from the SUV. She opened two of the three garage doors and cringed at the sight of the tow truck backing into position. Desperate to warn her friends, Erica rushed inside and locked the back door. Her pulse accelerated as she tossed her belongings on the kitchen island and scurried to the guestroom. She grabbed her phone off the nightstand and dropped onto the bed. Which of Gunter's other victims should she call first? She pressed a number.

Amanda answered. "I was about to call you."

Erica hesitated. "I have a question. Did Gunter buy or lease your car?"

"Let me guess, a leasing company repossessed the car you thought Gunter owned."

"Cars—his and mine."

"That makes five. One from my driveway and two from Wendy's condo. Which leaves her stranded without a vehicle."

"I wanted to smash his sports car to smithereens before the tow truck backed into position."

"A normal reaction. What about Abby's car?"

"It wasn't on the order. Hold on." Erica rushed to the kitchen and leafed through the remaining envelopes. "I don't see any mail from another lease company."

"Unless we hear otherwise, we'll assume our daughters' cars are owned free and clear."

"At least that would indicate Gunter's conscience isn't totally bankrupt."

"Before you draw that conclusion—" Amanda paused for a long moment. "If I remember correctly, you have a personal account. Right?"

"Yes." Erica swallowed the lump threatening to choke her. "Why?"

"You need to check your balance."

Cold fingers of fear gripped Erica as she forced her fingers to open her laptop and log onto her account. Her heart pounded wildly against her ribs. "That crook falsified your signature and stole your money too, didn't he?"

"All except three dollars."

"He didn't leave me enough to buy a box of donuts." Erica's nostrils flared. "I didn't report my ex for abuse because he's a cop. I can't think of one good reason why we shouldn't report his crimes."

"You and Morgan are on the same page."

"That man belongs behind bars." Erica cringed at her intense urge to exact revenge.

"I agree. But before we go down that path, I need to rescue Wendy, and the three of us need to figure out what we're going to do about the Blue Ridge properties. Take a deep breath and try to remain calm. I'll call you later today."

How could she remain calm? Gunter Benson had taken everything from her. "I'll try." Erica pocketed her phone. Now what? She trudged to the guestroom, counted her cash, and mentally added her next paycheck. After paying to keep the lights, heat, and phones turned on, she'd barely have enough left to buy food. Childhood memories of heart-wrenching stress over where their next meal would come from sent a shiver through her limbs. If she found a second job and sold everything except what she and Abby would need to furnish a small apartment, maybe she'd have enough cash for a deposit and a month's rent. Somehow, she had to summon the courage to break the bad news to Abby.

Following three hours of pacing, crying, and mentally cursing Gunter, Erica froze at the sound of the garage door opening. She silently prayed for composure, then squared her shoulders and strode to the kitchen.

Abby tossed her bookbag on the island. "What happened to the other cars?"

"We need to talk."

"You have more bad news, don't you?"

"Come with me." Erica grasped Abby's hand and led her to the porch swing suspended from the rafters in the glass-enclosed sunroom. The sun shone through the bare tree limbs and warmed the space. Dusty sprawled beside the glass. While continuing to hold her daughter's hand, Erica relayed everything she had discovered.

When she finished, Abby pulled away and sat on the floor beside her canine companion. "When do we have to move?"

Abby's calm voice failed to reveal the anguish Erica knew burned inside her child. "After Christmas." She knelt beside Abby and wrapped her arm around her shoulders.

"You'll need my car to go to work."

"Yes."

Tears erupted and tracked down her daughter's cheeks. "We won't have enough money for college, will we?"

Erica fought to rein in her emotions. "We'll apply for scholarships and grants, sweetheart."

Abby swiped her hand across her cheeks, then lifted off the floor. "I'll be right back."

Resisting the urge to follow her daughter, Erica returned to the swing. Unaware of the turmoil in the home yards away, a squirrel scampered down a tree trunk and dug at the ground. Erica's hands fisted. Why hadn't she continued to work full-time and open a secret savings account? Because she'd trusted the man she'd known as Brian Parker to take care of them.

Abby returned and dropped beside her mom. She placed a thick envelope on her lap.

Erica uncurled her fists. "What's this?"

"Cash left from my summer job."

Conflicting thoughts played havoc with Erica's emotions as she attempted to press the envelope back in her daughter's hand. "This is your money, sweetheart."

Abby gently pushed her hand away. "You've always taken care of me, Mom." Her voice cracked. "Now, we need to take care of each other."

Dusty padded over and laid her head in Abby's lap.

"You and I prevailed before, sweetheart." Tears formed and spilled down Erica's cheeks. "Together, we'll triumph again."

Chapter 27

Amanda filled a glass with ice water and swallowed mouthfuls to ease her parched throat. "Back to our Wendy dilemma." She faced Morgan. "Everything she owns is in her condo."

"Which is why we need to use my credit card to rent a truck tomorrow, then drive to Gulfport, pack her stuff, and bring her here until she decides what to do. I called Kevin and explained a friend needed to move. He volunteered to recruit a buddy and help us."

"Does he know Wendy can't pay them?"

"He's helping as a favor. I haven't told him anything about our situation and won't until I see where our relationship goes."

"When the house goes up for auction, our neighbors will know something's wrong." A crawling sensation crept up the back of Amanda's neck. "I don't know which is worse—having people believe I'm financially reckless, or that I was foolish enough to marry a loser."

"Other than your closest friends who will understand, does it matter what anyone thinks?"

"I've always valued my integrity."

"Which hasn't been compromised." Morgan touched her mother's arm. "Gunter Benson was a master at deception."

"True, but he never won you over."

"Because he wasn't Dad. I have an idea." Morgan withdrew her hand. "Before we have to move, invite your friends over, and we'll spin the Gunter story—"

"I don't want to lie or come across as a hapless victim."

"That's not what I'm suggesting."

"Then what do you mean by *spin*?"

"Tell the story in a way that makes you the strong, capable woman you are."

"I'll think about it."

"Good. Now let's find the best place to rent that truck."

"I'm glad you're home, honey."

"So am I, Mom."

Twenty-four hours after reserving the vehicle, Amanda trudged through the condo's empty living room and out to the balcony. She pulled her sunglasses from the top of her head and eased to the railing.

Wendy clutched a white teddy bear and her book, *Sugar Snow*, to her chest. "When I checked into the Blue Ridge Inn, I had no idea I was ten days away from being homeless." Her bottom lip trembled. "Last night I considered climbing over the railing and jumping. Until I thought about the baby growing inside me. There's no way I'd destroy an innocent child."

Amanda choked back tears as she slid her arm around Wendy's shoulders. "You're already a wonderful mother."

Morgan stepped out. "The guys just loaded the last piece onto the rental truck."

Amanda spun around and faced her daughter. "You go ahead. We need a few more minutes."

"Wait." Wendy twisted around and held out the teddy bear. "Will you take this for me?"

"Absolutely." Morgan cradled the bear in her arms. "I'll meet you two back at the house."

Wendy turned back toward the gulf.

Amanda inched closer to Gunter's youngest wife while drinking in the view. The surf lapped onto the shore, then receded after depositing salty foam. A flock of seagulls soared over the surf. One broke away from the crowd and dove to the surf to capture an unsuspecting fish. The seconds turned into minutes.

Wendy pushed away from the railing. "I'm ready to go now."

Amanda followed her inside. "Do you want to stop by the post office before we leave Gulfport?"

"What's the point?" Her voice faltered. "I already know how much I've lost."

Amanda laced her fingers with Wendy's. "The truth is, you've gained far more than you've lost, honey."

She faced Amanda, her eyes pleading.

"First you have one of God's precious children growing inside you. And second, you're a member of an exclusive wives club."

Wendy clutched her treasured book to her chest. "Promise you won't abandon me?"

Amanda's heart ached for Gunter's youngest victim as she traced an X across her chest. "I promise."

"I'm glad we met."

"So am I. Now, what do you say we head to New Orleans." Amanda escorted Wendy out to the hall and turned toward the elevator.

Mrs. Jones stepped out from her condo. "I have a little going-away gift for you." She pressed a sealed envelope into Wendy's hand.

"Thank you."

Her neighbor's expression hinted of compassion. "I wish you all the best."

Amanda and Wendy continued down the hall, then rode the elevator to ground level and made their way to the rental truck. Wendy climbed onto the passenger seat, peeled back the flap, and pulled a card from the envelope. "Oh my gosh."

"What is it?"

"A note thanking me for being a good neighbor, and a hundred-dollar bill. She must feel sorry for me."

"More likely, she valued your friendship."

"Do you really think so?"

"Absolutely."

Wendy sandwiched the money between the *Sugar Snow* pages, then laid the book on her lap.

After buckling her seatbelt, Amanda pulled out from under the canopy and headed west. As soon as they turned away from the gulf and drove toward Interstate 10, Wendy faced her. "Is Kevin Morgan's boyfriend?"

"They've only begun dating."

"He seems like a good guy."

"Indeed, he does." The remainder of the hour-long drive alternated between questions about New Orleans and long moments of silence.

When Amanda turned onto her driveway, Wendy pointed to the windshield. "Is that Gunter's truck?"

"It is."

"Did he let you keep it?"

"So it seems." Amanda peered at Wendy's pinched brow. "Only because he bought it before I met him."

"Did he also buy that house before you met?"

"He did." Amanda climbed out and escorted her guest across the yard and into the foyer. She tossed the truck keys in the bowl on the console.

Wendy set her book beside the bowl and turned in a slow circle before stepping into the formal living room. She ran her fingers along the back of the period sofa. "The modern furniture Gunter picked out for the condo is way different than what he bought for this place."

"Which makes sense." Amanda ambled to Wendy's side. "Gulfport is a beach town. This house is in a historic district."

"Did he ever call you Wendy or Erica?"

Amanda dug into her memory bank. "Actually, he almost never mentioned my name. Instead, he called me Hon."

"That's the same pet name he called me. I guess he didn't want to slip up."

"Gunter was smart and devious enough to live three totally different lives. Except for the gambling, which turned out to be his downfall."

"One time I played a slot machine in the Biloxi casino." Wendy lifted a vase off the end table. "After I won fifty dollars, the gambling bug bit me. I kept buying more tokens and ended up losing a week's worth of tips. I never went back." She set down the vase. "What about you? Did you ever gamble?"

If marrying the man who called himself Brian could be considered gambling. Amanda dismissed the thought and shook her head. "Fortunately, I never had the desire."

The front door opened, followed by footsteps and the pungent aromas of tomatoes, cheese, and sausage. Morgan carried a large pizza box. "After all our hard work, we deserve the ultimate comfort food." She placed the teddy bear on the console beside Wendy's book. "Don't worry about the money, Mom, I used the gift card Gunter gave me for my birthday. Ironic, because he most likely bought the card with the money he stole from your bank account."

Wendy's mouth fell open. "He stole money from your mother?"

"Sorry, Mom, I assumed you'd told her during your drive."

"What better time to explain another of Gunter's crimes than while indulging on pizza that's likely to give us serious indigestion."

"Good one, Mom."

After devouring the pizza, trashing Gunter, and watching two chick flicks, Wendy grabbed her childhood treasure and bear off the console and followed Amanda up to the second floor. She stopped beside a closed door. "Was that your and Paul's bedroom?"

Amanda nodded.

"Are you still sleeping in there?"

"I can barely stomach walking in, much less touch the bed."

"After I came home from Blue Ridge, I couldn't sleep in his bed either. Which is why I left it in the condo. Guess what was in that big garbage bag in the corner of the bedroom."

"Hmm. The sheets off the bed?"

"Cut to ribbons."

"Way to go, Wendy." Morgan set their guest's oversized suitcase at the top of the stairs, then pulled it down the hall.

Amanda elbowed Wendy. "Come on, I'll show you to your room."

Wendy followed her to the fourth bedroom furnished as a sitting room. She set the teddy bear and her copy of *Sugar Snow* on an antique rocker.

Amanda made up the sleeper sofa and cleared a space in the closet. "Tomorrow the three of us will begin mapping out our next steps."

Wendy embraced Morgan, then Amanda. "Thank you for helping me."

"That's what the Gunter Benson wives club is all about. Helping each other. Besides, you're family now." Amanda released her young friend.

"Let us know if you need anything." She followed Morgan from the room and pulled the door closed.

Her daughter nudged her arm. "What's with the wives-club comment?"

Amanda leaned close to Morgan. "That's what we call our little trio."

"Clever, and appropriate. Because in addition to the property in Blue Ridge, it seems you've inherited a second daughter."

"Which means I'll become an unofficial grandmother before I turn forty-five."

"A gorgeous, sexy grandmother."

Amanda's mind drifted to the lacy teddy she'd packed for the trip to Blue Ridge. "Remind me to burn it tomorrow."

Morgan's brow pinched. "Burn what?"

"The last remnant from my first anniversary with the fraud I married."

Wendy's eyes shifted from the landscape painting that graced the dark blue wall behind the sofa bed to a coffee-table book lying on the end table—*The Majesty of St. Charles Avenue*. She sat on the bed and traced her finger over the title, then lifted the cover and leafed through photographs of magnificent historical homes. Had the seven-bedroom house in Blue Ridge been as grand as those pictured in this book? Could it be again?

She set the book back on the table and ambled to the window overlooking the street. It would be fun to ride a streetcar to work every day. Her eyes drifted to an antique desk beside the window. How many thousands was that worth? Gunter had expensive taste, so the condo furniture should bring a good price. Except she'd need most of the pieces to furnish her own place. If she and Amanda became roommates, could they afford to rent an apartment on this street? Unless her friend's memories were too painful to stay in New Orleans, or to live with one of Gunter's other wives. Although she did say they were family.

Wendy opened her suitcase. After moving her laptop to an end table, she stared at the items she hadn't stuffed into boxes. How much money had she spent on expensive clothes since she'd married Kurt? She swallowed the regret threatening to choke her and pulled out pajamas. After changing clothes, Wendy switched off the bedside lamp and slid under the covers. Light from the streetlamp cast a dim glow across the room. She eyed the ornate gold ceiling medallion enhancing the combination fan and stained-glass light fixture. Did Gunter prefer the contemporary condo he'd furnished as Kurt, or this antique-filled house he'd decorated as Paul? What style had he chosen for Erica's home?

She rolled onto her side and peered at the white teddy bear propped on the chair. A fluttering sensation akin to a swarm of angry butterflies rippled through her chest. Tears erupted and dripped onto her pillow. How could she possibly earn a decent living and raise a child by herself?

Chapter 28

Erica pulled up to the curb in front of the high school and turned toward her daughter. "Are you still okay with the explanation we landed on last night?"

"Half my friends' parents have gone through a divorce, and a breakup is easier to explain than what's really going on." Abby placed her hand on the door handle. "Besides, our story is a version of the truth."

"At least we have that going for us."

"I'll ride home with Carrie." Abby blew her mom a kiss, then climbed out and retrieved her bookbag from the back seat.

Erica gripped the steering wheel as her daughter scurried up the sidewalk to join her circle of friends. How would Abby react when the full weight of Gunter's actions sent them spiraling from affluence back to financial hardship? After pulling away from the curb and easing past the school zone, Erica mentally prepared for her first day back to work since returning from Blue Ridge. She continued to rehearse the request she'd begun practicing while preparing breakfast.

By the time Erica parked behind the strip mall, tension gripped her neck and shoulders. She forced her legs to climb from her daughter's car and carry her to the upscale gift store's rear entrance. Inside, Erica stashed her purse in a cubby and peered around the storage space she had helped organize. She summoned every ounce of courage she could muster, then edged to the office and tapped on the open door.

The middle-aged store owner turned away from her computer screen. "Welcome back."

"Thank you. Do you have a moment?"

"For you, anytime." Janet Huffman motioned to a chair. "How was your trip?"

Erica sat across the desk from her boss. "The inn was wonderful and the town lovely." She crossed her legs at her ankles and folded her hands in her lap. Time to test the version of the story she and Abby had agreed upon. "One big discovery during the trip was how far apart my husband and I have drifted."

"The same thing happened in my marriage a decade ago. Sometimes I find it challenging being married to a dedicated FBI agent. Anyway, we worked out our problems. I hope you and Brian can mend whatever fences are broken in your relationship."

Except the man she'd known as Brian was a fraud. "Unfortunately, some fences are beyond repair."

"I'm sorry for you and your daughter. How's Abby taking the news?"

"She understands. The thing is, we need to move out on our own."

Janet's brows squished together. "Why doesn't Brian move out and let you stay in the house?"

A prickling sensation skittered up Erica's back. She hadn't anticipated that question. "Actually, we're not keeping the house."

"Losing your husband *and* your home is a bummer."

If only that was all she and Abby had lost. "Which is why I need to work a lot more hours."

"Our customers love you, and I wish I could bring you in full-time. But with the sluggish economy, I can only afford to add a couple of hours to each of the three days you're already working."

Erica struggled to conceal her discouragement. "That will help."

Her boss propped her forearms on the desk and laced her fingers. "I'd be glad to put you in touch with my sister-in-law. She's a professional marriage counselor with excellent credentials."

Should she share the more accurate story? That the man Janet knew as Brian was a criminal who'd stolen her last dime? To what end—other than invoking pity? Best to stick with the plan. "I appreciate the offer, but our marriage is beyond repair." *Because it never existed in the first place.*

"In that case, I wish you and Abby the best. If you'd like, you can begin the extra hours today."

"Thanks, I will." Erica stood and strode back to the cubby while mentally calculating how much six additional hours would provide—barely enough to buy a week's worth of groceries. The tension in her neck exploded into a killer headache. After digging into her purse for her pillbox and grabbing a bottle of water, she swallowed two over-the-counter pain pills.

With twenty minutes to kill before the store opened for business, Erica pocketed her cell phone, then headed to the front and rearranged a display of Christmas-themed items. Even though working retail was better than waiting tables, she'd made more money in tips than the hourly wage Janet could afford to pay. But that was six years ago, when the economy was booming. Would the same hold true today, and could she endure the hectic pace of restaurant work?

Erica ambled to the window and peered past the traffic to the bank across the street. Had desperation or a heartless soul driven Gunter to falsify checks and steal money from two women he professed to love? Would two part-time retail jobs provide enough income to survive? Her fingers curled, digging her nails into her palms. To protect Abby, she had to get a grip and keep people from learning the real reason Brian Parker would never again show his face in Asheville.

"Next week we'll offer a fifty-percent discount on all our Christmas stock."

Erica uncurled her fingers and spun toward Janet. "Good idea." If she arranged a garage sale, would she be able to sell everything she and Abby wouldn't need for more than pennies on the dollar? Would an estate sale bring in more money? How would she explain either to the neighbors without raising all sorts of questions?

"You seem a bit tense, which, given your circumstances, is understandable."

Erica forced her thoughts into submission. "I'm waiting for the aspirin to kick in and cure my headache."

"What a shame a few pills can't heal your marriage."

No kidding.

"If you don't have someone in mind, I can recommend a good divorce lawyer." Janet unlocked the front door. "She's one of my closest friends and as tough as nails."

Images of Chris spreading three photos on the Blue Ridge Inn dining-room table wrestled to the surface. "Thanks for the offer, but I've already talked to an attorney."

"Good for you. Time to go to work. Our most loyal customer just parked out front."

Erica pasted on her best smile and welcomed the woman whose frequent purchases hinted she either had endless resources or huge credit-card debt. For the remainder of her shift, she kept her anxiety at bay and took care of customers.

The tension exploded in her neck the moment Erica turned onto her driveway and spotted her inquisitive next-door neighbor heading up the front sidewalk. She parked beside the closed garage doors and breathed deeply to slow her racing heart. Erica climbed out and met the elderly woman on her front porch. "How are you, Mrs. Nesbit?"

"I'm fine, dear, but I'm worried about you."

Alarm bells erupted in Erica's head. Had her neighbor seen the tow truck hauling off their vehicles? Or had she noticed the empty spaces in the garage when she pulled out earlier? Did she dare ask?

"I read the notice in the paper about the public auction scheduled for next month."

Heat inched up Erica's neck and attacked her cheeks.

Mrs. Nesbit tilted her head. "There's nothing to be ashamed of if your husband's been laid off. The economic woes have affected far too many good folks around here."

Was she offering condolences or fishing for information? Either way, Erica needed to tread lightly. "Unfortunately, he lost his job." Technically that was true, although the reasons had nothing to do with the economy.

"What a shame." Mrs. Nesbit flicked a fly away from her face. "We hope your house doesn't sell for too much below market."

Who did she mean by 'we'? She and Mr. Nesbit? Had other neighbors noticed the tow truck or the public-sale notice?

"I haven't seen your husband around in a while. Is he looking for work in another town?"

If identifying victims to feed his gambling habit in some foreign country qualified as work. "Yes, he is."

"For your sake, I hope he finds something soon. When do you plan to move out?"

"Right after Christmas."

"You've been good neighbors. We'll be sorry to see you leave." Mrs. Nesbit stepped off the porch, indicating she'd achieved her objective.

Erica unlocked the front door, shuffled to the living room, and dropped onto the sofa. How many friends and neighbors would read the notice, recognize the address, and call or show up at her door to probe into her business? She'd moved from Baltimore to escape an abusive husband. Would shame force her and Abby to flee to another town? Could they find the strength to endure and move on with their lives in Asheville?

Dusty padded in and plopped her head on Erica's lap. She scratched behind the canine's ears setting the dog's tail to thumping the floor in a lazy motion. "You don't mind where we live, do you, girl?" If only the same held true for her and Abby.

Chapter 29

Following a restless night riddled with nightmares about bringing her baby home to a grungy tent under a bridge, Wendy forced her legs over the side of the sofa bed and stood. She slogged to the hall bathroom and stared at the hint of dark circles under her eyes. Her grumbling stomach and dry throat prevented her from returning to her room and crawling under the blanket. She trudged downstairs and followed the coffee aroma to the kitchen. "What time is it?"

"A little after nine." Amanda set her phone on the island and lifted off her stool. "The coffee's three-quarters decaf, if you'd like a cup."

"Do you have cream?"

"Vanilla-flavored."

"Then, yes." Wendy climbed onto a stool.

Amanda filled a mug and removed creamer from the fridge, then set both on the island. "Did you sleep okay?"

"A dream that haunted me before I married Kurt returned. Except this time it wasn't just me living under a bridge with other homeless people."

Amanda sat beside her.

Wendy cradled the mug in both hands and focused on the cream-colored liquid. "A week after my eighth birthday, I moved in with a new family. One of the other foster kids was a twelve-year old girl who had a nasty temper. The second time she slugged me, I ran away with nothing except the clothes on my back and *Sugar Snow*." Wendy's eyes remained downcast. "I spent that night in a convenience-store bathroom reading my book and imagining living with a mother and father who loved me."

"You were a brave girl to strike out on your own."

"I slept in that stall until my stomach grumbled so loud it woke me up. That's when I snuck into the store. The clerk caught me stealing a package of donuts and made me sit on the floor behind the check-out counter. When a police car parked out front, I thought the cops had come to take me to jail. Instead, they drove me back to the house." Wendy lifted her chin. "The next time that bully punched me, I slugged her in the face and gave her a bloody nose. She never hit me again."

"Which proves that bullies back down when someone stands up to them."

"Sometimes I wonder what happened to that girl." Wendy took a sip of coffee. "Know what I want to do this morning? I want to ride that streetcar."

"Good idea. In fact—" Amanda lifted off her stool. "After I fix you scrambled eggs to stop your tummy from protesting, we should ride down to Canal Street, then walk along the riverfront and treat ourselves to beignets at Café du Monde."

Morgan wandered in. "Sounds like you're planning to play tourist instead of figuring out what to do with your lives."

"You'll have to excuse my engineering-minded daughter." Amanda removed a carton of eggs from the refrigerator. "She's a stickler for digging into details."

"I learned from the expert." Morgan embraced her mother. "Seriously, shouldn't you focus on what's most important?"

"Waiting twenty-four hours won't matter all that much."

"Except we'll be one day closer to needing a place to live."

"Tell you what. Tomorrow morning, the three of us will meet right here and begin planning our future." Amanda cracked eggs into a pan. "By the way, I invited my three closest friends to join us for wine and cheese tonight."

"To party?" Wendy's tone hinted of surprise.

"Partly, but also to tell them the truth about the man they know as Paul."

"Good for you, Mom. I hope you don't mind me not joining you." Morgan stirred sweetener into her coffee. "Kevin and I are spending the day together."

"I like Kevin." Wendy clutched her mug. "He seems like one of the good guys."

A smile lit Morgan's face. "He is...in so many ways."

"I'm happy for you, honey." Amanda plated scrambled eggs while Morgan carried her coffee out of the kitchen.

After wolfing down breakfast and showering, Wendy slid the hundred-dollar bill from Mrs. Jones into her jeans pocket, then donned a denim jacket and dashed downstairs. "I'm ready to go."

"What a perfect day to explore my hometown." Amanda slid her miniature purse over her shoulder, donned sunglasses, and held the front door open. Three minutes after strolling to the corner, they boarded the dark green streetcar and found an empty seat.

Wendy propped her forearm on the windowsill and imagined crowds lined up along sidewalks ogling colorful parade floats. "My first foster dad gave me seven strands of Mardi Gras beads. He said a lady threw them off the balcony in the French Quarter. I kept them in a shoebox until I aged out of the system and gave them to a seven-year-old foster kid." Wendy fingered the delicate chain dangling a gold and diamond heart below her throat.

"That necklace you're wearing beats the heck out of plastic Mardi Gras beads."

"My first anniversary gift. I don't know if Kurt picked it out at a store or if Gunter stole it from Eleanor's jewelry box."

"Based on his gambling addiction, I'm guessing all the physical items he inherited from Eleanor were either liquidated in an estate sale or ended up in pawn shops."

"Everything except the Blue Ridge houses." Wendy lowered her hand. "Have you heard from Chris or the real-estate lady?"

"We've only been gone a few days."

"I know." Failing to mask her disappointment, Wendy focused on the passing scenery and imagined living in New Orleans. How much rent would she have to come up with? Was it safe to live downtown or near the French Quarter?

Moments after exiting the streetcar and crossing Canal Street to the sidewalk, Wendy cringed. A woman dressed in tattered clothes slumped against an abandoned storefront. What was her sad story? Had a heartless man abandoned her and left her penniless? Wendy forced her eyes to look away.

Five blocks and six homeless people later, they strolled past the aquarium and stopped at the edge of the muddy Mississippi river. "What do you suppose it's like to live on a boat?"

"Rocky and wet if you sleepwalk or forget you aren't on dry land."

"Even a rowboat would be better than living on the street."

Amanda nudged Wendy's arm. "Fortunately, we'll never have to experience either."

They resumed their stroll along riverwalk, until they stopped beside the Steamboat *Natchez* moored at the dock. "Did you ever ride on that boat?"

Amanda nodded. "A second-anniversary dinner cruise with Preston."

"Are you going to keep the name Sullivan or change it back to Smith?"

"Since Gunter and I weren't legally married, my name is technically still Amanda Smith. What about you?"

Wendy shrugged. "If I keep the name Peterson, at least people will think my marriage was legit."

"That makes sense. Except you'd have to legally change it."

"Chris can help me make that happen."

They continued meandering along the river until they crossed over to Decatur Street and walked a block to Café du Monde. After ordering, they settled at an outdoor table under the canopy. Wendy bit into a powdered-sugar-coated beignet while peering at other diners. "How many of these people do you suppose are locals?"

Amanda pushed her sunglasses up. "Considering this is one of the city's most well-known tourist destinations, and beignets aren't exactly what you'd call healthy, I'm guessing fewer than half."

"Blue Ridge is also a tourist town."

"On a much smaller scale."

"With a train instead of streetcars." Wendy's eyes drifted from a couple pushing a stroller to horse-drawn carriages lined up across the street beside a park. "Did you and Preston live far from here?"

"Within walking distance."

"What do you suppose your house is worth now?"

"A lot more than we paid for it."

"Do you wish you'd kept it after you married Paul?"

Amanda brushed sugar off her lips. "No, because the profit from selling that house paid for Morgan to attend LSU."

Wendy's head tilted. "How did you keep Gunter from stealing that money?"

"A secure education savings account."

"Smart move."

"Back then I didn't have a clue how smart."

A bird swooped down and plucked a crumb off the pavement. "If I'd had the money to go to college, I would have studied business and become an executive with a big company."

"An impressive goal."

One she'd never achieve. Wendy focused on passersby until she swallowed her last bite of beignet and drained her coffee. "Where did you first meet the man you thought was Paul?"

"A block from here." Amanda wiped her fingers with a napkin, then pushed her sunglasses down and stood. "Come on, I'll show you."

They made their way to the sidewalk. Just past Café du Monde, Wendy halted in front of Aunt Sally's. "Oh my gosh, they sell homemade pralines." She dashed inside.

Amanda caught up with her. "Are you suffering from a pregnancy craving?"

"My favorite foster mother made pralines." Wendy scooped two packages off a display and carried them to the counter. She pulled the hundred from her pocket and handed it to the clerk.

Amanda leaned close. "Are you sure this is how you want to spend your cash?"

Why was Amanda questioning her purchase? It wasn't as if she was spending money on clothes. "I'm gonna share the pralines with you and Morgan. Besides, I wouldn't have the money if Mrs. Jones hadn't given it to me."

Amanda shrugged. "That's true."

Wendy pocketed the change as they returned to the sidewalk.

They remained silent while strolling past more shops. At the end of the building, Amanda turned up a wide alley. She stopped beside a circular statue featuring six life-sized jazz musicians set in a pool of water. "This is where my tours began."

Wendy sat on the knee-high concrete barrier encircling the pool. "And Gunter was one of your tourists?"

"He was."

"Will you go back to being a tour guide?"

"I'm thinking about it."

Wendy twirled her fingers in the water. "Does that job pay well?"

"Ten years ago I made eighteen bucks an hour plus tips. I don't know about today."

"Did Gunter give you a big tip?"

"A fifty-dollar bill, which was more than the cost of the tour." Amanda scoffed. "If I'd only known where that money came from. But I didn't, and here we are—members of an exclusive wives club."

"What are you gonna tell your friends tonight?"

"The truth."

"I have an idea." Wendy popped up and dashed up the alley.

Amanda caught up with her. "Are you planning to buy more pralines?"

"Even better. We're gonna take a buggy ride."

"Hold on." Amanda grabbed Wendy's arm. "Those rides aren't cheap, and you're short on cash."

"You agreed that the hundred is my money, right?"

"Yes, but—"

"Then I want to treat us to a ride through the French Quarter."

Amanda released a sigh. "You won't let me convince you to keep that money in your pocket, will you?"

"Nope. But you can tell me all about the sights while we take that ride."

By eight o'clock, Amanda's guests had gathered in the formal living room, polished off a bottle of wine, and spent an hour chatting about their happy lives. During the first lull in the conversation, her oldest friend crossed her leg over her knee and pointed her empty glass at Amanda. "You haven't told us about your anniversary trip."

Words and thoughts collided in Amanda's head. "About that." She paused for a long moment to harness her courage, then nodded toward Wendy. "Actually, our houseguest is more than a friend." She breathed deeply, then launched into the Blue Ridge events, ending with news about the house, repossessed cars, and stolen money. When she finished, a stunned silence hung heavy. A fireplace log split and fell, sending sparks spiraling up the chimney.

Her closest friend set her glass on the coffee table. "First, thank you for trusting us enough to share the truth." She crossed her leg over her knee and pumped her foot. "And second, you should have that creep arrested and locked up without a key."

Another friend leaned forward. "We should start a go-fund-me campaign—"

"No!" Amanda cringed at the ferocity of her response. "For Morgan's sake, I don't want anyone else to know. Besides, Wendy, Erica, and I are capable of moving on without relying on charity." Amanda lifted a bottle of pinot noir off the end table, pulled the cork, and poured. "So, instead of wallowing in a pity party, let's enjoy Paul aka Gunter's last bottle of fine wine while we trash the bum."

Her friend lifted her glass. "Here's to three brave women who are members of the most unusual private club on the planet."

Wendy lifted her glass of ginger ale. "And to new friends."

Chapter 30

O n the way home from her second day of extended-work hours, Erica paid her utility and phone bills. At least she'd keep the lights and heat on through Christmas. Unlike her and her brother, she and Abby wouldn't have to survive on Raman-noodle meals. Although Hamburger Helper and peanut butter sandwiches would become menu staples.

Back home, Erica set her purse on the kitchen island, then pulled a box from under the counter and tossed Dusty a dog biscuit. "We won't let you go hungry either." She climbed onto a stool and checked her phone. No word from Amanda since she'd rescued Wendy. Resisting the urge to call, Erica pulled up her emails. Nothing worth reading.

She slid off her stool, filled a glass with ice water, and swallowed a mouthful. How long should they wait before calling Chris or the real-estate woman? A few more days? Until next week? She set her glass on the counter and cringed as she peered out at the spacious backyard. How could she and Abby leave this elegant house in Asheville's wealthiest neighborhood and move back into a cramped apartment without succumbing to bitterness? If she'd found a way to attend community college instead of marrying Jack, she'd have a marketable skill to fall back on. Her mind drifted to the first moment she'd cradled baby Abby in her arms and fell deeply in love. If she hadn't accepted Jack's proposal, the most important person in her life wouldn't exist.

Erica spun away from the window and stooped to stroke Dusty's back. "Life isn't always fair, is it, girl?"

The dog's tail thumped the floor in a lazy rhythm. Suddenly, Dusty's ears perked at the sound of Abby's voice drifting from the foyer. She sprang to her feet and scrambled from the kitchen.

The moment Abby strode in with Carrie by her side, her pained expression sent a shiver cascading down Erica's spine. "What's wrong?"

Abby dropped her bookbag on the floor. "The meanest, most conceited girl in school knows about our house going up for auction."

"I'm so sorry, sweetheart."

"By tomorrow everyone will know and make fun of me."

Carrie looped her arm around Abby's elbow. "Your friends will stick by you no matter what happens."

Abby pulled two bottles of flavored water from the fridge and a bag of chips from the pantry. "We'll be in my room, Mom." Dusty followed the girls out of the kitchen.

Grateful Abby and Carrie were close, Erica slid onto a stool. The time had come to channel her anger into positive action. She logged onto the internet and began searching for waitress job openings. An hour later she'd completed five applications, one at the restaurant where she'd met the man who had introduced himself as Brian Parker. At least she'd taken a positive step toward eking a living for her and Abby.

Desperate to remain task-oriented, she pulled up an Excel spreadsheet and began listing items she could sell. When finished, she forced her legs to carry her to the main bedroom. She stepped into the oversized walk-in closet and gawked at Gunter's clothes. How had he managed to live four separate lives without slipping up or calling one of his wives by the wrong name? Erica dug deep into her memory. When they began dating, he called her Hon, never Erica. After they married, every time he was in Asheville, he spent hours in his office with the door closed. She'd accepted his explanation about needing quiet to focus on paperwork. Was that the same excuse he gave Amanda and Wendy when he spent time in their homes?

A rush of adrenaline sent Erica dashing to the kitchen to grab a package of garbage bags. She scurried back to the closet, yanked a suit off a hanger, and stuffed it in a bag. Like a crazy woman on a mission, she filled six bags with his clothes and toiletries, then pulled the sheets off the bed and stuffed a seventh bag. When finished, she dragged every trace of evidence that he'd ever been in that room out to the garage.

Erica returned to the closet and began transferring her clothes and personal items to the guest suite. She wouldn't spend another night in the room where she'd slept with the man who had deceived her, until the time came to sell the furniture. Erica ambled to the kitchen and opened the under-counter wine chiller. In addition to a bottle of pinot noir, three bottles of chardonnay remained—all with the same label she'd shared with Amanda the day they'd met. Why not indulge now?

Erica pulled the cork from a bottle, filled a glass, and took a sip. As the golden liquid slid down her throat, memories bubbled up of the second time she and Gunter's other wives met in the library. She'd ripped her wedding picture to shreds after returning to her suite, then crawled into bed and cried herself to sleep.

Forcing the images aside, she carried her glass to the sunroom and took another sip. Had the man she'd known as Brian already conned someone else out of their money, or had he kept enough cash to bankroll his gambling habit?

Abby wandered in and plopped onto the swing. Dusty sprawled beside the glass. "Carrie invited me to spend tomorrow night at her house. But I don't want to leave you alone, so she's staying here instead."

"That's sweet of you, but you don't need to worry about me." Erica sat beside her daughter. "I applied for some jobs earlier today."

"Waiting tables?"

"It's honest work."

"And you're still hot enough to earn good tips."

Erica managed a grin. "I'll take your comment as a compliment."

Abby set the swing in motion. "Do you think you'll ever marry again?"

"Honestly?" Erica swirled her wine. "At this point, letting another man into our lives is so far down my list of priorities, it barely exists. Although, one fact is undeniable. I'll need to read a lot of books about how to tell the good guys from the jerks before I ever accept another date."

"Or you could write one on how to spot a con man."

"Not a bad idea." Erica swallowed another sip. "I'm proud of you for standing up for yourself at school."

Abby lifted off the swing, dropped to the floor beside Dusty, and wrapped her arms around her canine companion's neck.

A sense of trepidation exploded in Erica's chest as memories from her high-school days surged to the surface—the way teenaged girls in her poor neighborhood had a penchant to treat those outside their social circles with disdain. Would the same happen to Abby? She set her wine on a table, then knelt beside her daughter and sat back on her heels. "Do you want to talk?"

"About what?"

No need to allow her doubt to undermine Abby's confidence. "I just want you to know that we'll always have each other, sweetheart."

Chapter 31

After trashing Gunter Benson with her friends until midnight, Amanda fought the urge to pull the covers over her head. She forced her body to climb out of bed and slog to the bathroom. Hoping a bath would ease her tense muscles, she filled the tub and slid into the hot water. She leaned back and closed her eyes as images of her second date with Preston surged to the surface. How she was overcome with emotion when he shared that his parents' car had been swept away in a flash flood, turning their only child—a sixteen-year-old—into an orphan.

Tears tracked down Amanda's cheeks at the mental image of Preston curled up on the sofa cuddling baby Morgan on his chest. She swiped her fingers across her cheeks. *Gunter Benson should have lost his life to a drunk driver instead of her soulmate.*

Anger punctuated with remorse forced Amanda's eyes open. As Gunter's oldest fake wife, she needed to control her emotions. Especially since she and Wendy could no longer delay a serious conversation about their options.

Before the water cooled, Amanda stepped out of the tub. She dried her hair and slathered on body lotion, then donned a fleece sweatsuit. If not mentally, at least she'd be physically comfortable. She padded from the guestroom and eyed the closed door across the hall—Gunter's private room where he'd claimed to work the few days each month he'd spent in New Orleans.

Morgan walked out of her room and wandered over. "What are you thinking?"

"If I had invaded his space, I might have stumbled on the truth."

"That man was too devious to leave any clues behind."

"Are you saying that because you believe it's true, or because you want to protect my dignity?"

"It would have taken someone with a criminal mind to suspect Gunter of his lies."

"I suppose you're right."

Morgan nudged Amanda's arm as they headed toward the stairs. "How'd your friends react when you told them about 'Gunter'?"

"They called him every degrading name they could come up with while we polished off his last bottle of wine. And they adored Wendy."

"Because she's adorable." Morgan leaned close. "But a little naïve."

"True." At the bottom of the stairs, Amanda linked arms with her daughter. "How was your date with Kevin?"

"Amazing." They headed to the kitchen. "We sat on his parents' back porch and talked for hours. He's a lot like Dad."

"One of the good guys."

"Definitely." Morgan filled two mugs with coffee and handed one to Amanda. "I told him the real reason we packed up Wendy's belongings."

Amanda's brow pinched. What else had she revealed? She slid onto a stool and stirred sugar and creamer into her coffee. "Do you trust him?"

"I wouldn't have told him if I didn't." Morgan dropped two slices of raisin bread into the toaster. "Kevin agrees with me about turning Gunter into the authorities."

Because he was trying to impress her? "The problem is, he committed crimes in at least three states."

"Which most likely makes his a federal case."

"Do you honestly believe federal authorities would waste time searching for some con artist who fled to who knows where?"

"He shouldn't be allowed to get away with his crimes."

Amanda sipped her coffee. "He won't be the first or the last criminal to avoid prosecution."

Morgan buttered then plated the toast. "Are you saying you won't consider turning him in?"

"I will if Wendy and Erica decide that's the right move. Which reminds me—" Amanda unplugged her phone from the charger. "I owe wife number two a call." She pressed the number.

Erica answered before the second ring. "How's Wendy holding up?"

"About as you'd expect. What about you?"

"I picked up a few extra hours at the gift store, and I'll begin a second part-time job waiting tables next week."

"You've made a lot more progress than Wendy and me. Hopefully we'll make some decisions today."

"Have you heard any news about the Blue Ridge properties?"

"Not a peep."

Following five more minutes of conversation, Amanda ended the call with a promise to keep Erica updated.

Wendy wandered in, plopped onto a stool beside Amanda, and set a box of pralines on the island.

Morgan chuckled. "You and Mom obviously played tourist yesterday."

"She showed me where she first met Gunter."

"The infamous ring of jazz musicians." Morgan's tone screamed of sarcasm.

"You'll have to excuse my daughter's snarky tone. She never was a Paul Sullivan fan."

"Especially now that we know the truth about him." Morgan bit into a slice of raisin toast.

Amanda faced Wendy. "I hope you slept better last night."

"At least I didn't dream about living in a tent under a bridge."

"I'd call that progress."

"Speaking of progress." Morgan poured a glass of orange juice for Wendy. "I hope you don't mind me joining you and Mom during your brainstorming session."

Wendy shrugged. "Why would we?"

Amanda slid off her stool. "Before we tackle serious issues, we need to fuel our brains with a proper breakfast."

After devouring bacon and cheddar omelets, the trio strode to the paneled den smelling of evergreen from a scented candle. Wendy sat on the antique sofa facing the home's second fireplace and tucked her ankle under her knee. Morgan chose an accent chair angled beside the fireplace while Amanda settled on the sofa and balanced her laptop on her thighs. She stole a glance at Wendy chewing her fingernail. Her heart ached for the young woman Gunter had impregnated then left homeless and penniless. At least she wasn't alone now.

Amanda opened her laptop. "Why don't we begin by listing our combined assets."

"That'll be a short list," murmured Wendy.

"Now who's being the pessimist?"

"Sorry."

"You're forgiven." Amanda pulled up an Excel spreadsheet and typed *truck* in the first cell. Morgan remained uncharacteristically silent while she and Wendy completed the list, then launched into a lengthy conversation about finding jobs and renting apartments. When they reached a stopping point, Amanda faced her daughter. "Despite the fact you haven't uttered a word, I know something's going on in your brilliant mind."

"I've been listening to you two for the past hour and a half, and quite frankly I think you're going about this all wrong."

Amanda stared wide-eyed at her daughter. "In case you haven't noticed, we aren't overflowing with options."

"That's not the point. You're two smart women who have an opportunity to start fresh. So, why don't you forget about what you don't have and focus on what you want to accomplish?" Morgan scooted to the edge of her seat. "Beginning with you, Wendy."

"Well, I want to love my baby and make sure we live in a nice place."

"What about you personally? What do you want to do?"

"Hmm." Wendy pinched her chin between her thumb and forefinger. "I've always imagined being a businesswoman who people look up to."

"Which means you see yourself as a successful professional, right?"

Wendy shrugged. "I suppose so."

"Good." Morgan eyed Amanda. "What about you, Mom? What are your goals?"

Her brow pinched. Where was her daughter going with this?

"Humor me."

"All right." Amanda set her laptop on the coffee table, then crossed her leg over her knee. "I want to become financially independent and control my own destiny."

"That's exactly what I thought you'd say. So why have you and Wendy only considered going back to jobs you had before marrying Paul aka Kurt? Do you really want to wait tables or schlep around town entertaining tourists?"

"I know I don't." Wendy nudged Amanda. "What about you?"

Truth be told, she didn't relish the idea of guiding tours through the French Quarter's seedy streets. Amanda locked eyes with her daughter. "What are you suggesting?"

"First a question. How committed are you to staying in New Orleans?"

Amanda's brows knitted. She had never considered leaving her hometown. And yet, what compelled her to stay? Her father abandoning them? Cancer stealing her mother from her? Losing her soulmate to a drunk driver? Marrying a criminal?

"The bad memories outweigh the good ones, don't they?"

Amanda blinked. Had her daughter read her mind?

"More bad than good memories live in this town, Mom."

They were for sure on the same wavelength. "I know."

"Then I suggest you figure out a way for the wives club to save those Blue Ridge properties and turn them into a profitable business."

"Are you serious?"

"Why not?"

"For starters—" Amanda pumped her foot. "Winters are cold in Blue Ridge."

"True." Morgan held up her index finger. "There's also one big advantage the Georgia town has over New Orleans—no hurricanes wreaking havoc."

"The same is true for Gulfport." Wendy untucked her ankle and lowered her foot to the floor. "We were lucky our condo wasn't washed away during the last big storm."

Amanda faced the youngest member of the exclusive club. "Are you agreeing with Morgan's suggestion that we look forward instead of going backwards?"

Yeah. But first, we need to call Erica and convince her to jump onboard."

"Way to go, Wendy." Morgan gave her a thumbs-up. "You're already thinking like a successful businesswoman."

Wendy's face beamed.

Amanda leaned back and eyed the still-life painting over the mantel—the garage-sale find she'd brought from the shotgun house. Maybe Morgan was right.

Chapter 32

An hour after the gift store opened for business, Erica ignored her vibrating phone. Moments later a ping followed. Was Abby trying to reach her? She pulled her phone from her pocket. Prickles erupted at the back of her neck and surged down her spine as she read the text. Erica dashed to the checkout counter and pulled Janet aside. "There's a problem at school—"

"Say no more. Go take care of your daughter."

Erica rushed to the back room and grabbed her purse. Abby had never been in trouble before. She scurried to the parking lot and climbed into her child's car. The tires screeched as she pulled onto the road and turned toward the school. She clutched the steering wheel with an iron grip.

This was all Gunter Benson's fault. If she hadn't married him, they'd still live in a middle-class neighborhood. Her foot slammed on the brake the second her brain acknowledged the stop sign. She sucked in air to slow her pounding pulse and eased through the intersection. The last thing she needed was an accident, especially since she didn't know if Gunter had let the insurance lapse. One more problem to solve.

Erica's pulse accelerated as the high school came into view. She pulled into the parking lot. How should she respond to the text? Like a responsible parent, that's how. She hurried to the front entrance and pressed the buzzer. A woman responded. Erica explained the reason for her visit.

The door clicked open. She followed the sign to the counselor's office and knocked.

A woman pulled the door open. "Thank you for coming, Mrs. Parker. I'm Mrs. Johnston, the school counselor." She motioned Erica inside.

Abby slumped on a metal chair with her back against the wall, her chin touching her chest. Erica sat beside her and reached for her hand.

Mrs. Johnston leaned against her desk. "This is the first time Abby has caused any trouble. Unfortunately, her action resulted in property damage."

Erica frowned. "I don't understand."

"She smashed a student's phone against a locker and refuses to explain what prompted her to take such aggressive action."

Abby failed to lift her chin. "I just want to go home." Her voice was barely above a whisper.

"Your daughter has clearly suffered some sort of traumatic experience. Go on and take her home, Mrs. Parker. Call me tomorrow morning, and we'll talk about next steps."

"Thank you, I will." Heart-wrenching remorse fused with anger gripped Erica's chest as she escorted her child to the front entrance and out to the parking lot. She slid behind the wheel and glared at the parking permit on the windshield. Her daughter should have driven her car to school this morning, like every other day since the man they'd known as Brian bought it for her. Abby tossed her bookbag in the back seat and climbed into the front. The way she turned her head toward the side window made it clear she wasn't ready to talk.

During the ride home, Erica's mind filled with questions. Had one of Abby's friends made a derogatory comment? What about Carrie? Had she yielded to peer pressure and failed to stand by Abby? Something had forced her daughter to act completely out of character.

The moment she parked in the garage, Abby bolted from her seat and dashed inside.

Determined to remain calm, Erica filled her lungs, then slowly released the air as she peered at the empty parking spaces beside the car she and Abby now shared. She climbed out and pulled her daughter's bookbag from the back seat. Inside the kitchen, she laid her phone and the bag on the counter, then strode to Abby's room. Her daughter slumped in her beanbag chair staring at her phone. Dusty sprawled on the floor beside her with her head resting on her paws.

Erica settled on the desk chair. "Are you ready to talk about what happened?"

Tears erupted and spilled down Abby's cheeks.

Erica grabbed a tissue off the desk and handed it over. "Did one of the girls say something mean to you?"

"Worse." Abby blew her nose, then held out her phone.

Anger bubbled up inside as Erica glared at a photo posted on social media—two homeless women dressed in rags, crouched on a sidewalk littered with trash. Abby's head was superimposed on one figure, and hers on the other. *All these losers need is a tin cup* was scribed across the top. "Do you know who did this?"

Abby nodded. "She bragged about it to all my friends and said my loser dad is why we don't belong to the country club."

"Which made you angry enough to smash her phone?"

"I wanted to punch her in the face."

"At least you chose the better of two options." Erica set her daughter's phone on the desk. "About tomorrow—"

"I'm never going back to that school."

"You'll feel differently in the morning—"

"No, Mom. I won't." Abby stroked Dusty's back. "The girl who humiliated us is the richest and most popular kid in school."

"Maybe she acted out of jealousy."

"Over what?"

"You're probably a lot smarter than she is."

"Her father's a big-time lawyer and her mother's a surgeon, so she's plenty smart. Besides, I'm not the first person she's done this to." Abby's bottom lip quivered. "The last one was a sweet boy named Johnny. A week after she posted a picture of his head on a girl's nude body, he swallowed a bottle of sleeping pills...and never woke up."

Erica cringed at the cruelty teenagers could inflict on each other through social media. "If you still feel the same tomorrow, we'll come up with an alternative. For now, what do you say we order your favorite lunch and have it delivered?"

"Burgers, shakes, and fries?"

"With extra ketchup."

Forty-five minutes after placing the order, Abby slurped the last of her milkshake. "Know what I want to do now? Watch our favorite Christmas movie."

"*Miracle on 34th Street*?"

"Uh-huh."

Erica snapped her fingers. "Afterwards, let's spend the rest of the afternoon decorating that gorgeous, flocked tree we bought last year." Erica tossed lunch wrappers and paper cups in the trash. "Tomorrow, we'll make a big batch of sugar cookies."

Hours after watching their favorite holiday film, Abby plopped onto the living-room sofa and nodded toward the elegant tree adorned with an array of gold and blue ornaments. "Maybe you should forget about waiting tables and become an interior decorator, Mom."

"There's more to interior design than filling a tree with ornaments." Erica wrapped the quilted gold skirt around the tree stand.

"Not just decorating this place. After we moved to Asheville, you made our apartment look amazing on a shoestring budget."

"We'll talk about my career options later. Right now, I'll fix us a salad to balance our totally unhealthy lunch."

Abby followed Erica into the kitchen and climbed onto a stool. "I want you to teach me at home until I graduate, Mom."

Erica's hand froze on the refrigerator handle. How could she possibly work two jobs and homeschool a high-school senior? "You need a little more time to think this through, sweetheart."

"Carrie didn't come by after school today or text me."

"Maybe she'll reach out to you tomorrow."

Abby shook her head. "She might want to, but she won't. Especially since she's dating one of the most popular guys at school."

Losing her closest friend on top of everything else that had happened during the past two weeks was beyond unfair. Erica grabbed her vibrating phone off the desk. Amanda. Maybe she had news about the Blue Ridge houses. "Hey."

"I left you two messages. Is everything okay?"

"Abby and I spent the afternoon decorating for Christmas. What's going on?"

Erica's brow pinched as Amanda relayed the conversation she'd had with Wendy and Morgan. How could she possibly agree to another radical change that would further escalate the crisis that had invaded their lives?

"Wendy and I are considering this option and want your opinion."

Erica turned away from her daughter and peered at the moon hovering over the bare branches in the backyard. Was Amanda taking the brainstorm seriously or going along to appease Wendy? "I need time to think it through."

"We all do. How's Abby holding up?"

Another question she couldn't answer. "I'm about to fix supper."

"Abby's in the room with you, so you can't talk. Right?"

At least Amanda understood. "If you don't mind, I'll call you tomorrow."

"Take as much time as you need. We won't make a move until we're all in agreement."

Erica ended the call and set her phone on the counter. She spun from the window as Abby slid off her stool and ambled to the den. How big a role should her daughter's drama play in her decision? Erica removed the open bottle of chardonnay from the fridge and filled a glass. One fact remained crystal clear. She couldn't come to a conclusion until she discovered how adamant Abby was about not returning to school.

Amanda set her phone on the coffee table and slumped back on the sofa. A fire crackling in the hearth cast a warm glow on the den's paneled walls. "The only chance we'd have to turn those properties into a business is to move to Blue Ridge. I doubt Erica will agree to yank her daughter out of school halfway through her senior year."

Wendy sat cross-legged beside the fireplace sipping a cup of hot chocolate. "Maybe we could come up with enough money to pay the back taxes without her."

"Because she's an equal co-owner, we'd have to buy her out."

Wendy released a heavy sigh. "We'd have to rob a bank to come up with that much money."

"Regardless of what Erica decides, tomorrow we need to hire an estate-sale company."

Wendy lifted off the floor and moved to the window facing the narrow backyard. "Would you miss New Orleans if you moved to Georgia?"

"When I married the man I'd known as Paul, I knew his job required a lot of travel." Amanda moved to her friend's side. "Although I've never admitted this to anyone, I didn't mind him being away from home half the time."

"Because you didn't love him as much as you loved Preston?"

"We shared some passionate moments, but deep down I'm not sure I ever loved him at all." Amanda turned her back to the window. "Would I miss New Orleans or this house?" She pressed her palm to her heart. "No, because I'll always carry the happy memories with me."

"In that case, we need to figure out how to convince Erica to go along with our idea."

Chapter 33

Erica turned on the hall light and tiptoed into Abby's dark bedroom. Unlike every other school-day morning, Dusty remained on her spot on the bed. Did her daughter's faithful companion somehow sense Abby's need for more time to heal? Erica peered at the phone lying on the nightstand. Six-thirty-two and no alarm, which meant only one thing.

Now what? Wake her or let her sleep? Erica slipped out of the room, pulled the door closed, and followed the coffee scents to the kitchen. She poured a cup of caffeine and carried it to the sunroom. Christmas break would begin in two weeks. If Abby stayed out of school until the new year, she might abandon the idea of homeschooling. It would help if her closest friend found the courage to support her daughter. Although she understood the power of peer pressure, especially since Carrie had grown up in this community.

Erica sipped her coffee and dropped onto the swing. If only Gunter had waited six more months before fleeing the country, but he hadn't. She had fewer than four weeks to make a decision that would have a profound impact on their future.

The first hint of dawn crept into the dark sky. Erica had promised to make two phone calls this morning. One to the school counselor, the other to Amanda. No point tackling either task until she talked to her daughter. She set the swing in motion as her mind drifted back to the week she'd spent in Blue Ridge. The town was a fraction the size of Asheville. Even if they somehow came up with the money to pay the back taxes, they'd never generate enough revenue to turn the ramshackle house into any kind of business. The only logical move was to sell both properties and find other ways to move on with their lives.

At quarter past nine, Abby wandered into the kitchen and opened the back door to let Dusty out.

Erica forced a smile. "Good morning, sleepyhead."

"Did you call Mrs. Johnston?"

"I was waiting for you to wake up, so I'd know what to tell her."

Abby slapped her phone on the island. "Nothing's changed since yesterday."

Obviously, Carrie hadn't bothered to reach out. "Do you have finals between now and Christmas break?"

"Yeah."

"Do you want me to fix you breakfast?"

Abby shook her head, then grabbed a protein bar and trudged out of the kitchen.

Erica's shoulders slumped as she carried her phone to the den and plopped onto the sofa. Hoping the social-media incident would warrant Abby staying away from school for a few weeks, she called Mrs. Johnston. After discussing options, Erica plucked her daughter's bookbag off the kitchen island and headed to her room. Abby slouched in her beanbag chair reading a book. "I talked to your counselor."

"What'd she say?"

Erica set the bookbag on the desk, then lifted the stuffed bear off Abby's bed—the only toy her child had taken with her when they sought refuge in a Baltimore women's shelter. She fingered the pink ribbon tied around the bear's neck. "Mrs. Johnston will arrange for you to take tests and complete December's assignments at home."

She couldn't tell Abby that based on her experience with other bullying incidents, her counselor anticipated she'd miss her friends enough to return to school in January. If the woman knew the rest of their story, would she have the same expectation?

"When do I have to pay for the smashed phone?"

"You don't." Erica placed the bear back on the bed. "When the girl's parents learned about her prank, they told her she was responsible to buy a new one out of her allowance."

"So, her only punishment is paying for a phone she can use to wreck more kids' lives?" Abby's tone screamed of fury.

"Someday her actions will catch up with her."

"No, they won't. Because her family is rich."

Erica's heart ached for her child. At seventeen she'd learned far too many harsh lessons about the dark side of human behavior.

"Thank you for talking to Mrs. Johnston, Mom."

"You're welcome, sweetheart."

Abby lowered her chin and laser-focused on her book, making it clear she needed more time to recover. Erica ambled to the kitchen. Even if there was nothing more than a miniscule chance Abby would change her mind about finishing her senior year in school, she owed it to her daughter to reject Amanda and Wendy's wild idea. She carried her phone to the sunroom and pressed the New Orleans number.

Amanda answered. "I've been waiting for you to call."

"We need to talk."

Amanda stared at her phone as Erica ended the call. She understood the dilemma her friend faced as the mother of a teenager five months away from graduating. At the same time, she empathized with Wendy's new-found enthusiasm. She set her phone on the kitchen counter, then strode to the front porch where Morgan sat on the top step. "Where's Wendy?"

"Riding the streetcar again."

"I hope she remembers where to climb off." Amanda settled beside Morgan. "Erica called."

"Based on your expression, I'm guessing she hasn't bought into our idea."

"I don't blame her." Amanda plucked a twig off the step. "Although our idea qualifies as creative, in reality the concept of turning either of those properties into some kind of business is most likely a pipe dream."

"Every dream has its challenges, Mom."

"Even if all three of us agreed, we'd have a tough time making it happen." She snapped the twig in two and let the pieces slip from her hands. "Without Erica, it's impossible."

"Here's a question. What would you do if you were Gunter's only wife, and you had to make the decision all alone?"

Images of the once grand home fallen victim to years of neglect played like a slideshow in Amanda's mind. Someone with deep pockets and a vision could restore the property to its original condition. "Honestly? I don't know."

Morgan stared straight ahead. "Wendy and I talked for a long time before she boarded the streetcar. Her heart is set on using the houses to change her life."

"Are you trying to convince me not to abandon the idea?"

"I'm just saying, for Wendy's sake and yours, it's too soon to give up. Did you set a date for the estate sale?"

Amanda nodded. "A week from today. The woman in charge is one of the town's most well-known experts on antiques. She plans to meet us here this afternoon to give us an assessment."

Morgan swatted at a gnat. "At least then we'll know where we stand financially."

At two o'clock Wendy responded to the chime and headed to the foyer. Morgan and Amanda caught up with her as she pulled the door open. A tall, silver-haired woman clutched a soft briefcase. "I'm Adele Fontenot." She glanced from one to the other. "Which one of you is Amanda Smith?"

"I am. Please come in."

The woman stepped into the foyer. "Your home is lovely. Have you determined which pieces you want to sell?"

"We wanted to find out what the antiques are worth before deciding."

"Good idea. I'll need time to conduct an evaluation." Adele ran her palm over the console's surface.

Was she already assessing? "We'll wait on the back patio and give you all the time you need."

"Thank you."

Amanda led the way to the kitchen, then removed a pitcher of cherry limeade from the fridge and carried it out to the glass-top table.

Morgan filled three tall glasses, leaving one empty. "This was my favorite mocktail before I was old enough to drink real adult beverages." She handed a glass to Wendy.

"The pretty pink color reminds me of a sunset over the gulf." Wendy took a sip. "This tastes yummy." She set her glass on the table and eyed Amanda. "Did you talk to Erica?"

Amanda stole a quick glance at her daughter, then wrapped her fingers around her glass. "She called while you were riding the streetcar."

"What'd she say about us going into business together?"

How could she respond without fudging the truth or breaking Wendy's spirit? "At the moment, she's dealing with teenager issues."

Wendy ran her finger around her drink's rim. "I went to five different schools after I turned thirteen. Never stayed in one place long enough to make a best friend."

Amanda swallowed the lump rising in her throat.

Morgan reached across the table and touched Wendy's arm. "Now you have three best friends. Tell us about the best thing you saw during your streetcar ride."

During the following ninety minutes, Morgan steered the conversation away from anything relating to Blue Ridge or what was going on inside the house. Until Adele Fontenot appeared and pulled up a chair.

Amanda eyed the woman's nondescript expression. "May I pour you a glass of cherry limeade?"

"My favorite non-alcoholic drink. Perfect choice."

What did she mean by that comment? Amanda filled a glass and pushed it across the table. "I assume you've completed your assessment."

"I have." Adele took a sip. "While your home is filled with lovely pieces, every item except three are reproductions. A few are high-end, the others are more run-of-the-mill."

Amanda's jaw dropped.

Wendy clenched her bottom lip between her teeth.

Morgan's nostrils flared. "Are you saying it's not worth your time to handle an estate sale for us?"

"Not at all. Although my assistant would be in charge instead of me. As I shared with Amanda this morning, our fee is thirty-five percent."

Morgan planted her forearms on the table. "What does that pay for?"

"Excellent question. We handle all the advertising and promotion as well as contact our substantial client list. We'll provide the staff during the three-day sale and handle all the payments. And most importantly, we'll accurately price each piece to reflect the current value and help ensure a sale." Adele handed a sheet of paper to Amanda. "Those are the ten most valuable items listed in order—the first three are the authentic antiques. The number at the bottom of the page is an estimate of your profit if you decide to sell all the furniture and accessories."

Amanda stared at the estimate, then handed the paper to Morgan.

"Since the sale is scheduled to take place a week from today, I need to know if you still want my company to handle it for you."

Without professional help, they wouldn't have a clue how to price anything. Chances were they'd underprice items by more than the company's percentage.

Morgan handed the paper back to Amanda. "Even with the fee, we'll come out ahead using professionals."

Amanda nodded. "I agree."

"Excellent." Adele removed a contract and a pen from her briefcase. "All I need is your signature."

Amanda signed.

"Two days before the sale, my staff will be here to stage the house and price each piece you don't want to keep. When do you plan to move out?"

They'd need the money from the sale before they moved. "Not until after the sale ends."

"I noticed the rental truck in the driveway. It will help my team avoid mistakes if you pack everything you intend to keep except your beds and personal items."

A daunting task but doable. "We'll make that happen."

"Good." Adele took a sip of cherry limeade. "I appreciate your business and promise my team will serve you well." She stood. "I also wish you all the best on your new endeavors."

The moment the antique expert exited the backyard, Wendy grabbed the sheet of paper Adele had left on the table. Her eyes bulged. "That's our profit if we sell everything?"

Amanda slumped back in her chair. "Talk about one giant dose of reality."

Morgan sneered. "And one more example of Gunter Benson's scam."

Chapter 34

Memories muddled Erica's brain as she approached the table where she had first served the man who'd introduced himself as Brian Parker. Why hadn't she waited for an offer from another restaurant? Because she was desperate for cash, and this place had available time slots that fit her complicated schedule, that's why. Besides, it wasn't her customers' fault they'd been seated at a table laced with memories. She pasted on her best smile and greeted the young couple.

Throughout the evening, she continued to shake off images popping up from the nights she'd waited on Gunter. By the time her shift ended at ten-thirty, mental and physical exhaustion made her limbs feel like dead weight.

One of the young male waiters gripped her arm the moment she stepped out the back door. "You shouldn't walk out here by yourself after dark."

Another stark reality. Like a lot of cities, Asheville was no longer the safe haven it had once been. "This is the first time I've been downtown after dark since I last worked here."

"How long ago?"

"Six years."

"Were you a student at UNC?"

Did he really believe she'd been typical college age that recently, or was he being kind? "No, but I was new in town. What about you?"

"I'm halfway through my senior year. Most of the wait staff are students. Except for one old guy who comes in when we're short-staffed."

Great. She'd been reduced to working a job with kids close to her daughter's age. And what did he consider old? Two more servers joined them before he escorted her to Abby's car. Safety in numbers.

During the drive home, Erica replayed her conversation with Amanda. If Abby had already graduated, would she summon the courage to take another giant risk and agree to start over in Blue Ridge? Conflicting emotions churned her stomach. Wendy and Amanda couldn't follow through on their wild idea without her approval. At the same time, she desperately needed money from the sale of those two properties. No matter how much she cared about Gunter's other wives, her first obligation was taking care of her child.

After parking in her garage and closing the door behind the car, Erica clutched the steering wheel with an iron grip while she shook her head at the garbage bags filled with Gunter's clothes lined up against the wall. Reality slammed her chest like a fifty-pound sledgehammer. Asheville would always carry the stain of Gunter's deception, just as Baltimore was rife with memories of a painful childhood and first marriage. Maybe after Abby graduated, they should move to another town. Someplace with a college her daughter could attend on a budget. Until then she had to live with the hand she'd been dealt and overcome the guilt kindling inside over disappointing the other wives-club members.

Erica peeled her fingers off the steering wheel and trudged into the kitchen. After tossing her purse and keys on the counter, she ambled to the den and dropped onto the sofa beside Abby. "Did you prepare for tomorrow's test?"

Abby aimed the remote at the television, pausing the movie. "Are you worried I didn't study enough?"

"Since I'm now filling the role of teacher, I want to make sure you don't fall behind on your schoolwork."

Abby rolled her eyes. "Yes, Ms. Parker, I studied."

Erica slumped back and propped her feet on the coffee table. If her daughter refused to return to school, she'd be responsible for assuring she finished her lessons and passed all of her tests. Would it help if she called Carrie's mother and asked her to encourage her daughter to reach out to Abby? Or would that move make matters worse for her child? How had other parents handled bullying issues?

"How'd your new job go?"

Determined to put a positive spin on the situation, Erica nudged her daughter's arm. "I didn't spill any drinks or drop any plates. Even better, I earned enough tips to pay this week's groceries."

Abby turned off the TV. "If we rent an apartment close to a fast-food restaurant, I'll find a job and help out."

"We'll talk about that after Christmas." If Abby refused to return to her school, would she agree to enroll in another school to complete her final semester? Best not to broach that subject until January. "For now, we both need to turn in for the night."

Abby yawned. "I'm setting my alarm for eight."

"My shift at the store begins at ten tomorrow morning. Which means you'll need to finish your test before I leave."

"Not a problem." Abby kissed her cheek, then rose. "I'll see you in the morning."

Moments after her daughter and Dusty left the den, Erica made her way to the guestroom. She turned on the bedside lamp and peeled out of her uniform. How long before parents she knew from Abby's school showed up at the restaurant? Would they question why a woman who lived in an expensive house in the wealthiest community in town worked as a waitress?

Did it matter what they thought? As much as she hated to admit it, the truth was she cared how people viewed her and Abby.

Erica pulled back the covers and dropped onto the bed. Maybe she should talk to her pastor. Especially since she and Abby still attended the church close to their old apartment. Another decision for another day. She turned off the light and pulled the blanket up to her chin. Somehow, she had to find a way to make the best of whatever happened during the months ahead.

Chapter 35

Awakened from a dream about discovering a secret room filled with expensive antiques, Amanda rolled out of bed, crept across the dark hall, and gripped the doorknob. Her chest tightened as she stepped into Gunter's private space and flicked on the chandelier. A mahogany desk held center stage along a dark blue wall. One of the con artist's three authentic antiques seemed to mock her as she ran her fingers along the smooth top and breathed in the stale air. What had kept him hunkered in this room with the door closed all those hours? Was he gambling online or engaging in even more despicable activities?

Hoping to discover a clue, Amanda pulled the center drawer open. Surprised to find it empty except for a single key, she opened five more drawers. All also empty. One drawer remained. She gripped the bottom right-hand handle and pulled. It didn't budge. She grabbed the key and slid it into the lock, then pulled again. Her jaw dropped as she gawked at Gunter's private stash. One-by-one she removed four bottles of brandy and two of cognac.

"So that's why Gunter didn't want anyone invading his private space." Morgan wandered over and lifted a bottle of Remy Martin brandy off the desk. "This looks expensive."

"It is." Amanda spun toward two tall bookcases flanking the window facing the neighbor's house and eyed the array of assorted stemware set among books. "Those aren't just a collection of so-called antique glass-ware." She lifted a glass and sniffed the lingering woody scent.

Morgan set the brandy back on the desk. "Odds are the creep hid out in here to drink and gamble online—two activities that go hand in hand."

Wendy ambled in, yawning. "What woke you two up so early?" She blinked, then appeared to do a double take. "Oh my gosh. Did all those bottles belong to Gunter?"

Amanda nodded. "Did he also have a private room in your condo?"

Wendy shook her head. "But he always kept a bottle of brandy on the kitchen counter. I dumped it down the drain the day I returned from Blue Ridge."

"At least he didn't try to hide it from you." Morgan leaned back against the desk. "Like he hid all these from us."

Wendy lifted a small brass clock off the bookshelf. "Nearly every day when he was home, he'd take his laptop and leave for the afternoon. He explained that because I was too much of a sexy distraction, he preferred to work in a coffee shop. She set down the clock. "Since gambling was Gunter's real job, I'm guessing he spent all those hours away from home at the casino in Biloxi."

Morgan scoffed. "That's a guess you could bank on. At least we're all set if we ever develop a taste for brandy and cognac." She stepped away from the desk. "For now, we need to fix breakfast, then continue our chat from yesterday, make a decision, and decide what to keep and what to sell."

Amanda zeroed in on the painting featuring the Saint Charles streetcar hanging above the desk. Adele had only included one piece of art among the three antiques—a vase in the formal living room. Morgan was right. She and Wendy had to come to some kind of agreement. "I don't know about you two, but I'm in the mood for pancakes smothered with maple syrup."

Her daughter linked arms with Amanda. "Add a side of bacon, and I'm all in."

"Me too." Wendy followed Amanda and Morgan down the stairs toward the aroma of freshly brewed coffee.

Dawn cast a dim glow in the kitchen until Amanda flicked on the overhead light. While preparing the pancake batter and pouring it onto the griddle, she mentally replayed last night's debate. During breakfast she tuned out the inane chatter and reviewed her strategy. Logic was the only way to persuade Wendy and Morgan to face reality and abandon their wild idea.

After clearing plates off the island and loading the dishwasher, Amanda refreshed her coffee and climbed back onto her stool across from Morgan. Time to put her plan to the test. "Picking up where our conversation ended up last night, I'll review exactly where we stand."

Wendy huffed. "You haven't changed your mind, have you?"

"The facts didn't suddenly change overnight." Amanda drummed her fingers on the island. "Indulge me while I review what we know. First, even after selling the top-ten items on Adele's list, our estate sale would generate less profit than we'd hoped. At least we'd have enough cash to rent decent apartments and buy a used car for Wendy. Second, the third member of our crazy wives club isn't onboard with our wild idea. Third, coming up with enough money to buy her out is as unlikely as winning the lottery without buying a ticket."

Wendy elbowed Amanda. "Which is why we need to go to Asheville and convince Erica to go along with our idea."

"*Your* idea—"

"And Morgan's."

Amanda resisted rolling her eyes and eyed her daughter. "You're an engineering student, so you understand facts better than anyone."

"You're right. However, in addition to inheriting your nose for details, I also inherited a big dose of Dad's smarts." Morgan crossed her arms on the island. "The way I see it, you have two choices. Stay in New Orleans and take a giant step backwards. Or step out in faith and follow your dream to become financially independent and control your own destiny."

"Which is impossible without Erica."

"Even though I've never met her, based on everything you and Wendy told me, I suspect she also wants a better future for her and her daughter."

"Abby's still in school. What makes you think Erica would agree to pack up and move to Blue Ridge on some wild whim?"

"Because you and Wendy are her family now."

Amanda broke eye contact, then slid off her stool and peered out at the morning sun glistening on the glass-top patio table. Morgan had skillfully intermingled facts with dreams and turned the table on her position. Maybe a new adventure was exactly what she and Wendy needed.

Morgan eased off her stool and linked arms with Amanda. "You're reconsidering, aren't you?"

"There are no guarantees anything would work in our favor."

"Haven't you noticed how persuasive the youngest member of your club is?"

"Morgan's right." Wendy scooted beside Amanda. "Who talked you and Erica into going along with my idea to create a snow family in freezing weather?"

"Playing in the snow is a far cry from turning a ramshackle old house into some sort of viable business—especially without money."

"Look, I totally understand how much hard work and more than a little bit of luck it would take. And we might not succeed." Despite her admission, Wendy's tone oozed with optimism. "At the same time, the best way to make up for everything Gunter Benson has taken from us is to turn what he left us into a ginormous success."

"Well, what do you know." Morgan snapped her fingers. "The youngest member of your club has presented a compelling reason to go for it."

Amanda stared at Wendy's wide-eyed expression. "You never cease to amaze me."

"Because I'm blonde, or because I'm only twenty-three?"

"Know what?" Morgan's tone hinted of humor. "Even though our combined age is just one year older than Mom's, it seems we're on the verge of swaying her to our way of thinking."

"You mean you two ganged up on me."

Morgan thumped Amanda's arm. "Youth and enthusiasm trumps age and wisdom."

Amanda failed to stop an eye roll as she turned away from the window. She grabbed her phone off the counter.

"Let me guess." Morgan grinned. "You're calling Erica."

"Our fourteen-day commitment to call Chris is nearly over, so, I'm calling him first."

Wendy nudged her arm. "What are you gonna tell him?"

"To take both houses off the market until after Christmas."

Wendy high-fived Morgan as Amanda pressed the attorney's number. Moments after she left the message on voicemail, second thoughts niggled their way to the surface. Had she just made a huge mistake?

Chapter 36

After Erica rang up the wrong amount on purchases for three differ- ent customers, Janet pulled her aside. "You rarely make mistakes. What's going on?"

Overwhelmed by mental exhaustion and her latest dilemma, Erica erupted in tears.

"You obviously need to take a break." After motioning for the other salesclerk to take over, Janet led Erica to her office and closed the door. "Do you want to talk, or do you need a few minutes alone?"

News about the past-due car insurance collided with all the secrets Erica had kept bottled up inside and gushed out as if the dam had suddenly burst wide open. The moment the words stopped rolling off her tongue, an unexpected sense of relief washed over her, followed by guilt. "I'm sorry to burden you with my problems."

Janet grasped her hand. "You're more than an employee; you're my friend. Which is why I want to help you." She crouched beside her desk and punched a series of numbers on the safe keypad, then withdrew cash and placed the bills in Erica's hand.

"I can't take your money—"

"Consider this a loan." Janet folded Erica's fingers over the bills. "About the crimes Gunter Benson committed—you know my husband Roger is an FBI agent. If you give me permission, I'll share your story with him."

As Erica eyed her unadorned, left ring finger, she made a mental note to find the best place to sell used jewelry. "If it was just me—" She hesitated. "I appreciate your offer, but I can't make that decision without talking to Gunter's other victims."

"In that case, I'll wait until you give me the go-ahead. Are you up to finishing your shift, or do you need to take the rest of the day off?"

"I'm okay to continue working, and thank you for the loan." Erica stood. "I'll pay you back before the end of the year."

"There's no rush."

She walked out and slid the money into her wallet. Halfway to the front, a familiar ringtone sent her spinning around and rushing out the back door. She pressed her phone to her ear. "Hi, Amanda."

"You sound out of breath."

"I'm at work so I rushed out the back door." Cold air sent a shiver through Erica's limbs. "What's going on?"

"I scheduled an estate sale and discovered Gunter isn't a serious antique collector after all, but that's not why I'm calling."

Did she have news about their inheritance or more dirt on the con artist? "I'm listening."

"We have to move out the day after the sale ends. Since Wendy and I haven't secured a place to live yet, the three of us want to drive to Asheville and spend Christmas with you and Abby."

Why would they drive all those miles just to spend a few days together? Unless they believed they could convince her to go along with their idea. Whatever their misguided reasoning, at least she'd welcome the company. "Spending the last few days in Gunter's Asheville house with friends will help ease the pain of moving." Should she mention Janet's offer? Why not? "Actually, there's another reason I'm glad you're coming here."

"Now, I'm listening."

"My boss is married to an FBI agent—"

"She suggested we talk to him about Gunter's crimes, right?"

A mouse skittered across the parking lot and disappeared under a dumpster. "It wouldn't hurt to talk to him."

"Morgan would definitely agree. However, before you give your boss an answer, Wendy and I need to talk."

"Trust me, I won't do anything unless we all agree."

"My sentiments exactly."

Was Amanda referring to a discussion with the FBI or something else? "I have to go back to work." Erica stepped inside. "Call me after you and Wendy make a decision."

"Will do."

Erica slid the phone back in her pocket and returned to the front of the store. Relieved Janet's loan would cover the past-due car insurance and prevent her from breaking the law, Erica squared her shoulders and poured every ounce of energy she could muster into serving customers with a smile.

Wendy looked up from her phone the moment Amanda strode into the den. "Did you talk to Erica?"

"Yes. She's fine with our Christmas visit."

Wendy tilted her head. "What about our other idea?"

"That conversation is best done in person. Chris returned my call."

"And?"

"Both sales are on hold until he hears back from us."

Wendy set her phone on the end table. "How did Chris react to your request?"

"He didn't seem surprised." Amanda settled on the chair beside the fireplace. "He asked about you."

"Really?" Wendy imagined the handsome attorney smiling at her from across a table at a fancy restaurant. "What'd you tell him?"

"That you're doing well."

"The next time we need to share something important, I'll call him."

Morgan wandered in. "Are you talking about the handsome Blue Ridge lawyer?"

Wendy tilted her head. "How'd you know he's good looking?"

"Mom told me." Morgan propped her hip on the sofa arm. "Kevin and his friend agreed to come over tomorrow morning and help us load everything we plan to keep onto the rental truck. Which means we need to figure out what to sell."

"After we discuss a new development." Amanda relayed Erica's conversation about the FBI agent.

Morgan slid from the sofa arm to the seat. "What'd you tell her?"

"That I'd talk to you two."

"You already know I'm a hundred percent in favor of turning the bum over to the law, but the decision is yours and Wendy's, not mine."

"There's no question about Gunter deserving punishment for his crimes." Wendy pushed off the sofa and ambled to the fireplace mantel. She lifted a porcelain bowl that wasn't on the top-ten list. How could anyone tell the difference between real antiques and reproductions? "The thing is, I don't want my baby to know their father's a criminal."

Morgan propped her feet on the coffee table. "I can't imagine how your child would find out."

"What if we had to testify in court, or years from now, an FBI agent showed up at my door asking questions?"

"I understand your apprehension." Amanda lifted a broom off the brass fireplace tool set and swept ashes from the hearth into the firebox. "Before you decide, why don't you call Erica and ask her how Abby responded to knowing her father beat her mother?"

"That's not the same."

"Assault is just as much a felony as theft and bigamy. In fact, it might be worse."

"No man has the right to beat up a woman." Wendy resisted the urge to hurl the bowl across the room. "Erica didn't turn her ex over to the law."

Amanda returned the broom to the holder. "She should have, even if he was a cop."

"At least Gunter didn't physically abuse us. I suppose it wouldn't hurt to talk to the FBI guy."

"Are you sure, or do you need more time to think about it?"

"I wonder if Gunter has thought about any of us for one second since he wrote that letter and mailed it to Chris. Or has he been too busy targeting a wealthy Italian or French woman as his fifth wife?" Wendy set the bowl back on the mantel. "Go ahead and tell Erica to set up the meeting."

"I will, but first, what do you say we begin our what-to-keep-or-sell project?"

Chapter 37

The first flush of morning lit the sky as Amanda cradled her coffee mug and peered out the kitchen window facing the driveway. "If we haul that truckload of furniture all the way to Asheville and Erica stands firm on her decision, I'll turn around and drive right back to New Orleans."

Morgan wandered over, her hands propped on her hips. "There you go again, doubting your logical mind, and Wendy's power of persuasion."

"You're also underestimating a mother's desire to do what's best for her daughter. How would you have reacted if I had yanked you out of school halfway through your senior year?"

"Since rhetorical questions are impossible to answer, I'll use the last eggs to fix us an omelet."

"Clever way to avoid responding to my question."

"I'm a few months from earning a degree, which means I'm full of resourceful ideas." Morgan nudged Amanda's arm. "Now for this morning's most important question. Do you want regular or raisin toast with the omelet?"

She managed a half smile. "Raisin."

"Same for me, with honey." Wendy's cheery tone belied the early hour as she wandered in, opened the fridge, and removed a bottle of orange juice. "I'm now officially a college student."

Amanda spun away from the window. "How many courses are you taking?"

"Just one until we decide what kind of business to start." Wendy's face flushed with excitement as she filled a glass. "If I'd known free courses were available online, I'd have signed up a long time ago."

Morgan cracked eggs into a bowl. "Your timing is perfect for an up-and-coming business executive. Right, Mom?"

Despite her misgivings about the future, she wouldn't undermine Wendy's enthusiasm. At least not until they faced reality in Asheville. "Absolutely."

"You, Erica, and I can live in the little house while we decide what to do with the big one." Wendy took a sip of juice. "We can turn it into a luxury hotel, or a bed-and-breakfast like the Blue Ridge Inn."

"Do you suppose Erica will freak out when we drive up to her house in that giant U-Haul?" Amanda moved away from the window. "I can't decide if driving seven-hundred miles straight through without her commitment is the definition of unbridled enthusiasm or insanity."

Wendy chuckled. "It's a little bit of both."

Morgan glanced over her shoulder. "Since I'm flying back to New Orleans, we'll only need to buy gas for two vehicles."

"There is that." Amanda dropped three slices of raisin bread into the toaster. "The estate-sale crew is due to arrive in ninety minutes."

Morgan flipped the omelet. "Which means we need to decide whether to stay here or leave."

"Since we're gonna lock all our personal stuff in Morgan's room, I vote we leave." Wendy plucked the last praline from the package and took a bite. "Besides, I want to see the French Quarter and walk down Bourbon Street."

"We can't let you leave New Orleans without seeing what all the fuss is about. Especially if you enjoy street entertainers and jazz. Right, Mom?"

Amanda cringed at the thought of trekking for hours through narrow streets crowded with Saturday tourists and locals. "Tell you what. You two go sightseeing while I stay here and keep an eye on the sale."

"Works for me. What about you, Wendy?"

She shrugged. "Sure, why not."

"Then it's settled." The tension gripping Amanda's shoulders escalated as Wendy's comment about the little house struck her. After Morgan left for college, and Paul spent fewer and fewer days at home, she had come to appreciate time alone. How could she possibly adjust to living with two women she barely knew? Especially without Morgan around to keep Wendy entertained. Amanda buttered the raisin toast then climbed onto her stool. Why fret over a situation that had far less than a fifty-percent chance of happening?

Following breakfast and kitchen cleanup, Morgan and Wendy headed toward the streetcar stop while Amanda settled on the front porch. Adele had claimed the most serious buyers came early the first day. How many would show up this morning?

Twenty minutes before the official start time, a pickup pulled up to the curb. A middle-aged couple climbed out and made their way to the front porch. Should she speak to them? Why not. "Good morning and welcome."

They responded, then disappeared inside.

If they knew how much she needed the money, would they be willing to pay more for whatever piqued their interest? Fighting the urge to follow them inside and launch into a sales pitch, Amanda crossed her leg over her knee and pumped her foot as the second of a steady stream of bargain hunters arrived and dashed into the foyer.

When the first customers who'd completed a purchase walked out carrying a pair of end tables, a sinking sensation gripped Amanda's stomach. This was the second time the man she'd known as Paul had forced her to invite strangers to strip her home bare. The first sale had taken place at the home she'd shared with Preston the week before it sold. Now people she'd never laid eyes on traipsed through the house she'd lived in for the past nine years. No one cared about the story behind the sale. Maybe Morgan was right. She needed to stop acting like a victim. No matter how risky, it was time to begin forging a future as a survivor. For her sake as well as the other wives club members.

The second Amanda noticed her across-the-street neighbor heading in her direction, she grabbed her purse from under her chair, then rushed through the house and out the back door. She peered at the front porch from behind the rental truck. After the neighbor stepped inside the house, Amanda headed straight to the streetcar stop.

Unwilling to answer questions from nosy neighbors or anyone else she might know, she waited for the streetcar to arrive. Once onboard, she volleyed her attention between gazing out the window and mentally creating stories about locals and tourists as they climbed on and off the iconic ride. Each time they passed Gunter's house, she counted the vehicles parked along the street. Watching strangers load furniture she'd admired onto trucks seemed akin to a bizarre out-of-body experience. Following the last ride by the house, Amanda closed her eyes and allowed images from the past twenty-five years to play across her mind.

"Let me guess. You've been riding the rails all day."

Amanda's eyes popped open as Morgan sat beside her, and Wendy settled across the aisle and slid to the window. "If this was a freight-train boxcar, I'd be well past Mississippi by now. How'd your day go?"

"I'm all walked out. Which is why I booked a Steamboat *Natchez* jazz cruise for the three of us tomorrow. Don't worry about the money, Mom. Treating us is the least I can do before we bid New Orleans a final goodbye."

"You're obviously not expecting to land a job in your home state?"

"The best industrial engineering jobs aren't in Louisiana."

Amanda glanced at her daughter's personally-designed college ring. "You have such a bright future ahead of you, honey."

"So do you, Mom."

"During the past few hours, I've had plenty of time to reflect on the last twenty-five years. Especially those we enjoyed with your dad. I also remembered the final months of Mom's illness, when she tried to assure me that God never gives us more than we can handle. Even though I've survived losing two people I loved, I doubted her, but now, I'm beginning to understand what she meant."

"You've been gifted with a sharp mind and a big heart, Mom." Morgan squeezed Amanda's hand. "Which means you're meant to accomplish something important."

"Raising you to become the amazing woman you are has been my most important mission."

"Which you did almost perfectly."

"I see." Amanda thumped her daughter's arm. "And why *almost* perfectly?"

Morgan leaned close. "One of these days, I'll fess up to some of the shenanigans I pulled off without you finding out. Nothing illegal or cringe-worthy, mind you."

"Since we have a few minutes before our stop, you could begin now."

"Nah, I'll wait until my college days are over. Just in case a few more opportunities pop up."

Amanda chuckled. "Opening that door without letting me peek in conjures all sorts of mental images."

"In that case, I'll tell you one."

By the time Morgan finished her humorous story, memories from Amanda's own youth bubbled up. "Would you believe I did the same thing when I was a teenager?"

"Of course, after all I am your daughter."

A block before their stop, Wendy popped off her seat. Amanda and Morgan followed her off the streetcar and onto the sidewalk. As dusk settled over New Orleans, they climbed onto the front porch and walked into the foyer. The marble-top console and the gilded mirror were both gone.

The woman in charge of the sale strode in from the back of the house. "The first day is always the most active." She swept her arm in an arc toward the nearly empty living room, then across to the formal dining room. "As you can see, the more valuable items have already sold. Clients who purchased some of the larger pieces—including the dining-room table—have arranged to pick them up tomorrow."

Wendy plucked a candy wrapper off the floor. "What about the antique desk upstairs?"

"A dealer bought it a half hour ago."

"For a good price?"

"Good enough." The woman tucked an iPad under her arm. "If all goes well, we'll finish up before noon on day three."

Amanda eyed the painting still hanging over the fireplace mantel. Two more days of this, and she'd walk out of this house for the last time—hopefully with a sizable check in hand.

Chapter 38

S truggling against the tension gripping her shoulders, Erica pulled into the church parking lot. Before today, she had never requested a private meeting with her pastor, or any pastor for that matter. Would the man she listened to on Sunday mornings judge her, then slip into preacher mode and quote a lot of scripture? Or would he share practical words of wisdom to help her make a decision? Was he even aware that she and Abby had attended his church and sat in the back row nearly every Sunday morning for the past ten years?

Erica pushed her apprehension aside, peeled her fingers off the steering wheel, and climbed out of Abby's car. She forced her legs to carry her across the parking lot and into the administration building.

A pleasant-looking woman Erica recognized greeted her, then escorted her down a hall and knocked on a door standing halfway open. "Mrs. Parker is here."

Erica's breath caught. The last time someone had spoken that name she'd had no idea it was a sham, or that the man she'd married had stolen everything from her.

The woman stood aside.

Erica stepped into the professionally decorated space awash in shades of blue and pale gray.

A warm smile lit the pastor's face as he rounded his desk and offered his hand. "Welcome."

Erica accepted. "Thank you, Pastor Newsom."

"Please, call me Jeff." He released her hand and motioned toward the upholstered sofa. "Do you mind if I call you Erica?"

"Not at all." Surprised yet pleased with his easygoing manner, she crossed one ankle over the other.

"Would you like a soft drink or water?"

Aware her throat might become seriously parched at any moment, Erica nodded. "Water, please."

He removed a bottle from a mini fridge set in a built-in cabinet and placed it on the coffee table, then sat in a casual chair across the table from the sofa. "How's Abby enjoying her senior year?"

How did he know her daughter's name? "I...um..."

"Abby's one reason you're here, isn't it?"

The compassion in his eyes, as well as his gentle tone, helped ease Erica's tense shoulders and gave her confidence a much-needed boost. She laced her fingers in her lap as the events of the past few weeks tumbled off her tongue in one lengthy monologue. When she finished, a huge sigh escaped.

"First, let's address your question about forgiving Gunter versus pursuing justice." Jeff leaned forward. "The fact is, those are two entirely different issues. God has called each of us to forgive those who hurt us, just as we've been forgiven. At the same time, when his children break the law, they must face the consequences of their actions."

"Are you saying I should follow through and schedule an appointment with the FBI agent?"

"Do you believe you'd be making the right decision, and if so, why?"

Her last conversation with Amanda bubbled up. "The three of us don't want Gunter to hurt any more women."

"There's your answer. However, you need to forgive him in your heart before you meet with the agent."

"What about Amanda and Wendy?"

"They each have to make that decision. Of course, it might help if you explain to them why you consider forgiveness important."

"What about after we talk to the FBI agent?"

"Leave justice to those called to uphold the law."

Erica glanced at the painting of the sun rising over the ocean adorning the wall opposite the sofa. Could she find it in her heart to forgive the man whose actions had led to high-school girls tormenting Abby and her closest friends to abandoning her?

"Are you questioning whether or not you're able to forgive Gunter?"

"The truth is, it took a long time to forgive my first husband for the abuse he inflicted on me and Abby. For years, when something reminded me of him, bitterness seemed to creep back in."

"Forgiveness isn't natural. Summoning the courage to absolve others for the pain they've inflicted requires a lot of prayer as well as self-reflection."

Erica uncapped the water bottle and took a long drink to ease her dry throat. At least he'd provided one answer. Time to seek a second. "About the property Gunter left the three of us...even if we're able to raise enough money to pay the taxes, I have no idea how we'd turn them into a profitable business."

"When an opportunity arises, it's important to weigh the pros and cons. In your case, staying in Asheville is predictable, while moving to Blue Ridge is the opposite. I urge you to seek divine wisdom as you consider one very important question. Which town offers the most promising future for you and your daughter? When the answer becomes clear, cast your fears aside and step out in faith."

Images of her first nights back at waiting tables played in Erica's mind. The long hours. Needing an escort to walk across the parking lot in the dark. "It seems I'm facing a big dose of soul-searching."

"Today, you've taken an important step in that direction." After praying for her, Pastor Jeff stood. "Please don't hesitate to call if you need to talk again."

Grateful part of the weight bearing down on her shoulders had been lifted, Erica rose to her feet. "Thank you for your time and your advice."

"I'll always be here to listen and help guide you." He escorted her to the door. "Let me know what you decide about your future."

"I will." After returning to the car, Erica drove straight to the gift store. A sense of calm washed over her as she approached Janet. "Can we talk for a minute?"

"Sure." She led Erica to the back room. "What's up?"

"My friends and I have decided we want to talk to your husband. Unless he considers our case too unimportant to pursue."

"A couple of years ago, a scoundrel his sister trusted cheated her out of a lot of money. Believe me, once you tell Roger your story, he'll jump at the chance to bring Gunter to justice. I'll ask him to contact you to arrange a time and place to meet."

"Thank you, Janet. You're a good friend." Two hours after giving her boss the go-ahead and returning to work, Erica responded to a text and called the number provided. Agent Huffman answered after the third ring.

"I'm Erica Parker."

"Thank you for responding. My wife believes you have a legitimate case; however, I need to hear the details before I agree to meet with you."

"Do you have time to listen now?"

"I'll make time."

Erica signaled Janet, then strode to the back room and shared everything she had learned about Gunter Benson's deceptions and crimes. "What's your opinion? Do we have a case?"

"I only have one question. How soon can I meet with you and his other two victims?"

Chapter 39

At one-thirty on day three of the estate sale, Amanda stood in the living room staring at the check in her hand. Her eyes met Morgan's. "Although we didn't make enough to cover the taxes, the profits are better than I had anticipated."

"One more indication you and Wendy are on the right track."

"Except we still don't have a clue whether or not Erica will go along with our plan."

Wendy lifted a vase off the mantel. "We'll figure out a way to convince her, even if she decides to join us in Blue Ridge after Abby graduates."

"That's a possibility, except we'd still need to come up with more cash."

"You gals will figure it out." Morgan's phone pinged a text. "Kevin and his friend are on the way over to load everything else onto the truck. He offered to keep my car at his house until I return to New Orleans, and he'll pick me up at the airport."

"If you ask me, he's crazy about you." Wendy grabbed a sheet of newspaper. "Based on everything I've seen, he's a keeper."

Morgan smiled. "I agree."

Amanda folded the check and slid it into her wallet.

"Are you comfortable carrying a check worth that much money in your purse, Mom?"

"There's no way I'll deposit it and take even the slightest chance Gunter could find a way to access my checking account."

"What about parking it in my account?"

"Call me skeptical, but I wouldn't put anything past that scoundrel."

"I can't say I blame you. Just make sure you protect it until you open a new account under your legal name."

"You don't need to worry about me. If some thug attempts to snatch my purse, he'll experience the full fury of a woman scammed."

"After I moved to Gulfport and started working night shifts, I took a self-defense course and learned how to deliver a swift kick and a left hook where both count."

"Well then, Mama Bear—" Morgan thumped Wendy's arm. "I'm assigning you as my mother's personal secret-service agent."

"Together we're a force to be reckoned with, both in business and on the street." Wendy set the wrapped vase in a box along with other random items that failed to attract buyers.

Amanda shook her head and ambled into the empty dining room. She peered up at the ornate gold and crystal chandelier.

Morgan moved to her side. "What are you thinking?"

"Kevin's an electrical engineering student. Do you suppose he'd know how to remove that?"

"You want to take it with you?"

"A lot of good memories happened in this room. Think about all those times you and I prepared a meal together, then dined on our culinary creations under that light."

Morgan slid her arm around Amanda's shoulders. "Just you and me, without Paul aka Gunter."

"Which made those meals extra special." Amanda patted her daughter's hand. "Twice a year after you left for college, my friends and I continued that tradition. So yeah, I want the chandelier to go where I go."

Wendy strolled into the room. "If I have a girl, I hope we'll be as close as you two are." She looped her arm around Amanda's elbow. "After I'm successful, maybe I'll track down my mother so I can tell her about her grandchild and find out why she left me. That is, if she's still alive. Until then, you're my baby's only grandmother."

"An honor I proudly accept."

Responding to a knock, Morgan withdrew her arm from around Amanda's shoulders. She rushed to open the front door and welcomed Kevin. "Mom added a new task for you guys to tackle after you help us finish loading the truck."

An hour after arriving, Kevin carried an eight-foot stepladder into the dining room. He lifted his chin while scratching his head. "That chandelier looks fragile and heavy."

Amanda crossed her arms. "Any problem taking it down?"

"Piece of cake. Packing it for safe travel is another story."

"We have that covered." After the guys disconnected and lowered the fixture to the floor, Morgan helped Amanda secure the treasure with layers of bubble wrap and a heavy quilt. When they finished, Kevin and his friend placed it in Gunter's pickup beside the women's luggage. "Looks like you're ready to roll."

"By this time tomorrow, we'll be more than halfway to Asheville." Amanda secured and locked the cover over the truck bed.

Morgan stood on her toes and kissed Kevin's cheek. "Thanks for all your help."

His face lit with a smile. "For you, any time. Where are you staying tonight?"

"Mom's closest friend invited us to stay at her house." She handed Kevin her car key.

"Promise to call me during the trip and after you arrive?"

"I promise."

Kevin turned toward Amanda. "I've enjoyed working with you, Mrs. Smith. I'm eager for you to meet my parents at graduation."

Grateful he hadn't call her Mrs. Sullivan, Amanda stole a quick glance at Morgan, then smiled at Kevin. "I look forward to meeting them." After he climbed into Abby's car and backed out of the driveway, she nudged her daughter. "Wendy was right about that young man being wild about you."

"Believe me, the feeling's mutual."

Images floated up from Amanda's happy memory bank. "After two dates with your dad, I knew he was the one."

"Is that your way of telling me you approve of Kevin?"

"Does he make you happy, honey?"

"Deliriously happy."

"Then yes, I approve." Amanda linked arms with Morgan as they headed to the back door. "Are you ready to bid this house one final goodbye?"

"More than ready."

Inside the kitchen, Wendy stood at the island with her laptop open. "I've been doing some figuring." She handed Amanda a sheet of paper. "If we open a bed and breakfast and average a seventy-five-percent occupancy rate for a full year, that's how much money we'd make before expenses."

Amanda stared at the number, then gave the paper to Morgan. "What do you think?"

"Impressive."

Wendy's face beamed. "The number or that I figured it out?"

"Both."

"Even after expenses, a three-way split is more than double what your mom and I would earn waiting tables or guiding tourists around New Orleans."

"Know what else I think?" Morgan set the estimate on the island. "You've just increased your chance of persuading the third member of the wives club to ditch Asheville by at least twenty-five percent."

Amanda eyed the number again. If the calculations were anywhere close to accurate, and if they came up with enough cash, maybe their inheritance would open the door to a bright future. "Good job, Wendy. Let's take one more look around the house to make sure we didn't miss anything."

Wendy's smile faded as her eyes followed Amanda and Morgan walking away from her. Had she over or underestimated the potential profits? Even if she'd been dead-on accurate, how could they turn a dilapidated house into a viable business without a heap of cash? Life had been a lot easier when no one expected much from her—the pretty blonde who earned decent tips and landed a rich husband. A quiver rippled through her chest. Except she'd married a fraud who preyed on vulnerable women.

She closed her laptop. If she hadn't met the man she'd known as Kurt, would she still be waiting tables, or would she have married some other guy? Better to accept reality than to mull over what-ifs. Gunter's betrayal had set her feet on a path that both challenged and intimidated her.

Wendy pressed her hand to her tummy. Was it her imagination, or did she feel the first hint of a baby bump? Either way, her child deserved a mother who had inner strength, like her new friends. She grabbed the estimate off the island and stared at the number. With a little luck and a lot of hard work, she and her new friends would turn what little Gunter had left them into a gold mine. She folded the paper and stuffed it into her purse. As she moved from waitress to businesswoman, would she give up when things got tough?? Wendy squared her shoulders, touched her tummy, and lifted her chin. Absolutely not.

Chapter 40

The morning sky remained pitch black as Amanda released her closest friend from a tearful embrace and stepped off the front porch. A knot of hesitation nestled in the pit of her stomach the moment reality set in. She was minutes from abandoning the town she'd called home for forty-three years to forge an unknown future with women she hadn't known existed a month earlier. Despite second thoughts running rampant through her brain, it was too late to back out now.

Amanda followed Wendy to the pickup and climbed behind the wheel while Morgan eased the rental truck onto the street. Her pulse pounded as she backed out of the driveway and pulled behind Morgan. Would Preston's memory secured in her heart make up for never again visiting his grave?

"Is it hard for you to leave New Orleans?"

Amanda stole a quick glance at Wendy. How should she respond? Truthfully, that's how. "The town not so much. The good memories...yeah, it's difficult."

"I hope one day good memories will outweigh the bad ones." Wendy paused for a long moment. "I've never told anyone other than a social worker what happened the night before I moved out of my last foster home." Wendy's tone hinted of profound sadness. "My foster dad stumbled into the bedroom reeking of alcohol and cigarettes. He stopped beside the twin bed closest to the door. The second he unzipped his pants and yanked the covers off my thirteen-year-old roommate, something inside me snapped. I grabbed the lamp off the nightstand and slammed it across his head. He collapsed onto the floor cursing in pain. My roommate and I climbed out the window and spent the rest of the night huddled on a park bench."

"Oh my gosh, Wendy. You saved that young girl from a lifetime of torment and shame."

"The next morning we reported the incident to a social worker. After we got our meager belongings and the money I'd saved from a summer job, the social worker promised never to send another child to live in that house. That afternoon, I bought a bus ticket to Biloxi and never returned to Mobile."

Respect for her young friend multiplied fivefold as Amanda followed Morgan onto Interstate 10 and headed east. "You're a real-life hero, as well as a survivor."

"The way I see it, you, Erica, and I were meant to show the world that no matter how difficult the situation is, women who pull together can overcome anything to create positive futures."

Subtle shades of pink and blue lit the sky. "You're absolutely right. And there are no other women on the planet I'd rather have as my partners on this journey."

Responding to Morgan's ringtone, Amanda answered. "What's up?"

"How's everything going back there?"

"Couldn't be better."

"A half hour down, eleven to go. Let me know when you two need a pitstop."

"Will do."

Garlic, tomato, and cheese scents wafted across the kitchen as Erica's phone pinged a text from Amanda. "Updated ETA six-thirty-five." A half hour until their guests arrived. She tapped the screen. "Will have supper ready."

Abby wandered into the kitchen. "Did you tell your friends I dropped out of school?"

Erica set her phone on the counter. "You didn't drop out; you simply changed venues." She stirred the spaghetti sauce. "The answer to your question is no, I haven't told them."

"Why do they want to spend Christmas with us?"

Should she tell Abby about their wild idea? No need to stir up that hornet's nest, especially if Amanda and Wendy had come to their senses. "I imagine they need a little down time before finding new places to live."

"Maybe they want to move to Asheville." Abby lifted a cookie from a glass jar and took a bite. "Anyway, I'm glad we're gonna have company for Christmas."

The unmasked gloom in her child's tone weighed heavy on Erica's shoulders. Abby had always enjoyed spending time with her friends during her winter break. Now she spent hours alone in a house slated to be sold out from under them. Maybe the Christmas spirit would touch her friend Carrie's heart and prompt her to reach out to Abby.

"Do you want me to set the table with the Christmas dishes, Mom?"

Why not? Even if she had purchased them with the con artist's credit card. Besides, a party atmosphere would help ease the tension. "Yes, along with wine glasses. Also turn on the Christmas-tree lights and some background music." Erica filled the pasta pot with water and set it on the stove. Would Amanda and Wendy arrive in a festive mood or depressed over losing their homes?

Abby rushed into the kitchen. "A giant rental truck and a pickup just drove onto our driveway. Maybe they're moving to Asheville after all."

So much for her friends coming to their senses. Erica turned on the oven and the burner under the pasta pot.

"Do you want me to let them in?"

"We'll go together." As they headed to the foyer, Erica breathed deeply to forestall a pounding headache. She opened the door moments before the three women climbed onto the front porch. "Welcome to Asheville."

Wendy dashed in and gave Erica a quick hug. "Our last pitstop was three hours ago."

"That's a long stretch between bathrooms. Abby will show you to the powder room."

"Good, because my leg-crossing strategy won't work much longer."

Amanda stepped into the foyer. She embraced Erica, then stood back. "You and Abby could easily pass for sisters."

"The same is true for you and your daughter."

Morgan smiled as she extended her hand. "It's a pleasure to meet you."

"The pleasure's all mine." Erica smiled at the pretty young woman as she released her hand and faced Amanda. "How was the drive?"

"Long but pleasant." Amanda peered into the living room. "Gorgeous decor. Your work or Gunter's?"

"Mine. The house was pretty much empty when Abby and I moved in."

"I like your style, which is both elegant and inviting."

"Thanks. I imagine you'd both like to freshen up before supper."

"You read my mind."

After guiding them to a guestroom suite, Erica returned to the kitchen, unwrapped a package of garlic bread, and placed it on a baking sheet. How soon would her friends launch into a serious sales pitch? Why hadn't she given Abby a heads-up? Because her daughter already had more than enough to deal with. She pulled the last bottle of red wine from beneath the counter.

Amanda ambled in. "Based on the tomato and garlic scents, I'm guessing spaghetti is on the menu."

"Homemade, mind you." Erica slid the bread into the oven and set the timer. "I haven't told Abby about your idea."

"Wendy and I agreed not to bring the subject up tonight." Amanda lifted the lid off the saucepan and sniffed. "This looks as delicious as it smells." She set the lid back on the pot. "I'd like to talk to you privately tomorrow morning."

Erica's brow pinched. Had Amanda changed her mind? Did she intend to recruit her as an ally to counter Wendy? "Is six too early?"

"Not at all."

"Good. Because our FBI agent is scheduled to meet us here at ten."

"Have you told Abby about him?"

"She knows." Erica pulled the cork from the wine. "I have two bottles of chardonnay if you prefer white."

"Red is perfect."

"Good." Erica slid spaghetti noodles into the boiling water.

Wendy followed Abby and Morgan into the kitchen, with Dusty trailing behind. "Oh my gosh, everything smells yummy."

"When you taste Mom's spaghetti and Caesar salad, you'll swear she's Italian."

Morgan slid her arm around Amanda's shoulders. "It seems both our moms have mastered the art of spaghetti sauce."

Wendy lifted a cookie from the jar. "Store-bought or homemade?"

"Slice and bake." Abby pulled a bowl from the cabinet. "The cooked version is almost as good as the raw dough."

Wendy took a bite. "One of my foster mothers kept rolls of cookie dough in the fridge."

Abby's eyes widened. "How many foster moms did you have?"

"Seven."

"That's a lot."

"Tell me about it."

Erica sliced and plated the bread, then transferred the noodles and sauce to the bowl and added freshly grated parmesan. "Are you ladies ready to dine?"

"I'm more than ready." Wendy carried the bread platter to the formal dining room. Amanda followed with the spaghetti and the wine while Abby removed the salad from the fridge.

The moment her guests were seated, Erica returned thanks. When she finished, Amanda pressed her palms together. "That was the perfect blessing. Thank you."

"You're welcome." Erica passed the spaghetti to Wendy while Abby handed the salad to Morgan. During dinner, all five women joined in on the lively conversation as if they'd been friends for years. Erica marveled at how well Morgan engaged Abby. After finishing the meal, everyone pitched in to help with kitchen duty.

At ten-fifteen, Wendy released a yawn laced with a sigh. "I don't know about y'all, but I'm ready for a good-night's sleep."

Amanda yawned. "So am I."

"That makes three of us," added Morgan.

After their guests retrieved overnight bags from the pickup, Erica escorted Wendy to one guestroom suite and Amanda and Morgan to the other. Grateful they'd enjoyed each other's company without a single word about the Blue Ridge properties, she slipped into Abby's room. "I hope you don't mind me bunking with you."

"Of course not." Abby climbed onto her twin bed and pulled the covers up to her chin while Dusty sprawled on the floor between the beds. "I like your friends, Mom."

"So do I, sweetheart." After setting her phone alarm for five-thirty, Erica crawled into the other bed and turned off the light. She'd be ready for whatever happened tomorrow.

Chapter 41

Amanda's eyes popped open five minutes before her alarm was set to go off. Careful not to wake Morgan, she eased out of bed and tiptoed to the bathroom. After splashing her face with cool water, she donned her robe, then slipped into the hall and followed the enticing aroma to the kitchen.

Erica sat at the island cradling a cup of coffee. "I hope you slept well."

"Better than the night before we left New Orleans." Amanda filled one of the empty cups beside the coffee maker and stirred in sugar and creamer. "Abby's a lovely girl."

"So's Morgan."

"We're both blessed to have such wonderful daughters." Amanda slid onto the stool beside Erica. "Yesterday during the drive, Wendy and I talked a lot about the two Blue Ridge properties. We also discussed how important it is for you to do what's best for Abby."

"A week ago, Abby dropped out of school."

Amanda peered at her friend's profile. "What do you mean by dropped out?"

Erica focused straight ahead while relaying the details. "At least for now, I'm playing the role of both mother and teacher."

"Does Abby want to return to school after Christmas?"

"At this point...no. Unless her friends stop ignoring her and show some compassion." Erica turned toward Amanda. "You haven't changed your mind about moving to Blue Ridge, have you?"

"Believe me, I've waffled back and forth a dozen times." Amanda sipped her coffee. "Wendy enrolled in an online business class."

"Seems our young friend isn't backing down."

"That's an understatement." Amanda removed a sheet of paper from her pocket, then unfolded it and set it on the island.

"What am I looking at?"

"Wendy's estimated annual profit from a bed and breakfast."

Erica's mouth fell open as she stared at the paper. "You're all in, aren't you?"

"Even if she missed the number by half, split three ways that's more income than we'd earn shlepping food to customers or guiding tourists through narrow streets."

"Did your estate sale generate enough money to pay the back taxes?"

Amanda shook her head. "We're still short."

Erica remained silent for a long moment. "Yesterday when you drove up in that rental truck, I assumed you'd taken this detour to persuade me to buy into your idea. But then when you asked to talk privately, I thought you wanted me to help change Wendy's mind. Now, I understand why you believe starting over in a new town is worth the risk."

"What about you, Erica? Have you had a change of heart?"

"The first night at my new waitressing job, I considered myself a failure. Not because of the work, but because I neglected to take control of my own future by relying on the man I thought was my husband." Erica slid off her stool, skirted the island, and refilled her mug.

Resisting the temptation to probe, Amanda remained silent.

Erica stirred her coffee while facing the window. "Abby and I moved to Asheville to escape her abusive father, only to fall victim to a different kind of abuse."

"You, Wendy, and I are survivors, not victims."

"Deep down, I know you're right." Erica whipped around and faced Amanda. "I can't commit to leaving Asheville, but I'll help raise the cash we need." Erica removed items from the desk drawer and dropped them on the island. "My wedding rings from Jack and Brian. I have no idea how much they're worth."

Amanda lifted the diamond-studded band and examined the inside. "Twenty-four-carat. At least the gold's real." She paused. "Was your 'cash *we* need' comment a slip of the tongue or a commitment?"

Erica set her mug on the island. "A couple of days ago, Abby commented about my eye for decorating—"

"She's right. Even the guestroom looks professionally decorated."

"So, maybe at some point I'll put those skills to use and help you and Wendy transform that grand old house into a gorgeous inn."

Amanda reached across the island and touched Erica's arm. "Our little wives club is destined to turn what Gunter left behind into one of the best B and B's in North Georgia."

"I haven't committed, so please don't say anything to anyone until I've had a chance to talk to Abby."

"Understood. Speaking of Wendy, she created a things-to-sell spreadsheet complete with estimates. We'll add your rings to the jewelry she and I listed yesterday during our drive."

"Seems the youngest member of our crew is becoming one savvy businesswoman. Which calls for a celebration." Erica moved a box from the counter to the island and lifted the lid. "The best donuts in Asheville."

"The universal comfort food—" Images of the second meeting with Chris floated up from Amanda's memory. "And the perfect way to celebrate our new partnership, no matter how long it takes you to join us."

Morgan wandered in. "Are you two up early to raid the donuts or talk about your futures?"

How should she respond? Amanda locked eyes with her daughter. "Erica and I have had a heart-to-heart."

Morgan sat beside Amanda and eyed Erica. "Let me guess, you've bought in?"

"Financially, yes. But I'm not in a position to commit physically."

"Because of Abby?" Morgan's head tilted. "I'm curious. What changed your mind?"

"Let's just say, Wendy's calculations tipped the balance. But mum's the word until I say otherwise."

"Got it." Morgan selected a chocolate-covered donut and took a bite. "Cream-filled. Perfect."

"Would you like coffee or milk to wash that down?"

"Save the milk for Wendy. I'll take the hard stuff."

Erica filled a mug and set it on the island. "Speaking of hard stuff, I've already told Agent Huffman everything I know about Gunter."

Amanda grabbed a blueberry donut. "Based on the detective shows I've watched over the years, I assume he'll want to corroborate your story and gather new details from Wendy and me."

Morgan lifted her mug and aimed it at Amanda then Erica. "Gunter Benson is about to discover that he picked the wrong women to mess with."

At ten o'clock sharp, Erica escorted Agent Huffman into the dining room. Following introductions, she motioned to the chair at the opposite end of the table that Brian had claimed as his seat. Her heart pounded against her ribs as she settled beside Abby and reached for her hand. In a few short weeks, her daughter had discovered that the stepfather she adored was an imposter. A criminal. Despite Abby's quiet demeanor, her clenched jaw hinted of the turmoil churning inside her.

Agent Huffman set a notepad on the table and flipped to a blank page. "Thank you for agreeing to meet with me. Erica shared what she knows about Gunter Benson. Now I need to hear from each of you. No detail is too small, and don't worry about repetition. Patterns are important." He paused and glanced at each woman. "Who volunteers to go first?"

"I do." Amanda crossed her arms on the table and began with details about the day she met the man who introduced himself as Paul Sullivan.

Erica's emotions volleyed between anger and empathy while the con artist's other wives detailed their relationships with the man they'd married, as well as their spin on the events in Blue Ridge. Gunter had obviously mastered the art of deception. Had he already targeted other innocent victims?

Following Wendy's story, Agent Huffman asked a series of pointed questions and continued taking copious notes. When finished, he set down his pen.

Morgan drummed her fingers on the table. "Now that my mother and her friends have bared their souls, do you have enough evidence to pursue this case?"

Agent Huffman closed his notepad. "Gunter Benson preys on innocent women because he believes he's invincible. I intend to prove him wrong." He pushed away from the table. "I'll keep you ladies updated on my progress."

After escorting Agent Huffman to the front door, Erica linked arms with Abby. "We need to talk." She escorted her daughter through the den and out to the sunroom with Dusty padding behind them. Erica pulled the glass door closed.

"What's going on, Mom?"

"Amanda and Wendy didn't drive that rental truck all the way from New Orleans because they're moving to Asheville." Erica breathed deeply and slowly released the air, then sat beside her daughter and revealed the real reason for their trip. "I haven't committed to anything other than helping my friends raise the money."

"Because of me, right?"

Erica patted her daughter's arm. "You're the most important person in my life, sweetheart."

Abby remained silent for a long moment. "I need the car." She popped off the swing and headed toward the door.

"Wait!" Erica rushed after her child and grabbed her arm. "Where are you going?"

"To take care of something I should have done days ago." She locked eyes with Erica. "Don't worry about me, Mom. I promise I won't do anything stupid."

She peered deep into her daughter's eyes. "I trust you, sweetheart."

Abby kissed her cheek, then dashed out.

Erica pulled deep breaths into her lungs and let them slowly release, then strode into the den.

Amanda relaxed in a club chair. "Your daughter just ran through here as if a swarm of hornets was chasing her. Is she all right?"

"She will be."

Wendy crouched beside the combo bookshelves and cabinet flanking the fireplace. "I found the perfect movie to watch. *Legally Blonde*—one of my all-time favorites."

"Excellent choice." Grateful for the distraction, Erica set the disc into the DVD player, then settled on the sofa and propped her feet on the coffee table. More than an hour into the film, Abby strolled in and squeezed beside her.

"Do you want to talk?" Erica whispered.

"When the movie's over."

The moment the final scene ended, Erica aimed the remote, shut down the system, then lifted off the sofa.

Abby grabbed her arm. "Stay here, Mom. I want to share something with everyone."

Erica hesitated. "All right." She lowered back onto the seat.

Abby rose, then headed to the fireplace and lifted a photo of her and her mom off the mantel. "When Brian moved Mom and me into this neighborhood, I tried to fit in with all the rich kids. I believed I'd succeeded, until one of the most popular girls turned on me. I was embarrassed and ashamed. Then last night during dinner and again today, when you shared your stories with Agent Huffman, I witnessed real friendship. One that isn't based on wealth or status or whether or not a person belongs to a fancy country club. Less than a month ago, Mom, you, Amanda, and Wendy were strangers—and now the way you're supporting each other and stepping out in faith to change your lives has inspired me to take a stand."

Abby set the photo back on the mantel. "When I left a while ago, I drove straight to Carrie's house and told her she was a sucky friend, and even though I forgave her, I no longer needed her friendship. Then I confronted the girl who posted that ugly meme all over social media. I told her my mother and her business partners are the most courageous and capable women on the planet, and that their daughters don't need to tear other people down to feel good about themselves."

Morgan applauded. "Way to go, Abby."

Erica's chest puffed as she rose and embraced her daughter. "I've never been prouder of you, sweetheart."

Amanda pressed her hand to her chest. "You and I have raised exceptional daughters, Erica."

"I confronted one bully with my fist and another with a lamp." Wendy lifted off the sofa. "You used your brain, girlfriend."

"Yes, she did." Erica smiled at her daughter.

Abby laced her fingers with Erica. "We need to figure out how we're gonna raise enough money to pay those taxes and turn the houses into a huge success."

"I'll get my laptop and meet y'all in the dining room." Wendy dashed from the room.

Amanda stood and stretched her arms over her head. "It seems our first official board meeting is about to begin."

Chapter 42

Wendy aimed her two-carat diamond solitaire at the dining-room chandelier. "I always loved how this sparkled." She handed her engagement and wedding rings to Amanda. "What do you think? Do they look like the real deal or a good fake?"

"Definitely real, although I'm not an expert." Amanda set the rings on the table, then pushed a diamond-studded, white-gold wedding band to Wendy. "You can also add that one to our list."

"From Gunter?"

Amanda nodded. "Unless we come up short, I want to keep all my jewelry from Preston."

Erica added two wedding bands to the mix.

"If we're lucky, these five rings plus the diamond studs Gunter gave me will add enough cash to pay the property taxes at least." Wendy tapped her keyboard, then turned her laptop toward Erica. "This store claims to buy jewelry for top dollar."

"Assuming they offer us a fair price, we need to figure out how much furniture to take with us."

"That makes sense." Wendy tapped her finger to her chin. "Whatever we keep will save money in the long run."

Erica nodded. "Exactly. To start, there are eight empty bedrooms be-tween the two houses, and we have no idea how many pieces in the other three bedrooms are salvageable. Abby and I can fill four of those rooms."

"We have one complete set from the New Orleans' house," added Amanda.

"Plus, enough furniture from the condo for two bedrooms—except for the bed I shared with Gunter. I left that in Gulfport along with the shredded sheets."

"So that's what you stashed in that big garbage bag?" Morgan snickered. "I suggested burning the sheets off Gunter's bed, but Mom donated them to a homeless shelter."

Abby nudged her mother. "Since we're talking about bedrooms, how many are in the house we'll live in?"

"Four."

Amanda snapped her fingers. "Know what I think? We need to give you and Dusty the main suite. It's the biggest bedroom, and it has a private bath."

Abby's eyes widened. "Are you sure?"

"Absolutely. Right, Wendy?"

She nodded. "After you stood up to those mean girls, you deserve the best room in the house. Plus, there's a fenced backyard for Dusty."

Abby tilted her head "What about after your baby's born?"

"We have six months to figure that out. In the meantime, we have more rooms to fill. My living-room furniture will look awesome in the B and B." Wendy swept her arm in a wide arc around the dining room. "So would everything in here."

"You have a good eye, Wendy. Since we sold most of the New Orleans furniture, we'll need items for the ranch-house den."

Abby propped her elbow on the table and twirled a lock of hair around her finger. "Will our den furniture fit in that room?"

"With your mom's decorating talent, we'll make it all fit." Amanda laced her fingers. "Which brings us to the gorgeous furniture in your living room."

"Before we decide what else to keep, we need to find out how much our jewelry's worth." Erica pushed away from the table. "Who wants to go with me?"

"Why don't you three partners go, while Abby and I decide what to do about supper."

Amanda unlaced her fingers. "I'm game."

Erica lifted off her chair. "I'll find a box for the rings."

"I'll get my diamond earrings." Wendy rushed to her room and removed the box from her suitcase side pocket. As she lifted the top, her mind traveled back to the day they'd celebrated their first-year anniversary in Gulfport's most exclusive restaurant. The way Kurt smiled while she unwrapped the box to reveal earrings sparkling in the candlelight like miniature fireworks. Wendy's brow pinched. Had Gunter bought her gift with money he'd borrowed on Erica's house? Were the diamonds even real?

Wendy pulled another box from the suitcase and peered at the gold and diamond heart attached to a delicate chain. Assuming the gems weren't fake, this was her only other piece of real jewelry. She slid the necklace back in the suitcase and dropped the earrings in her purse, then joined her partners in the kitchen.

Erica lifted her keys off the island. "Are you ladies ready to discover how much closer we are to paying those taxes?"

"As ready as ever." Amanda slung her purse over her shoulder as they followed Erica to the garage.

Wendy slid beside the driver's seat and pointed to garbage bags lined up along the wall. "Gunter's stuff?"

Erica nodded.

Wendy clutched her purse with an iron grip. Which wife had her husband slept with the week before their wedding? What about the week after?

Erica backed out of the garage.

The sudden onset of nausea accosted Wendy. "Stop."

Erica braked. "Did you forget something?"

"I'll be right back." Wendy climbed out, dashed to the kitchen, and grabbed a can of ginger ale from the fridge. She sipped until the nausea subsided, than carried the can back to the car. "Sorry for the disruption."

Erica reached across the console and patted Wendy's arm. "No need to apologize. Amanda and I understand."

What did they understand? That anger at Gunter or pregnancy had made her sick to her stomach? "I'm okay now." Wendy forced her mind to focus on the future, until Erica pulled into the jewelry-store parking lot. "What if Gunter's gifts are as fake as his identity?"

Amanda opened her door. "Let's hope they're not."

Wendy swallowed sips of ginger ale then followed her partners inside.

After Erica asked to speak to the person in charge, a gentleman approached and introduced himself as the owner. She explained their mission, then placed the rings on the counter.

Wendy reached into her purse, withdrew the earrings, and set them beside the rings.

The owner carried all five pieces to a desk.

Moisture erupted on Wendy's upper lip as the man weighed then examined each piece with a jeweler's loupe and jotted a note. Minutes passed. Why was he taking so long?

His expression remained neutral as he returned and faced them. "This is how much I can offer you." He placed a sheet of paper on the counter.

Wendy's heart pounded against her ribs.

Amanda's brows peaked. "Are you serious?"

Erica cleared her throat. "We'll take it."

The owner nodded. "I'll give you half in cash and half in a check."

Five minutes later, Erica backed out of the parking lot and turned onto the street.

"Where are we headed?"

"To my bank to cash that check."

Wendy pulled her phone from her purse. "Do you two mind if I call Chris?"

Erica glanced in the rearview mirror. "What do you think, Amanda? Should Wendy make that call now or wait until we break the news to Morgan and Abby?"

Chapter 43

Erica followed Amanda and Wendy to the kitchen and slapped an envelope on the island. "At least Gunter isn't a total scumbag."

Abby's eyes darted from her mom to the envelope. "Were your rings worth enough to pay the taxes?"

"Thanks to Wendy's solitaire, we ended up with more than four grand to spare."

"Oh my gosh." Morgan pressed her palms together. "You ladies are awesome."

"After we left the jewelry store, I called Chris." Wendy's face lit with a smile. "Our inherited properties are now officially off the market. He's gonna reserve rooms for us at the Blue Ridge Inn beginning two days after Christmas. And because they don't allow pets, he'll take care of Dusty until the ranch house is move-in ready. He'll also have a guy check out the HVAC and water heater."

"Talk about going above and beyond." Morgan snickered. "How old is this guy?"

Wendy shrugged. "Twenty-something?"

"Hmm." Morgan tapped her finger against her cheek. "It seems your young attorney is either single-handedly attempting to put an end to bad-lawyer jokes, or he has a serious crush on the blonde member of the Blue Ridge wives club."

Wendy's cheeks pinkened. "He's nice, that's all."

"He's way more than nice."

Images of Chris and Wendy's obvious flirtation played in Erica's mind. That was a conversation for another day. She set her keys on the desk. "Assuming we'll need to spend a good bit of the extra cash on making the ranch house livable, the three of us decided to advertise a pre-Christmas sale for this coming weekend."

"Talk about pressure." Morgan shook her head. "We definitely have our work cut out for us."

"Starting first thing tomorrow morning." Wendy's tone radiated excitement. "Tonight, we're celebrating over dinner at a Mexican restaurant."

"Because Gunter hated Mexican food," Abby and Morgan responded in unison, triggering laughter.

An hour after the laughter died down, the women sat at a round table in a corner booth. Morgan held up her glass. "As Abby so eloquently informed her friend, here's to the three most courageous and capable women on the planet."

Erica and Amanda lifted their adult beverages while Wendy and Abby raised glasses of lemonade.

Amanda took a sip then set her glass on the table. "No matter how much we add to our bottom line this weekend, turning the other house into a guest-worthy inn will cost a fortune. That is, if we don't spend it all on the ranch house."

Wendy drummed her fingers on the table. "There you go again, being all pessimistic."

"There's a big difference between pessimism and practicality." Amanda sighed. "I'm just saying we need to keep reality in perspective."

"The reality is, even if Gunter aka Kurt used the money from Erica and Abby's house, he loved me enough to spend a fortune on expensive jewelry." Wendy planted her forearms on the table. "I could've sold my rings and earrings on my own and moved to Florida, but I didn't because we're a team. So, cheer up, partner. We'll find a way to raise the money we need."

Erica scooped guacamole onto a chip and stared at the chunk of avocado. "A couple days ago, I asked my pastor whether or not we should move to Blue Ridge. He suggested I consider the pros and cons, then step out in faith. No matter how many challenges we'll need to overcome—" She reached for her daughter's hand. "Abby's courage proves our vision is divinely guided."

"One thing I've learned as an engineering student is the importance of careful observation." Morgan leaned forward. "Although Gunter didn't have a clue, he chose three women who possess the necessary skills for an effective partnership. In the months ahead, will you squabble? Absolutely. But in the end, Mom's attention to detail, Erica's commitment to completing tasks, Wendy's unbridled enthusiasm, and Abby's bravery will lead you to enormous success."

"I always wanted to be a cheerleader, but I was never in one high school long enough to try out." Wendy stroked her left ring finger. "Now I understand that cheering for business partners is far more important than cheering for sports teams."

"You're right." Abby reached for a chip. "In my opinion, we need a college grad on the team. So, I suggest we make Morgan our official consultant."

"That's a great idea." Amanda nudged her daughter's arm. "Are you game?"

"Absolutely. Although you, Wendy, and Erica are exclusive members of the Blue Ridge wives club—"

"At least as far as we know," added Erica.

"Even if other wives are lurking somewhere out there, Gunter willed those two houses to you three." Morgan held up her index finger. "As my first official consulting act, I recommend we come up with a different name for our new enterprise."

"Great idea." Wendy leaned forward. "Who has a pen?"

"I do." Erica pulled a pen from her purse and handed it to Wendy as their server arrived with their dinner. While they brainstormed potential names and debated the reason for Gunter's derision of Mexican food, Wendy doodled on a paper napkin. After polishing off her burrito, she slapped her palm on the table. "I figured it out."

Erica tilted her head. "Why Gunter refused to eat Mexican?"

"No. What to name our company. His wives' first names begin with an A, a W, and an E. Right? In addition to the three of us, two daughters are now part of our team, and their initials are A and M. Which is how I came up with this name." Wendy held up the napkin.

Morgan's brows raised. "Talk about creative."

Abby grinned. "I love it."

Amanda's mouth curved into a smile. "You continue to amaze me, Wendy. I can't think of a more appropriate name."

"Well then, since we all agree, I suggest we toast Wendy for officially naming our business." Erica lifted her glass. "Here's to Awesam."

"And to the ladies who are way more than business partners." Tears pooled in Wendy's eyes. "I love you all like sisters."

Warmth radiated through Erica as she lifted her glass. "To our Awesam family, who's destined to create something special."

Chapter 44

Early Christmas morning, a subtle pecking noise awakened Wendy. A warm sensation radiated through her chest as she eyed the yellow and black bird perched on the sill. "Well, hello there." The feathered creature jerked its head toward the window. "Are you looking at me or admiring your reflection?" The bird hesitated for a long moment as if considering how to respond then flew away. "Come back anytime."

Wendy climbed out of bed and headed straight to the bathroom. After showering and towel-drying her hair, she followed the vanilla and nutmeg scents to the kitchen. "What smells so yummy?"

"Warm homemade eggnog with rum flavoring instead of the real stuff." Amanda dipped a ladle into the saucepan, then filled a mug and sprinkled the beverage with nutmeg. "A Smith-family, Christmas-morning ritual." She handed the mug to Wendy. "Now an Awesam family tradition."

Wendy sipped. "This is yummier than Mountain Mama's dessert coffee."

Abby removed a sheet of croissants from the oven and set it on the island. "What's Mountain Mama's?"

Erica slid her arm around her daughter's shoulders. "The best coffee lounge in Blue Ridge."

Morgan set a charcuterie platter on the island. "Sounds like a fun place."

Memories bubbled up as Wendy lifted a plate off the island. So much had happened since Chris first revealed details about the father of her child. Her heart swelled as she filled her plate with goodies. Now she was celebrating Christmas with amazing women who had chosen to transform Gunter's lies into a promising new adventure.

Abby pinched the end off a croissant. "Even though we sold all the living-room furniture, how about we enjoy breakfast around the Christmas tree before we open our gifts?"

"Perfect." Wendy carried her plate and mug to the living room. She sat cross-legged on the floor and counted six wrapped gifts under the tree. "Who's the sixth present for?"

Abby strolled in. "Dusty."

"Of course." Morgan sat beside Wendy. "We can't forget the family pet."

Wendy plucked a strawberry off her plate. "Figuring out how to spend our agreed-upon budget for the secret name I drew was a lot more fun than shopping for stuff I don't need."

Morgan chuckled. "One look in your closet back at the condo made it obvious you wear the bulk of that stuff."

"I suppose I've been making up for all the years my entire wardrobe fit into a medium-sized suitcase. Which made moving between foster homes easy enough." Wendy bit into her croissant.

"One fact is certain." Amanda lowered to the floor. "Shopping is a much better coping mechanism than eating or drinking too much."

"Amen to that." Erica sat beside her daughter.

"I have a ton of cute jeans." Wendy aimed her mug at Abby. "Since we're the same size, I'll share them with you."

"Really?" Abby's eyes widened. "You're a way cooler friend than Carrie."

Wendy nudged Abby's arm. "You mean, sister."

"That's what I meant to say."

Amanda set her mug on the carpet. "This reminds me of the first Christmas after Morgan was born. Preston and I had spent our yearly gift budget fixing up the nursery, so our presents to each other were toys for our new baby."

Wendy pressed her hand to her chest. "That's so sweet."

"The first Christmas after Abby and I moved to Asheville, we splurged on a Biltmore candlelight tour."

"I imagined being rich and living in that ginormous house." Abby giggled. "Except I couldn't decide which bedroom would've been mine. After Awesam is successful, we should all come back and visit the Biltmore together."

Erica smiled at her daughter. "Great idea, sweetheart."

Conflicting emotions released a tingling sensation in Wendy's chest as her new family shared memories of past Christmases and visions of future holidays. Eager to move on, she carried the plates to the kitchen the moment everyone finished eating, then dashed back and stooped beside the tree. "I hope you don't mind if I share my gift first." She reached for a bag and gave it to Erica. "I picked this out especially for you."

Erica removed the tissue paper, then pulled out two scented candles. She wrapped her fingers around the first glass container and sniffed. "My all-time favorite scent."

"I know, because I checked the candle in the den which is almost burned to the bottom."

"Thank you, Wendy. They're perfect, and you're right, I was down to the last burn. I'll go next."

Amanda accepted the gift from Erica. "Hmm, I wonder..." She peeled off the wrapper, opened the box, and removed a pair of leather gloves. Laughing, she held them up. "The perfect gift for a New Orleans native."

"I don't want my new partner to suffer from frostbite."

"Are you assuming another snow village is in our future?"

Erica nodded. "That's a distinct possibility, except you'll need a different pair of gloves to handle wet snow."

"I'll keep that in mind." Amanda set the gift aside, then reached for a gold bag and handed it to Abby. "For the youngest member of our team."

Abby reached in and withdrew a bottle of perfume. "Yay. My favorite scent."

"I know." Amanda grinned. "Your mom told me."

Abby hugged Amanda, then lifted a gift and set it on Morgan's lap. "I hope you like what I picked."

Morgan ripped off the paper and opened the box. "Oh my gosh, Abby." She held up a royal blue sweater. "This is gorgeous."

"It's not quite one of LSU's colors."

"Close enough. I love it. Thank you, Abby." Morgan removed the last bag from beneath the tree and placed it on the floor in front of Wendy. "Especially for you, girlfriend turned sister."

Wendy's pulse accelerated as she yanked the tissue from the bag and removed a teal green tunic. "Wow. My first maternity shirt."

"The first of three."

Wendy pulled out a blue, then a black and white tunic. "These are perfect. Thank you, Morgan."

"Awesam's business mogul has to look the part."

"We have one more gift." Abby tossed the wrapped present to Dusty. The canine family member ripped the paper off with her teeth then carried the giant chew bone to the corner and sprawled on her belly.

Amanda faced Wendy. "We've all shared some of our favorite Christmas mornings. Now it's your turn."

Wendy's eyes drifted to the elegantly decorated tree as past Christmas mornings surfaced in a nondescript blur. Happy tears erupted and cascaded down her cheeks. "Today is my favorite." Her heart drummed in her chest as her family gathered around her. For the first time in as long as she could remember, she understood the true blessings of Christmas.

Chapter 45

Erica paid the two guys she'd hired to load the second rental truck, then headed into the empty den and reached for her daughter's hand. Memories from the past six years flooded her brain. "The last time you and I fled to a new town, we faced an unknown future." She squeezed Abby's fingers. "The same holds true today with one big difference. This time we aren't alone."

Amanda walked in from the garage. "Morgan boarded the plane a half hour ago, and I already miss her." Her shoulders slumped. "LSU is an hour's drive from New Orleans. Blue Ridge is nearly nine hours away."

Erica released her child's hand then looped her arm around Amanda's elbow. "You'll Facetime her every day, and you'll be together when she graduates in May. Chances are she'll find a job closer to Georgia."

"Are you trying to cheer me up?"

"Yes, is it working?"

"A little."

Wendy wandered in from the kitchen. "Chris plans to meet us at the inn and take Dusty to his house."

"We'll leave after I take one more look around." Erica released Amanda's arm then roamed from room to room conjuring memories. Who would buy this house? A family? An investor? She stopped at the main-bedroom door and peered into the room she'd shared with the man who had lied to her—who'd stolen from her. The same man whose one compassionate gesture—no matter how unintended—offered her and Abby a bright future. *If* they raised enough money to refurbish the mansion. Erica released a heavy sigh and pulled the door closed. She met her travel companions in the kitchen then scooped the envelope stuffed with the garage-sale proceeds off the island and tossed the house keys on the counter. "It's time to take the Awesam caravan on the road."

Five minutes later, she backed the rental truck down the driveway and pulled behind Abby in her car and Wendy in Gunter's truck. Amanda took the lead in the other rental. During the drive, Erica mentally ticked off a long list of tasks to make the ranch house livable. By the time she pulled into the inn's parking lot at dusk, the tension in her shoulders had crept up the back of her neck and lodged in the base of her skull. She climbed out of the truck and rolled her shoulders, hoping to ease the pain.

Wendy rushed to meet Chris at the porch steps, then escorted him across the lot. Amanda and Erica strode over. Abby opened her car's back door and clipped a leash to her pet's collar. Dusty jumped onto the pavement and responded to Chris's head pat with an enthusiastic tail wag. Abby stooped and wrapped her arms around Dusty's neck. "This nice man will take care of you for a few days."

Chris smiled. "Beginning tomorrow, I'll bring her to the ranch house so she can be with you during the day, then I'll take her home at night until you move in."

"Thank you." Abby popped the trunk. "Her bed's back there."

Chris removed an envelope from his jacket pocket. "Before I leave with Dusty, I have estimates on several items." He handed the envelope to Wendy. "After you ladies look everything over, give me a call."

Erica cringed. What did he mean by several items?

Wendy stuffed the envelope in her jeans pocket. "Do you mind if I call you after supper?"

"Not at all. By the way, I assumed you'd be tired, so I ordered pizzas and salad to be delivered in half an hour."

Amanda lifted an eyebrow. "My daughter was right about you going above and beyond."

"I'm glad to help." Chris gripped the leash. "What do you say, Dusty? Would you like to meet Duke, my black lab?" He led Abby's pet to his sedan and opened the back door. Dusty sprang onto the seat, a clear sign she trusted her dog sitter.

Wendy pressed her hand to her chest. "Chris is the nicest guy, and he loves dogs."

Amanda linked arms with Wendy. "I'm guessing he also has his eye on a certain blonde newcomer."

"He probably has a girlfriend."

"I suspect you'll find out soon enough." Amanda and Wendy followed Erica and Abby to the inn's back door.

Faith greeted them with a big smile. "Welcome back, ladies, and Abby. Your miniature snowman is still intact, Wendy."

"Thanks for saving it."

"Our chef will miss her little friend after you move to your new house. Anyway, I'm putting you and Amanda in the Sycamore suite. Erica, I have you and your daughter in the Appalachian room. Did Chris tell you he ordered supper for you?"

"He did." Wendy turned toward Erica. "We'll meet you and Abby in the dining room in twenty minutes."

Erica nodded. "Bring that envelope."

"I will."

Faith opened the Sycamore suite then escorted Erica and Abby to their room. "I'm delighted you're moving to Blue Ridge. We're a close-knit community where folks look out for each other." She faced Abby. "My daughter, Hannah, is a senior at the local high school. She's eager to meet you tomorrow at breakfast. Until then, you and your mom let me know if you need anything." Faith set the key on the bed then left them alone.

"Just think, sweetheart, by this time tomorrow, you could have a new best friend."

"Maybe." Abby plopped onto the sofa and pulled her phone from her pocket. Her thumbs raced across the keypad.

Erica unzipped her suitcase and began hanging clothes in the closet. "Are you texting or posting?"

"I'm deleting sucky friends from my social-media accounts."

"That's a big move. I'm proud of you, sweetheart."

"Things didn't work out so well in two big towns." Abby set her phone on the coffee table. "Maybe living in a small town will turn out better."

"If Chris and Faith are any indication, we've definitely made the right move." While Erica unpacked, her thoughts shifted to the envelope. How much would the estimates set them back? A few hundred? Thousands? She'd find out soon enough.

"Twenty minutes is up, Mom."

"You're right." Images of the day Chris laid three wedding photographs on the table bombarded Erica's mind as she escorted her daughter from their room. She halted at the dining-room entrance and blinked to block the mental pictures.

Abby touched her arm. "Are you okay?"

Erica patted her daughter's hand. "I am now." She turned toward foot-steps striking the floor behind them. Wendy held the envelope from Chris in her right hand. Should she ask or wait?

Faith responded to the back doorbell. Spicy tomato and sausage aromas wafted around the delivery guy as he carried two medium-sized pizza boxes and a salad bowl into the dining room.

Erica and Abby settled across from their partners. Wendy laid the envelope on the table then lifted the box lids. "One loaded, one cheese and pepperoni."

"That's a lot of pizza." Amanda distributed plates.

Erica forced her eyes away from the envelope. "If you don't mind, I'd like to bless our meal."

Amanda nodded. "Please."

When she finished, Amanda smiled at her. "When we move into our new home, we'll take turns giving thanks."

"Great idea." Wendy scooped salad onto her plate. "Amanda and I read the estimates."

Erica stared at her. "Good news or bad?"

"A little of both. On the plus side, the stove just needs scouring, and the roof is fine for now. Unfortunately, the heating and air conditioning system, the water heater, the refrigerator, and the dishwasher are toast."

Erica trilled her lips. "How much is replacing all that gonna cost?"

"Nearly all of our cash reserves." Wendy lifted a slice of loaded pizza onto her plate. "I hope you don't mind, but considering we can't move in until those items are replaced, I made an executive decision and gave Chris the go-ahead."

Why had Wendy made the decision on her own? Erica caught Amanda's eye. Were they on the same page?

Amanda broke eye contact. "Like any well-managed company, we need specific roles for each partner."

Yeah, they were definitely on the same page. "The question is, what roles, and how will we decide who fills which one?"

"During our ride to the airport, Morgan offered to create an organizational chart and email it to me later tonight. With that in mind, I suggest the four of us meet in our suite tomorrow morning before breakfast to consider our consultant's suggestions."

Erica nodded. "I agree. What about you, Wendy?"

She shrugged. "Fine with me."

"Then it's settled." Amanda set a slice of pizza on her plate. "Our first official board meeting will begin at seven-thirty tomorrow morning."

Chapter 46

Amanda settled on one of the wingback chairs in the Sycamore sitting room, set her laptop across her knees, and eyed Erica. "Is Abby joining us?"

"Not until breakfast."

"All right then." Keenly aware her partner's eyes laser-focused on her, Amanda opened her daughter's email. How would they respond to Morgan's suggestions? She squared her shoulders. "Our consultant wants you to know that she put a lot of thought into these recommendations." Amanda glanced at Wendy then Erica. No reaction. So far, so good. "I'll begin by describing the three key positions. The first is a President who will oversee our vision as well as set and track goals for our operation. Next is a Chief Executive Officer in charge of strategic direction, organization, and building a successful team. Last but not least is a Chief Financial Officer who will play a significant role in how we manage our income and expenses."

"That's only three." Wendy's brow pinched. "Counting Abby, there are four of us."

"Given that she'll be a full-time student, Morgan has a special role for her, which I'll explain in a few minutes. First, I'll share Morgan's recommendations for each position. In case you're wondering, the roles are equal in importance and authority."

Amanda turned toward Wendy. "Based on the fact that you've enrolled in business classes, and considering the initiatives you've already taken regarding our finances, she suggests you assume the role of CFO."

"Hmm." Wendy tapped steepled fingers on her chin.

Amanda studied their young partner's pinched expression. Did she consider the suggestion a compliment? What if she objected? Were they on the verge of their first major disagreement? She held her breath.

"Wendy Peterson, Chief Financial Officer." The young partner tilted her head. "I like the sound of that."

Amanda exhaled. "Then you accept?"

Wendy shrugged. "Why wouldn't I?"

"No reason." Amanda shifted her attention to Erica. "Morgan recommends you assume the role as our Chief Executive Officer."

Erica folded her hands in her lap. "Taking on that important a role is a big move for a former waitress and salesclerk."

"True." Amanda set her laptop on the coffee table. "However, we're each assuming unfamiliar positions that will challenge us to dig deep and draw on our innate abilities."

"She's right." Wendy crossed her leg over her knee. "CEO is the perfect position for you."

"It's definitely a step above interior decorator." Erica paused. "Okay, I'll go along with it. Which makes you our president, Amanda. What about Abby?"

"Morgan suggests she assume the role of Vice-President. Which means she'll have a title but little responsibility."

Erica nodded. "That makes sense."

"Good." Time to address the first subject. Amanda opened her laptop. "Given that our roles are equally important, I propose that beginning today the three of us discuss all issues before making decisions."

Wendy pumped her foot. "What happens when we disagree?"

"We'll talk it through as a team, then we'll vote."

"Will our votes need to be unanimous, or will two out of three be okay?"

"Good question, Wendy."

"If I may." Erica scooted to the edge of her seat. "I suggest unanimous regarding decisions with major implications, and two out of three for those that are less important."

Way to go, Erica. "Who's in favor of our CEO's suggestion?"

Wendy raised her hand. "I am."

"Which makes our first decision unanimous." Amanda lifted off her chair. "Why don't we head over to the dining room and celebrate with coffee."

"Works for me." Erica stood.

Wendy uncrossed her legs. "Me too."

While making their way across the hall, Amanda pictured the daunting task that lay ahead. How could three women who had limited experience possibly raise enough money to turn their vision into reality? That was a discussion for another day.

Six other guests who had gathered around the dining-room table beside the window greeted them. Amanda prepared a cup of coffee and carried it to the table close to the entrance.

Abby ambled in and plopped beside her mom. "Did you figure everything out?"

"We did." Erica touched her daughter's arm. "Including making you our vice-president."

"Cool."

Faith strolled in with a pretty, dark-haired teenager. "Abby, I'd like you to meet my daughter, Hannah."

Abby lifted off her chair. "Hi."

"Back at you." Hannah moved close to Abby. "Some of my friends are waiting for us at Mountain Mama's."

Abby eyed her mother.

"Go ahead, sweetheart."

Hannah linked arms with Abby. "I already connected with you on social media."

"Really?"

Erica pressed her hand to her chest as her eyes followed the girls strolling into the hall and around the corner. "Thank you, Faith."

"Meeting your daughter was Hannah's idea. We're a small town, so the kids all know each other. Believe me, by the end of the day, Abby will no longer be a stranger."

As Erica pressed her hand to her chest and again expressed her gratitude, a question arose in Amanda's mind. How much, if anything, did Faith know about their situation?

Two more guests moseyed in, settled at their table, and introduced themselves. Mouthwatering maple and bacon aromas wafted around the chef as she carried a tray from the kitchen.

After enjoying breakfast and chatting with the other guests, Amanda and her partners excused themselves. The moment they stepped into the hall Abby dashed in from Mountain Mama's—her face flushed. "Hannah invited me to spend the day with her and her friends. Is it okay if I skip working at the house?"

Erica faced her partners. "What do y'all think? Should we let our VP take a day off?"

Amanda tilted her head. "One of a vice president's most important functions is establishing community relationships, so yeah."

Wendy grinned. "Assuming your mom agrees, we've made our second unanimous decision."

"Y'all are the best." Abby spun around and rushed back to the lounge.

"We just made my daughter enormously happy."

"Abby is the reason the three of us are standing here this morning." Amanda touched Erica's arm. "I can't think of a better way to thank her."

Wendy pulled her phone from her jeans pocket. "Chris and an AC guy are meeting us at the house at noon."

"In that case, we need to head to the bank and open a business account." Amanda nudged Erica. "Wendy and I will meet you in the parking lot in five minutes."

"Got it."

An hour later, Amanda parked the pickup in the ranch-house carport.

"Chris left the back unlocked." Wendy climbed out and headed straight to the door.

Amanda snickered. "We should begin counting the number of times Wendy mentions our attorney's name."

"Assuming we can count that high." Erica climbed from the back seat and followed Amanda into the kitchen.

Wendy nodded toward the end of the counter. "Chris already had the old refrigerator hauled away."

Amanda swallowed a giggle. "Which room do you gals think we should tackle first?"

"Definitely the bathrooms then the kitchen." Erica forced open the window over the sink, emitting a breath of fresh air.

Wendy's eyes gleamed the moment a vehicle drove into the carport. "They're here."

Unable to resist the temptation, Amanda nudged their CFO's arm. "Who's here?"

"Chris and the AC guy. Who do you think?" Wendy pulled the door open.

Erica removed her phone from her pocket and headed to the den.

Dusty bounded in and sped through the kitchen. Chris followed and introduced the AC guy.

Dusty returned with her tail tucked. Wendy stooped down and patted the canine's head. "Abby isn't here, girl." She straightened and smiled at Chris. "She's spending the day with Faith's daughter."

"Ah." The attorney's expression mirrored Wendy's. "Hannah's a great kid." He cleared his throat as if he'd suddenly become aware of his reaction to the pretty blonde. "The water heater and your new appliances are scheduled for delivery this afternoon."

Wendy's head tilted. "Thank you for taking care of everything."

"My pleasure." Chris glanced at his watch. "I have to run, but I'll check back with you later today."

Wendy stood at the open door while their attorney returned to his vehicle.

Suppressing the urge to comment on their obvious attraction, Amanda moseyed into the den.

Erica pocketed her phone. "Agent Huffman already has a solid lead on Gunter's whereabouts."

"This soon?" Amanda scoffed. "Seems the notorious con artist isn't so clever after all."

Chapter 47

Four days after the partners initiated a serious cleanup campaign, Amanda stood in the kitchen and breathed in the fresh lemon scent. "Tomorrow night, we'll prepare our first meal in our new home."

Wendy entered from the carport and set a box packed with items from her condo kitchen on the counter. "Chris hired two guys to help us move in tomorrow."

Erica faced the window above the sink. "Dusty has already claimed the backyard as her territory."

Amanda moved beside Abby as she tossed a frisbee to her canine companion.

"After we're settled, we need to address our biggest challenge—how to raise more money." Erica spun away from the window. "First, I suggest we conduct an in-depth assessment of Eleanor Harrington's vacation home."

Amanda nodded. "Now's as good a time as any."

Erica entered the den and slid the glass door open. "We're heading over to the big house, sweetheart. Do you want to come with us?"

"Sure." Abby clapped twice. "Come on, Dusty, we're gonna check out our new adventure." The family pet padded beside the women as they traipsed across the side yard and driveway then stepped onto the cracked sidewalk.

Erica brushed her fingers through her hair as they climbed onto the front porch. "At least the outside doesn't look any worse than it did a month ago. The inside could be a different story."

Amanda opened the door and stepped into the once-grand foyer.

Dusty rushed past her and embarked on a serious sniffing mission.

Abby scrunched her nose. "We'll need a dozen candles to kill that smell."

Wendy pointed to spiderwebs stretched across the foyer chandelier. "First thing we need to do is call an exterminator." She headed toward the back of the house.

Dusty's paws clicked the wooden floorboards as she bounded back to the foyer and up the stairs. Abby followed her. "I bet she's on the hunt for some kind of critter."

"She'll find at least one." The moment Amanda stepped into the living room, dust mingling with the pervading musty aroma triggered a sneeze.

Erica lifted a vase off the fireplace mantel. "Based on your experience with the shotgun house, and assuming we'll do a lot of the work ourselves, how much cash will we need to refurbish a house this big?"

"A small fortune." Amanda's attention drifted to the broken window and water-damaged floorboards. "For the past few days, I've contemplated a question Morgan posed the day she left Asheville." She ran her finger over a dust-encrusted end table. "Is it possible the three of us are destined to use our inheritance to impact lives?"

Erica shrugged. "That's why we shared our story with Agent Huffman."

"Perhaps we're meant to do more than help bring about justice." Amanda moved beside the fireplace and focused on the landscape painting depicting the sun rising above a mountain range. "—such as how we use this house."

Erica's brows raised. "Are you suggesting we abandon our bed-and-breakfast idea?"

Amanda shook her head. "I'm saying we need to consider expanding our vision."

Erica set down the vase. "Unless we raise a small fortune, whatever vision we end up with will never see the light of day."

A ladybug landed on the mantel, compelling Amanda to scoop the tiny insect into her hand. "Maybe we should pray for a miracle."

Erica released a sigh. "That's a mighty big prayer."

Footsteps and paws striking the staircase made it clear their vice president and her canine assistant had concluded their second-story appraisal. Abby rushed in from the foyer. "There are definitely critters living up there."

Amanda eased to the broken window and released the ladybug to the front porch.

Wendy dashed in. "I know where we can store the furniture we're saving for the inn." She motioned the partners to follow her then led them through the house and out the French doors to the patio. "Over there." She rushed to the free-standing, triple garage and opened the side door.

Amanda followed and entered the dark space then pushed up the main garage door. A vehicle shrouded with a gray cover filled the first bay of the otherwise empty building. "At least two-thirds of the space is available."

Wendy blew dust off the tarp. "What are the chances that whatever's under here runs?"

"Let's find out." Abby gripped a corner of the tarp. "Hey, Wendy, how about giving me a hand?"

The two young women peeled back the cover to reveal a vintage red convertible that at first glance appeared in pristine condition. Erica ambled to the front and touched the hood ornament. "I don't know how old this is, but it's definitely a Cadillac."

Wendy palmed the fin extending from the door to the taillights. "What do you suppose an old car like this is worth?"

Amanda stooped and flicked a bug off a whitewall tire. "Depends on how rare it is."

Abby climbed onto the passenger seat, opened the glove box, and removed a leather binder. "According to the owner's manual, I'm sitting in a 1960 Eldorado." She pulled her phone from her back pocket and tapped the screen. Her eyes bulged as her mouth fell open. "Oh my gosh. This old car is worth more than a hundred grand."

Erica's brows lifted. "Are you serious?"

"Dead serious." She held up her phone.

Erica stared at the screen. "Talk about a miracle."

Wendy yanked her phone from her jeans pocket and tapped the screen.

"Let me guess." Amanda sidled over. "You're calling Chris."

"Who else do you think will help us find a buyer?" Wendy rolled her eyes, then pressed the phone to her ear. "The call's going to voicemail." She waited. "Call me. We just uncovered a gold mine."

Twenty-four hours after discovering the Eldorado, Amanda hung the last of her clothes in the closet. A lump rose in her throat as she closed the door and eyed her new bedroom. Gunter Benson's deception had plunged her into a life far different than the one she'd lived five weeks earlier, but what he didn't anticipate was that it was better—more honest, more fulfilling.

A smile formed as she spread the comforter on the bed she and Preston had shared. He'd be proud of her for taking control of her destiny. She arranged the decorative pillows then took a quick glance around and walked out. Halfway down the hall, sniffles perked her ears. She peered into the room beside hers.

Wendy sat on the bed clutching her copy of *Sugar Snow* to her chest. Tears tracked down her cheeks. Amanda stepped in and sat beside her friend. "We've been through a lot of emotional ups and downs during the past few weeks."

"Every time a case worker dropped me off at a new foster house, I prayed I'd finally have a family." Wendy laid the book on her lap. "I thought that happened when I married Kurt. Except it turned out he's a fraud."

Erica paused outside the door. "Are those happy or sad tears?"

Wendy swiped her fingers across her cheeks. "This is the first time I've moved into a house with a real family."

"An extra-special family." Erica ambled in. "Since the day we first met at the Blue Ridge Inn, we've faced challenges no woman should ever have to endure. And yet here we are, taking control of our lives and turning adversity into opportunity."

"What if we fail?"

"Are you kidding?" Erica dropped on the other side of Wendy. "There's no way the members of our exclusive wives club will do anything other than achieve enormous success."

"I want my baby to be proud of her mother."

Amanda smiled. "Is *her* a slip of the tongue or wishful thinking?"

Wendy pressed her hand to her belly. "Last night I dreamed about dressing a little girl in a frilly pink dress and taking her for a ride on the train."

Amanda nodded. "Definitely wishful thinking."

Abby walked past then backed up. "Is this some kind of meeting?"

"More like a family gathering." Erica motioned her to come in. "Are you all settled in your new room?"

"Uh-huh." Abby approached with Dusty at her side. "Hannah's sleeping over after a bunch of us watch a movie at the Swan Drive In."

Wendy's eyes widened. "I didn't know drive-in movies still existed."

"Swan is one of the few left." Erica nudged Wendy's arm. "The three of us should go sometime."

As the conversation about outdoor movies continued, Amanda peered around the room filled with furniture from Wendy's condo. Six weeks ago, she'd had no idea the women gathered in this room existed. Now they were family. It was Eleanor Harrington's hidden gift that had made Awesam possible, not the maneuvers of the gambler who used wives for his own demented gratification.

Amanda squared her shoulders and lifted her chin as she stretched her arm around Wendy's shoulders. No matter what happened in the days ahead, somehow justice and her new family would prevail over Gunter Benson to stop him from defrauding any more innocent women.

Thank you for reading Blizzard at Blue Ridge Inn, the first book in what will be a multi-book series. The story continues in The Inheritance as Amanda, Erica, and Wendy struggle to overcome the past while facing new challenges and uncertain futures.

Afterword

Beginning a new series is always exciting. This book was especially fun because while the story and characters are fictional, the Blue Ridge Inn is real. Perhaps one day you'll visit Blue Ridge and stay at this beautiful, historic bed and breakfast.

Although writing is a solo activity, the road to publication requires a team. A special thank you to all who travel this road me.

To Sherri Stewart, my editor whose keen eye and expertise make my writing better.

To my beta readers, Pat Davis, Carlene Dunn, Bev Feldkamp, Kitty Metzger, Kathy Warner, Nancy Wirth, and Sandra Abernathy for reading my manuscripts and providing feedback and suggestions.

To my friends at American Christian Fiction Writers North Georgia Chapter, for their inspiration and for providing speakers who share their experiences and knowledge. To my friends at Word Weaver's International Greater Atlanta Chapter, whose critiques and encouragement are invaluable.

To John Lavin, owner of the Blue Ridge Inn, for his gracious hospitality.

To my readers, newsletter subscribers, and launch team, for joining me on this journey.

To all who posted or plan to post reviews on Amazon, Goodreads, BookBub, and other sites. Your reviews are the best way to thank authors.

To my amazing family, who are the wind beneath my wings.

To the citizens of Blue Ridge, Georgia. Visiting your lovely town inspired me to write this series.

Above all, I thank God for His amazing grace, unconditional love, His Son, and the gift of eternal life.